The Jack the Ripper
Walking Tour
Murder

Other Books by Albert Borowitz

A Gallery of Sinister Perspectives: Ten Crimes and a Scandal

*The Woman Who Murdered Black Satin:
The Bermondsey Horror*

Innocence and Arsenic: Studies in Crime and Literature

The Jack the Ripper Walking Tour Murder

· Albert Borowitz ·

A
Joan
Kahn
BOOK

ST. MARTIN'S PRESS · NEW YORK

Copyeditor: Linda O'Brien

Library of Congress Cataloging in Publication Data

Borowitz, Albert, 1930–
    The Jack the Ripper walking tour murder.
"Joan Kahn book."
    I. Title.
PS3552.O7547J3   1986   813'.54   85-25159
ISBN 0-312-43944-X

First Edition

10 9 8 7 6 5 4 3 2 1

For Joan Kahn, an intrepid literary
explorer who discovered me twice.

The Place: London
The Time: August 1988

· **1** ·

Paul Prye put up the collar of his ancient Burberry and tugged on the peak of his Greek seaman's cap. The sunny intervals that BBC had cautiously promised for the day had been few and far between. But at least it had stopped raining.

From the bench where he sat in front of the Tower Hill tube station he gazed across at a weedy patch of ground that had been grandly named Trinity Square Gardens. He wondered who tended it—Incapability Brown?

Paul was always early. This was one of the banes of his wife Alice's existence: the hours they wasted waiting for the theater doors to open, or for countless flights to exotic climes to be called before their ticket counter was ready for passenger check-in.

If Paul was ever destined to be late, or to arrive breathless at the last possible moment like his braver friends he admired so much—who could always find one more parking space and trample on a whole row of symphony subscribers' toes without a blush—today would not be the day. For today, on this Thursday in August 1988, Paul Prye, for the very first time in his life, was going on a Jack the Ripper Walking Tour.

It was the right year for the tour, no doubt of that, the centennial of the Ripper's crimes, which had run their bloody course between August 31 and November 9, 1888. In many of the museums of London, Ripper exhibitions were being presented, and of course the newspapers and magazines were full of potboiling accounts of the old horrors. Paul Prye wouldn't have missed the season of Ripper observances for the world. (Oh, to be in England—on Jack's big anniversary!) For though Paul was a professor of urban history at Columbia University, his real passion was true crime. He delivered tidy little lectures on his favorite cases to the indulgent members of a New York City bibliophiles' society, but most of all he read and reread his favorite authors, from Thomas De Quincey on, and compulsively amassed a huge library of books, manuscripts, and ephemera that related even marginally to crime history.

Why had Paul become obsessed with crime? To friends who asked politely, he recalled that as a child he had collected detective stories with his father. But he had heard other theories expounded about his odd hobby. Paul was tall and, before too many European vacations had left their mark, had been thin. He had a long head (whose dark brown hair was beginning to turn gray now that he had entered his forties), a nose that was aquiline and perhaps not too small, and he sometimes sported a deerstalker's cap; need more be said? It was obvious that he had a Sherlock complex, people would say with a grin. And then, of course, his family name had preordained him as a sleuth. Paul would try to look amused whenever this observation was made, but somewhere it is written, "Don't make a joke about a man's name. He's heard it before." Occasionally, a less flattering hypothesis was posed. Once, when Paul finished reading his fellow club members a murder lecture of which he was particularly proud, a psychiatrist rose under the pretense of asking a question: Didn't the speaker think that people preoccupied with criminal cases harbored a secret hostility? Paul answered that he was not certain. It was an interesting point. But of one thing he felt quite sure: psychiatrists who asked such questions at book club meetings harbored open hostility. A lawyer in the audience sprang to Paul's assistance: Was the speaker able to account for the fact that there were so many more doctor-murderers than lawyer-murderers? Paul acknowledged that the medical profession had a clear statistical lead. But, he added, he was not at all certain that it was a matter to be explained on the basis of relative malice; more likely, it meant only that it is easier to poison a man than to talk him to death.

Even Alice Prye couldn't produce a satisfactory explanation of her husband's preoccupation with violent death. Time and again she would be asked how it felt sitting, every day of her life, across the breakfast table from a man who read avidly about poisons. The truth was that she didn't mind in the least. She was herself an ardent devotee of Agatha Christie, and Paul had even induced her to tackle some of the true-crime classics. "There's nothing like a good domestic poisoning," she would respond to her friends' mocking concern, "but frankly, I don't see myself as the 'murderee' type."

Paul would have had to be certifiably insane to want to dispose of Alice, by poison or otherwise. She was professor of art history on the faculty of New York University. Her beautiful oval face and swanlike neck inspired even new acquaintances to murmur comparisons to Modigliani and Botticelli, and Paul would often confide to her that she looked "more like an artwork than an art historian." "That's what Proust calls idolatry," dark-haired Alice would protest, pursing her lips in feigned annoyance. "You don't identify paintings with someone you like, you approach them on their own terms."

Much as Alice tolerated, and to some extent shared, Paul's interest in Jack the Ripper and all the other bad-tempered people who were the subjects of his lectures, she was not about to waste a precious day in London on a walking tour. Most likely she was gallery hopping, or hunting for dress fabric at Liberty's.

So Paul was waiting alone for the tour group to gather. He looked at his watch: 1:45. For perhaps the tenth time he took out of his coat pocket a copy of *Time Out* and reread the telegraphese advertisement:

> 1880's: East End Murders: Jack The Ripper. Meet 2pm. Tower Hill tube. £1.75. Look for red badge or carry a copy of *TO*.

From time to time Paul would flash his *Time Out*, but no red badge had so far answered his signal.

He passed the time watching the busy pedestrian traffic on Tower Hill. As an unwary tourist emerged from the mouth of the tube station, a long-tailed squirrel monkey would be clapped on his shoulder by one of four photographers who offered to snap a picture of man and beast for the old folks at home. The monkeys were dressed in two-piece knit outfits in pink-and-white stripes or other equally immodest designs. It struck Paul as remarkable how closely the styles favored by the little creatures matched those of the tourists with whom they posed. When the photos arrived home it would be hard to tell where tourist ended and monkey began: a disembodied dark-faced homunculus would seem to be hovering in midair over the shoulder of a grinning hunchback.

Paul wondered which of the people who filled the benches of Tower Hill or were crowded around the ice cream and souvenir stands might prove to be his tour companions when the magic hour of 2:00 struck. His speculations were interrupted when an orderly troop of boy scouts streamed out of the tube station. Oh, no, groaned Paul, they can't be here for the Ripper walk! He was reassured when they were marched through the square toward the steps that led down to the Tower of London across the road. They would spend a wholesome afternoon with their nation's history; instead of retracing the scenes of Jack's slaughters, they would visit the pleasant green where Anne Boleyn was beheaded.

In the midst of the square, Paul finally spotted some of his companions: three fair-haired young men in woolen jackets and jeans who held copies of *Time Out* at stiffly extended arm's length. In a few moments others rallied one by one to their standard. First to join them were an enormous man whose round face was circled by a piratical red beard, and a tall, elderly man with a slight limp that he tried to disguise with a vigorous, thrusting walk. Paul next caught sight of a trio of women, who stood slightly apart from the men. One was a tweedy middle-aged woman with an imperious, not to say imperial manner, which may have been enhanced by the boxy purse that hung from her arm. Paul guessed that she had come in from the suburbs on the pretext of a visit to Harrod's (he noticed the distinctive gold-lettered olive shopping bag in her other hand) but that she had quickly sneaked away from the store to join this faintly disreputable tour. She was conversing politely with a pleasant-looking woman with large rimless glasses and heavy gray hair brushed straight back behind her ears. Close by them, but apparently ignored by both, was a young blonde in a black leather miniskirt and a voluminous matching jacket with fantastically overstuffed shoulders. Paul thought that if she was waging a solo campaign for the return of the miniskirt, she was making a very persuasive case.

He looked again at his watch. It was 2:00. As he got up to join the group, he was passed by a slightly built man who was hurrying out of the tube station. The man had fine brown hair combed from side to side to hide a bald spot. He had a sandy mustache that drooped over a receding chin, and his watery eyes blinked weakly behind gold-rimmed glasses. Damned if he isn't the image of Hawley Harvey Crippen! Paul thought. But the man wore a red badge. He was their guide.

As if his arrival had been a prearranged signal, it began to rain again.

•

The guide invited the group to take temporary shelter in the lobby of the tube station while he sold them their tour tickets. As if they had been saving their last ounce of energy for the walk, about half a dozen bedraggled, raincoated figures at last eased themselves from benches where they had been waiting inconspicuously, and trailed the procession indoors.

Paul stood at the end of the ticket queue because he had a personal request to make and didn't want to interrupt the collection of money from the others. He was an amateur criminologist, he told the tour leader after he had paid for his ticket, and on his return to New York he planned to lecture about the tour at his book club. Could the guide give him his name and telephone number, so that he could call him if he found his tour notes were muddled (or soaked through) when he got back to his hotel room? Under the impatient glares of the waiting group, the guide took a printed card out of his billfold, held its edges fastidiously between thumb and index finger as if to avoid leaving a fingerprint, and handed it without comment to Paul. He then turned to address the tour members: "Now, ladies and gentlemen, we are ready to begin our Ripper walk. My name is Frank Collins. For the benefit of those among you who are already accomplished Ripperologists, I should explain that the tour itinerary is arranged in accordance with a geographical rather than a chronological scheme. We shall visit three of the murder sites—one in Aldgate and two in Spitalfields."

"What!" exploded the English giant with the pirate's beard. "Do you mean to say that we're not going to Buck's Row and Berner Street?"

"I'm afraid not, sir," Collins responded in a tone somewhere between passable courtesy and indifference. "That would be a long walk indeed. Those sites are within the territory of my colleague who leads a walk at 7:30 this evening from the Whitechapel tube. It's called 'The London of Jack the Ripper.' You might like to join that excursion as well."

Indignation was beginning to turn the "pirate's" face the color of his beard. Paul thought he saw the word *refund* forming on the angry man's lips. Why is it that I find it so much harder to express consumer outrage than the English? he wondered. A few years ago Alice and he had gone to the Coliseum to watch Hans Werner Henze conduct his opera *The Bassarids*. The performance did not begin on time, and finally a diffident junior manager stepped before the curtain. He announced that the installation of the set was being delayed by industrial action on the part of the stage crew. He was still in mid-sentence when a tall gentleman, with the commanding mien of a C. Aubrey Smith, rose in wrath and held two ticket stubs aloft in a V for Victory sign. "Money back!" he shouted twice, and stormed out toward the box office.

But the red-bearded Ripper expert decided to settle for the three sites, and the leader continued his introductory comments. The man's a docent, Paul decided contemptuously; he's learned his whole speech by rote.

". . . The years go by, but somewhere in a dark corner of the English psyche, it is always the autumn of 1888, when the Ripper stalked his prey in the fog-bound streets and byways of the East End."

What tripe! Paul wrote in his notebook. But if he had been more honest with himself, he would have remembered having spouted similar nonsense in his own lectures. He had, however, at least emphasized to his audience that the "fog" traditionally claimed to have obscured Jack's murder scenes was pure invention. The Ripper had generally chosen brightly lit locales, as if he were flirting with discovery.

Frank Collins shepherded the weather-defying walkers back into Trinity Square, and the tour began. Paul meticulously charted their route in his notebook. Turning their backs on the Tower, they walked north up Cooper's Row and Lloyd's Avenue toward Fenchurch Street. When they reached this busy thoroughfare, they pursued its eastern course to Aldgate, where the group, following Frank's lead, dodged across the road. Running to the northwest was a street with a name that bore a bloody memory of Jack the Ripper: Mitre Street. On the eastern side of the street they reached their first destination, Mitre Square, a small cobblestoned courtyard, perhaps twenty by thirty yards in size. It was bounded by a modern office building and the red brick school of the Sir John Cass Foundation, established by a London alderman in the early eighteenth century for the poor of the East End. It was long after the schoolchildren were safe in their beds that Jack the Ripper, in the square below, claimed his fourth victim, Catherine Eddowes, in the early hours of a Sunday morning. This was the Ripper's most daring attack, for Mitre Square, lined on two sides by tea warehouses and by far the busiest and most respectable of the locales chosen by the murderer, was patrolled by a policeman every fifteen minutes.

As they stood in the middle of the courtyard under a light drizzle, Collins gave a reasonably accurate version of the strange fate that had brought Kate Eddowes at last across the path of the murderer. At nineteen, after being educated at a London charity school much like the one that stood as silent witness to the Mitre Square atrocity, she had run off with a soldier, to whom she bore three children. In time the couple broke up, and Kate supported herself on the streets of the Spitalfield slums. Occasionally she would choose a more honest occupation, such as hop picking in Kent in the summer of 1888. It is remarkable that she could have sustained such arduous exercise, for an autopsy showed her to be suffering from such an advanced stage of Bright's disease that, even had she eluded the Ripper, she could not have lived on for more than a year. Collins added a curious anecdote offered the police by a market porter named John Kelly, who had lived with Kate for the last seven years of her life. She had told him that she knew the Ripper by sight.

Collins paused for dramatic effect. He had obviously been trained by the tour agency to milk this doubtful tale for all it was worth.

"Who knows? Perhaps when Kate made this boast to Kelly, she was signing her own death warrant. There was nothing in the porter's life to impress his mates at the local when they traded stories over a beer or gin. But suppose he told them one night that the woman he lived with knew Jack the Ripper. And suppose further that they passed the word along to the company in another tavern, and that in their midst, listening silently, was a stranger—we've been told what he must have looked like—a rather tall man, with a dark complexion, and a partiality to deerstalker caps, like his celebrated fictional contemporary, Sherlock Holmes. He remembered Kate Eddowes, or Kate Kelly, as she called herself. He knew her address, and he bided his time."

Mitre Square itself was much as it had been in the late nineteenth century, except that the three-story boarding house where the prostitute Catherine Eddowes had lived was gone. Paul was struck, as he had often been before in visiting the scene of a famous murder, by how little the spirit of evil seemed to linger in the place. Frank Collins did his best to conjure up the horror that the name of the discreet square had once evoked. He quoted a popular rumor that Catherine Eddowes's body was found at the precise spot where, in 1530, a woman had been murdered by a mad monk named Brother Martin.

The tour group, having passed through the square, filed two abreast through St. James Passage, which led into Dukes Place. On the left side of the passage was the Village Snack Bar, perhaps the modern successor, Collins said, of one of Jack's evening haunts. It was along this passageway that Police Constable Edward Watkins came, not suspecting anything unusual until his bull's-eye lantern picked out Eddowes's lifeless body, her slashed throat and frightfully mutilated face. None of these facts, as Collins recounted them, were new to the bearded Ripper buff, and so, to the mounting irritation of the rest of the group, he insisted on adding details of his own to their guide's narrative. The tall, elderly man with whom he had been standing on Tower Hill abruptly strode out of earshot, and seemed to make his point: the Ripper expert fell silent, and Collins resumed control.

Collins led the walkers back to Aldgate High Street. The group was closely bunched around their leader, except the three young men in blue jeans, who lagged somewhat behind. One of them seemed to be taking notes on the events in Mitre Square. The Ripper aficionado, attempting to recover from his recent setback, prattled on about Kate Eddowes's private life. When it became clear that nobody was listening, he sulked and tugged at his beard. The main body of the tourists did not seem to be taking Jack the Ripper very seriously.

They were in a holiday mood, chatting lightly with whichever of the group's members happened to be at their side as the line of march changed. Paul noticed that the rather elegant gray-haired woman with the rimless glasses had long since lost the tweedy suburbanite in the crowd and had become the center of attention of a number of the men. The miniskirted beauty, not to be outdone, had quite attached herself to Collins, demonstrating wide-eyed appreciation of his every word.

When they passed the foot of Middlesex Street, the site of the Petticoat Lane market, Paul wondered where they were being taken. Ahead was the western beginning of Whitechapel Road, but Collins had said they would not see the sites in the Whitechapel district, whose name was synonymous with the Ripper's crimes. Paul had not brought a map or any of his Ripper books and was close to losing his bearings. A firm sense of direction was not one of his endowments. Alice had already threatened not to let him out of their room at the Piccadilly Hotel unless he bought a compass. He was flattered: the woman to whom he had been married for more than twenty years wanted to see him again.

Just as Paul started to ask him about their route, Collins turned left and headed north along Goulston Street. Paul now knew where they were going. The next stop would be the most dreadful scene of all, the infamous Miller's Court.

•

They came to a halt at the corner of White's Row. Before them rose a huge multistory car park, which had ruthlessly obliterated the street's Victorian past.

"Here the Ripper's final victim, the beautiful Mary Jane Kelly, met her gruesome death," Collins told them.

Why are all female victims always "beautiful"? Paul entered in his notebook. He always made one exception from this skeptical appraisal: the Rubenesque young prostitute Mary Paterson, whom Burke and Hare murdered and sold as an anatomical subject when they ran out of graves to rob. Her body was so beautiful that artists congregated at the medical school to make sketches. Unfortunately for her killers, one of the medical students who also came for a look recognized Mary, and had good reason to know that she had only a few nights before been in the full bloom of vitality.

When Paul's mind returned from its wanderings (he really had a soft spot in his heart for Mary Paterson), Collins was well into his story.

"Miller's Court was no more than a narrow passage between the house backs. Leonard Matters, one of the first writers on Jack the Ripper, visited the place before it was torn down. He described it as a 'dirty, damp and dismal hovel, with boarded-up windows and a padlocked door, as though the place had not been occupied since the crime was committed.'

"The murder of Mary Kelly was the only crime of the Ripper's that was committed indoors. It was a butchery almost without parallel in the history of crime—as if Jack, having for once no fear of interruption, could plumb the very depths of his sadism."

The suburban lady deftly made her way to the front of the group. Something had piqued her curiosity.

"Mr. Collins," she asked, "was Mary Kelly related to Catherine Eddowes's John Kelly?" Genealogy was obviously another one of her passions.

"I understand it's not an uncommon name in Ireland," the disaffected Ripper buff said sourly from the fringe of the group before the guide could reply. But Collins ignored him.

"You raise an interesting point, madam. There has been considerable speculation about a possible link between the two last victims. The problem is further complicated by the fact that Kate Eddowes sometimes was known as Mary Ann Kelly.

"Let me tell you what we do know about the Ripper's final victim. Born in Limerick, Mary Kelly was much younger than the other women murdered by Jack, probably about twenty-five years old. She was a tall woman with blue eyes and dark hair that fell in profusion to her waist, accounting for her nickname, 'Black Mary.' We are told that she plied her trade not far from here, outside the Ten Bells pub in Commercial Street, and was such a terror at hair pulling that competitors were disinclined to poach on her territory."

He paused for a moment. Paul thought he was making a rapid assessment of whether he was holding his audience's attention. The rain was beginning to come down harder and some of the group were becoming restive; spirits were beginning to be affected by the inclement afternoon. In fact, a brief dispute broke out between a tall, slender couple among the raincoated figures who had made up the rear guard that had mustered when Collins appeared at Tower Hill. The woman kept repeating the same phrase in an angry tone; it seemed to Paul that if he strained he could almost make out her words, but they eluded him as if muffled by the heavy air.

In quest of a reassuring smile, Collins looked about for the leggy blonde who had been his most devoted listener by far. But for the moment she seemed to have fallen back in the ranks; her place at his side had been taken by the three sober young men in blue jeans. Perhaps the girl's interest had been blunted by Collins's rhapsodizing about the charms of the raven-tressed Mary Kelly.

Giving up his search for his fickle devotee, Collins continued his tale of Mary Kelly's brief life.

"Mary Kelly, like all the other prostitutes on her Dorset

Street beat, had lived in fear of Jack the Ripper. Illiterate herself, she had a costermonger read her all the newspaper articles on the Ripper murders, and despite the fact that she was a celebrated street brawler among the women, she shuddered.

"Black Mary was last seen alive at eleven-forty-five on Thursday night, 8 November, by one of her competitors, the widow Cox. Mary was in the company of a thirty-eight-year-old man who had a mottled complexion and a reddish mustache and was carrying two pails of beer. When the widow saw the couple enter Mary's miserable room in Miller's Court, she heard the girl singing a sentimental ballad of her homeland, 'Only a Violet I Pluck From My Mother's Grave.'

"That night, as I daresay you will not be surprised to hear, it rained intermittently. The next day was to be the occasion of a double celebration in London, since it was both the date of the Lord Mayor's Show and the birthday of the Prince of Wales. At about ten in the morning, while preparations for the Lord Mayor's procession were at a feverish pitch, a chandler named McCarthy sent an assistant to Miller's Court to collect Mary Kelly's overdue rent. The messenger found her door locked, but peering through a crack in the windowpane, he saw a horrible sight."

As Collins was about to embark on a description of the dismemberment of Mary Kelly, Paul Prye walked a little way off under the pretext of examining a building facade. It was only in the 1970s that the police photographs of the Ripper's victims had at last been generally published. Paul still did not understand why publication had been necessary, since generations of readers had been quite content to exercise their own imaginations on the lurid details left by Victorian journalists. Yet there was a morbid side to the fascination with crime; Paul would have been the last one to deny it. When, many years ago, he had taken part in a group tour of the Black Museum at Scotland Yard, he was astonished to learn that the grand finale of each visit was a display of photographs of the victims of the most notorious atrocities of the day. Paul had hidden ignominiously behind one of the display cases while the pictures were passed around. This squeamishness had made Paul a figure of fun at his book club. The president had said of one of Paul's lectures that "there was a good deal of analysis in it, and very little blood." Though reluctant to admit it, Paul had preferred this mocking critique to the highest praise.

When Collins had completed his survey of Mary Kelly's remains, as if he were counting the shards at an archeological dig, it was time to walk on to the final site. Collins led them east along White's Row until they reached the corner of Commercial Street, where they turned north. Just as they reached the Spitalfields Market, there was a sudden cloudburst with a dramatic accompaniment of thunder. Collins brought them into the entranceway of the market, where they huddled, waiting for the storm to pass over. Here, ignoring the unfriendly looks and unceremonious elbows of porters who waded through the group carrying bushels of the hard green apples Paul loved to buy on the streets of London, Collins told them about the Ripper's second victim, Annie Chapman, who was murdered only a short distance away in Hanbury Street. It seemed to Paul a disservice to Annie to recount her murder so soon after the supreme horror of Miller's Court, for the life and death of every murder victim should be respected as unique, and yet Annie's tragedy, presented out of order for the convenience of Collins's route, could not fail to come as an anticlimax, not to say a disappointment. Ironically, the two women's nicknames almost seemed to mark them as rivals: Kelly was "Black Mary" to friends and clients, and Chapman was always "Dark Annie." A forty-seven-year-old widow, Annie prided herself on her respectable past as the wife of a veterinary surgeon, whom she tended to turn into a doctor when she was in an expansive mood. Her claims to bourgeois propriety gave her at least one posthumous advantage over the Ripper's other victims: some writers denied that she was a prostitute. But the neighborhood where she lived suggested otherwise, despite the fact that she supplemented her earnings on the street with the sale of matchboxes and artificial flowers.

Collins told them that when one of Annie's female friends saw her on Friday, 7 September 1888, she was shocked to see how ill she looked. Annie explained that she had not eaten or had a cup of tea all day. Later the landlord of the dubious establishment in which she lived, at No. 35 Dorset Street, saw her sitting by the fire. When he asked her whether she wasn't going up to bed, she replied that she had no money. This brought the landlord's show of sympathy to an abrupt end; if she did not find the money somewhere, he told her, she would have to move on. She took to the streets in the early morning, and near daybreak, a market porter (almost an inevitable figure in the Ripper murders) found her body in the backyard of the building at No. 29 Hanbury Street.

By the time Collins had traced this murder story to its end, the rain had stopped again.

Paul finished a note on Annie Chapman and looked up to see that the walkers were about to cross Commercial Street and that he must leave the shelter of the market to catch up with them. They were already massed at the curb and Collins, circumspect as ever, was surveying the traffic before beckoning to his charges to proceed. As he raised his hand in signal to them to follow, something went terribly wrong—in fact, a succession of things.

First it was only the sounds that Paul's ears painfully registered without comprehension of their source or direction: a chain of sputtering explosions that became a steady, abrasive roar. Then a nightmarish vision took shape, in which some details were preternaturally clear: a blindingly bright Cyclopean eye, a swelling metallic body of deep crimson striped with black like the pelt of a bloodshot tiger. The scattered impressions suddenly coalesced into a realization of danger. A motorcycle streaked up the street and veered without warning toward the front ranks of the group, missing contact by the narrowest of margins as it swerved to avoid them at the last instant. Before the driver righted his course, a number of the tourists—their arms flailing as they were tripped or pushed down in the panic-stricken crush of bodies and limbs—had fallen back against the curb or into the street. For a moment they lay stunned and strangely silent, as the bike roared off, until a faint cry was heard from among them, as if in an afterthought of pain. One by one, they disentangled themselves like the separating heads of a wounded hydra. To Paul's immense relief, they all were soon back on their feet, showing no signs of serious injury.

The more leisurely walkers, like Paul, who had been well out of the rider's path, drew back a respectful distance to allow their companions to regain their composure; many of them were still recovering in their own private ways from shock and bewilderment. Among those who had had a narrow escape was Frank Collins. An impassive man, he seemed to show little effect of the accident, except that at some point in his fall or in the melee of bodies he had lost his official red badge. Paul also noticed the giant Ripper specialist ostentatiously dusting off his knees and staring resentfully at Collins. His unspoken words of reproach were as palpable as if encircled by a comic-strip balloon above his now disheveled head: "What do you expect to happen to you on a second-rate Ripper tour that doesn't even go into Whitechapel?" Nearby, Paul spotted the slim raincoated couple comforting each other in a tender manner that to his old-fashioned mind indicated marriage; their recent quarrel in White's Row, whatever had sparked it, was now forgotten in their close brush with disaster.

The sociable gray-haired woman had been the last to rise from the street. She picked up her rimless glasses from the curbside; remarkably, they were undamaged. But she obviously had been the most shaken by the near catastrophe. Lightly rubbing her right thigh, she glared down the street where the cyclist had disappeared from view. "The damn fool almost hit me," she said in a strangled voice.

Frank Collins was completely at a loss. He evidently was not prepared by training or disposition to cope with anything that was not planned in advance in the tour agenda, and how could anyone, even if more resourceful than he, have dealt gracefully with this dangerous mishap? Paul, in fact, rather admired the way he tried to take up the frayed thread of his lecture.

"I am very sorry, indeed, that this reckless cyclist has given us all a fright, but I take it that no one has suffered any permanent damage, except possibly a few more gray hairs." Paul cringed a little at Collins's choice of words as he watched the pleasant middle-aged woman (had he heard someone call her Margaret?) polish her miraculously surviving glasses. "If you're willing to continue, I'm quite certain we can now cross the street in safety to look at Hanbury Street, and to talk about the mysterious fate of Jack the Ripper." But Margaret (yes, Paul was quite sure he had heard her addressed by that name) had

had enough. In a distinctly Bostonian accent, she asked Collins if he would be good enough to find her a taxi. They walked off together down Commercial Street, while the remainder of the group waited at the corner of Hanbury Street. Paul noticed that on the north side of the street, where Annie Chapman's body had been found, commercial buildings had, like the car park in White's Row, shouldered aside all memories of the past, but the houses across the way did not appear greatly changed in their depressing aspect from the days and nights of poor Annie.

In a few minutes, Paul Collins returned alone. He conscientiously completed his script, telling them of the many attempts to unriddle the mystery of Jack the Ripper's identity. Was he a mad lawyer, the Duke of Clarence, a Jewish ritual butcher whose love for his profession had gone awry, or a transvestite midwife who killed to cover up for a botched delivery? As a good feminist, Paul was more than willing to cede England's most famous crimes to a woman. But the list of suspects Collins had reeled off for the walkers was hopelessly out of date. He had left out one of the latest theories that was among Paul's favorites, despite the fact that it resembled some of the elaborate puns he would sometimes try out on Alice only to be told that they were "complicated, but not good." The new hypothesis, broached a decade ago by Joseph Sickert, son of the painter Walter Sickert, attributed the murders to Sir William Gull, physician to Queen Victoria and the Royal Family. According to Sickert, Gull's slaughter of Mary Kelly, with the assistance of a brutal coachman, was part of a cover-up of a surreptitious marriage of the Duke of Clarence to Ann Elizabeth Crook, a girl in a tobacconist's shop in the Cleveland Street area that housed the notorious male brothel supposedly frequented by the duke. Gull, Sickert claimed, had secretly committed Ann Elizabeth to an asylum until her death in 1921. Mary Kelly, a servant girl, who had had the misfortune of witnessing the wedding, was cruelly dispatched at Miller's Court. But why would Gull have dealt so violently with the witness and spared the bride? And how did this high-society conspiracy explain the Ripper's earlier murders? When Paul ended his murder lectures with riddles like these, there was only one fully satisfactory solution—to escape from the podium before the question period could begin.

When the tour was over, Paul felt more keenly than ever before his most glaring failure: he was better at asking questions than answering them.

•

Alice Prye gave Paul a distracted greeting when he returned to their hotel room. She had not removed her poplin rainhat and her coat was still draped from her shoulders; she squinted intently down at the bed cover where she had neatly overlapped the day's purchases of Chinese fabrics—slubbed silks of red, plum, and dull green; black faille; and a gold brocade of an exotic pattern with dragons or their next of kin.

Paul said, "You seem to have done pretty well for yourself. Happy birthday!" It was a standing joke between them, but they were both such avid shoppers that neither was in a very good position to complain about the other's extravagance. Their shared self-indulgence was also favored by the happy coincidence that they were both spoiled children of prosperous stockbrokers.

"I've had a lovely day!" Alice exclaimed, her voice rising with the characteristic enthusiasm she brought both to shopping and art scholarship. "Would you believe it? I've found every fabric I need for my kimono at Liberty's." It was going to be one of Alice's most bizarre creations. "The red and green are for the sleeves, and the plum's in the middle."

Alice ran on about her plans for the kimono. Suddenly she became aware that Paul didn't seem to be listening. She broke off, and asked him, "How did you do today?"

"I think I was a witness to a murder attempt."

Alice said brightly, "Then you've had a *lovely* day too.

The theater season in London was unusually thin, and the Pryes had never had so much difficulty making up their evening programs. There was, of course, the mandatory long-running British sex farce intended primarily for the American tourist. The present offering, which had transferred the usual bedhoppings to a Mormon setting, was titled *Hanky Hanky Hanky Panky*. Paul and Alice had little difficulty in deciding to pass it up. *The Mousetrap* was still playing, as it would until the Day of Judgment, when not only the play's murderer but everyone who has ever lived would be pronounced guilty. The Pryes had never seen a professional performance of the play, but had suffered through many community-theater productions in the United States. Alice kept insisting that some year they must see it in London, but, as always, this was not to be the year.

It was, therefore, to quite a different show that they rushed breathlessly upon Paul's return from the walking tour. He had not taken the time to change his clothes, which embarrassed him hugely, for Alice had put on one of her antique beaded dresses and was turning heads from the moment they emerged from the lift. The show they had chosen was the new musical by Andrew Lloyd Webber, the smash-hit successor to *Cats* and *Starlight Express*. So far as the distracted Paul had been able to gather from the first act, there was not a single human character in the play. All the performers were playing the parts of pencil sharpeners and other pieces of office equipment. Between musical numbers, Paul whispered to Alice: "Cats, trains, and plug-compatible computer equipment. What next?"

Alice was always inclined to take a longer historical view. "It's really very Victorian, darling," she whispered back. "Remember the lovesong of the magnet and the churn in *Patience?*"

Now it was the interval and Alice, who had a very orderly mind, was at last ready to talk about the "murder attempt."

"Tell me the story from the beginning and don't leave anything out," she insisted. One of her constant complaints about Paul was that he was always impatient to get to the main point. When he would come home like a happy terrier with a bloody piece of faculty gossip in his mouth, she would always slow him up by saying that before he told her his news, he must recall for her in detail how his informant "managed to bring up the subject."

She also made it plain to Paul that she intended to make her own judgment on the events of the walking tour. "No editorializing, please," she demanded. "You can do that later, at the book club."

Compliantly, Paul gave her an unadorned account of what had happened in Commercial Street. When he finished, he could read disappointment in her face; Alice was much too vivacious to have played a good hand at poker. "I wish I could show more enthusiasm for your afternoon adventure," she told him. "It doesn't strike me as anything out of the ordinary. Do you remember the TV talk show you watched last week in Paris?" Paul was fighting a perennial losing battle to improve his French on their short trips abroad and was perfectly willing to listen to any trivia on television as long as the speakers talked reasonably slowly and avoided the subjunctive. Alice, who had no difficulty with the language, was amused by his ineffective training sessions. She continued: "The host was leading a public campaign against mopeds and was showing charts with shocking statistics on pedestrian injuries. You've probably forgotten because for you it was just a free Berlitz lesson. Therefore, when you come close to witnessing just the kind of accident that's happening all over Europe, you jump to the conclusion that the motorcyclist was trying to kill somebody."

Paul shook his head more in sorrow than in anger. "The trouble is, obedient as ever, I've told you the story without 'editorializing.' All I have to show for my submissiveness is that you've completely missed the point. The man was a reckless idiot and has no business being on the road. But he didn't try to kill anybody."

"Then what does that do to your 'murder attempt'?"

"If you had been listening more carefully instead of jumping to your own conclusions, I think that would have been obvious to you from the start. One of the walkers—I wish I knew who and why—tried to push Margaret into the path of the motorcycle."

Alice shook her head. "You poor deluded man, I see that we really must discuss this later or you will never get to sleep tonight."

For the time being they had to break off the conversation; the bell had rung and the audience was returning to take their seats. It was hard for Paul and Alice to switch their minds back to the show, but they did their best. As the curtain rose, a pair of amorous pencil sharpeners appeared on stage to sing a duet that had become a runaway best-seller on records. Paul bent forward to listen, but did not completely trust his ears. He believed, though, that he had just experienced something new in London lyrics: a couplet in which "cravings" was rhymed with "shavings."

It was while waiting for their after-theater dinner that they came back to the subject of the walking tour. They sat virtually alone at a small table on the second floor of Wheeler's, having given their customary order for Dover sole Capri. They supposed that this was probably the gastronomic equivalent of *The Mousetrap*, but no rigorous gourmet was watching them and they really did like the chutney and bananas—probably more than England's in-offensive national fish. "Let's look at it sensibly," Alice began. "What makes you think Margaret was pushed?"

"Because I saw it happen."

"How is that possible? I thought you were lagging be-hind keeping up with your precious notes."

"I had finished my last lines on Annie Chapman and when I looked up I saw that the group was getting ready to cross Commercial Street. I was starting to catch up with them."

"And how far behind them were you when the motor-cycle just missed them?"

"Probably several yards."

"But how could you have seen Margaret at all? By your account, you must have had well over a dozen people in the tour, and they must have been pretty well bunched around Collins."

Paul thought for a moment and shook his head. "No, I don't think I was the only straggler. I think a few others had lingered with me in the market. One of them was the limping man I mentioned. You know, Alice, I wish I knew their names. I'm beginning to make this sound like a Sherlock Holmes story: 'The Adventure of the Limping Man.'"

The idea appealed to the mystery reader in Alice.

"I'm glad they're anonymous. Don't you see that if you're right about what happened (and I don't for a moment admit that you are), you have stumbled into a real-life version of the classic Agatha Christie murder setting. She brings together a dozen assorted personages for dinner at an isolated mansion. But, of course, we're told precisely who the house guests are. There is the retired colonel home from India service, the irresponsible flapper (rather anachronistic, I think, when we get past the Second World War), and the swarthy fellow up to no good whom Anthony Shaffer has endearingly called the 'Oily Levantine.' You've been to an Agatha Christie party with a difference—you don't know anyone's name (except perhaps Margaret), and if you were your usual absentminded self, you probably can't even tell me what anybody looked like. It would be a wonderful murder case. How I wish it had actually happened."

She held up a monitory finger to signal that she intended to keep the floor. "Well, let's recapitulate what you've said. You were a few yards away from the scene. You think that maybe a few walkers were trailing behind with you, so let's give you the benefit of the doubt. I'll assume that there wasn't such a crowding at the curb that it would have been impossible for you to spot Margaret. By the way, how did you happen to pick her out?"

"I think that it must have been her glossy gray hair. She was one of the few women in the group brave enough to go bareheaded."

"I'm beginning to get the feeling you're giving me only part of the story. You probably thought she was pretty. You know how I can't leave you for a moment at a cocktail party without finding you in deep conversation with the best-looking woman in the room. But I'll scold you about that in the morning. Let's assume, as I say, that you could have made her out as she walked off the curb. If everything happened so suddenly—the unexpected boom of the motor, the speeding motorcyclist, and then your Margaret in an ungainly heap with the others—how in the world could you have stood there calmly, senses all alert, and distinctly seen her pushed at just the right instant? Or I guess I should say *almost* the right instant, since the lucky woman escaped."

"I wish I had a good answer for you, Alice, but I don't. It was like an image in a dream that I can recall with great precision the next morning but can't hope to explain." Paul was not sure he was getting through to Alice, for though he had very vivid dreams that he could recount to her at breakfast with abundant detail, she either slept dreamlessly or had a gift of oblivion.

Since Alice was no dreamer, Paul added a footnote from her world of art. "It seemed to me like a moment borrowed from surrealism. What I find most dreamlike about Dali's melting clock is not that the clock is melting, though I don't suppose clocks usually become liquescent in temperate climates. It is that the clock is outlined so sharply and becomes the center of our vision, when in real life we'd never give it a look unless we needed to know the time; it would stand or hang in a room as an indistinct object while our thoughts were focused elsewhere.

"Well, it was a little bit like that at the moment the motorcycle charged the walkers. At first, the noise and sight of the oncoming cycle held me frozen, but only for an instant. Without my being aware that I'd adjusted my focus, the foreground of the scene asserted itself. In the midst of the mass of bodies at the curb my eyes unreasonably seized on a single isolated detail: an arm thrusting Margaret forward.

"This isn't the first time I've had this kind of experience. Do you remember the collision between the commuter train and the car at the crossing in Brookline when we lived there? I had just gotten off the train and was walking toward the traffic light ahead. A car was turning left across the tracks when the train went past the red signal light and hit it broadside.

"Now it might easily have been asked on that occasion, since the accident had happened with such startling suddenness, how could I be certain that the light had not turned green? In fact, you'll remember I was asked that quite effectively in cross-examination when I testified for the car driver in traffic court. The prosecutor had a lot of other good questions for me as well. Why was I looking at the light while I was walking along the track? Where was the light located? Was the pedestrian crosswalk of cement or wood? Although we had already lived for ten years only a block and a half from that crossing, I could not answer a single one of those questions. Yet of one thing I was positive: the train had crashed the red light and negligently caused the collision.

"Even though you'd do just as good a job cross-examining me on what I saw at the curb of Commercial Street, and how I could see it standing where I was, I am equally certain that what I told you really happened: someone tried to push Margaret under the wheels of that motorcycle."

"You still haven't convinced me," Alice said. "But let me argue with you when we get home. Your Dover sole is getting cold."

The Pryes had a nightcap when they returned to their room. Paul did his usual bartending with the plastic travel bottles of scotch and vodka that they carried on their travels in a little brown canvas bag carrying the legend EXECUTIVE LUNCH. As soon as he handed Alice her vodka, she returned to the charge.

"Your problem is that you just haven't read enough Agatha Christie. If you had, you would realize that at Commercial Street you fell for just the kind of illusion that made her famous. Time and again in her books you see something take place in full view (which is more than you could have had, no matter how hard you try to persuade me otherwise). But despite the fact that when you read her or see her plays you witness everything that's happened, you completely misinterpret it because your judgment is clouded by psychological preconceptions."

Sipping his scotch, Paul had become mellower than he'd felt since the Ripper walk had taken its dangerous turning. He was in a mood to hear Alice out to the end of her argument. "For the uninitiated, could you supply an example?"

Alice couldn't have been happier to comply. "Captain Hastings, looking out on the street below Hercule Poirot's window, sees a richly dressed young woman being shadowed by three men and a middle-aged woman. They have been joined by an errand boy who points after the young girl, gesticulating as he does so. Describing the scene to the detective, Hastings poses what seem to him to be the only two alternative solutions to the melodrama down on the street. Is the girl a crook, and are the shadowers detectives preparing to arrest her? Or are the pursuers scoundrels planning to attack an innocent victim? In fact, as Poirot quickly recognizes, neither of these thrilling solutions is correct; the young woman is, instead, a famous actress being followed by a crowd of fans who have recognized her."

Paul liked the story but still managed to look insulted. "I don't see what resemblance that anecdote has to my experience today. In the scene you have described, nothing really happened and Hastings's problem was an overheated imagination. Men like that have no business looking out the window at all. He reminds me of what they used to say about the gossipy Viennese of the turn of the century. If they saw a man and a woman walking together on the street, they assumed they were having an affair. If they saw two men together, they assumed they were homosexuals. And if they saw a man walking alone, they concluded that he masturbated."

Alice was undaunted. "If you're not impressed with that example, I have two others that you'll have more trouble with. Case No. One. In one of Christie's plays, a young woman in full view of the audience is seen handling a poisoned cup of coffee. What conclusion are we expected to reach? Quite naturally, that she is trying to poison someone. What is the fact? That in desperation over the apparent threat of a blackmailer, she is considering taking her own life to spare her husband embarrassment."

Paul was about to protest, but Alice warded him off by making a short arc with one finger. "No, you're not playing fair. Let me give you my last story. Two children, A and B, are involved in a violent quarrel. A beats B's head against the ground, and their mother, coming upon them, trembles and says, 'That is dangerous.' What does an onlooker make of the mother's comment? Isn't it obvious? What is dangerous is that A may do B a serious injury by beating his head against the ground. But it turns out that the mother meant just the opposite: that B has a lot of pent-up hostility and that A would do well not to incite him to retaliation. Ultimately, B turns out to be a murderer."

Despite the fact that he was well on his way through a second scotch, Paul threw his eyes up to the ceiling, one of his stylized signals of marital despair. Alice was quick to deal with this familiar show of resistance. She went on:

"I can see you're getting impatient with me, Paul. But if I'm not worth listening to, learn from Agatha Christie. It is very easy for the eyewitness to confuse the actor with the person who is being acted upon and to infer hostility when it either does not exist at all or may reside elsewhere."

Paul started taking off his tie, a discreet hint that he hoped his day was almost over. "Now I've listened both to you and to Agatha Christie. Would you mind telling me how I misread the simple fact that someone pushed Margaret and came close to getting her killed?"

"I'm not criticizing you, Paul, because I know you believe what you've told me. But I think you've arrived at the least plausible conclusion without considering the alternatives. And why? Simply because of one of your most endearing traits: you're really very protective of women. You think you see a woman pushed and the first explanation that pops into your mind is that someone must be trying to harm her with malice aforethought. By the way, Paul, do you realize that we have been talking about this case on and off for more than three hours and you still haven't told me whether Margaret was pushed by a man or a woman?"

Paul had thrown his tie aside but made no further progress in undressing. He was going to have to let her finish, that was plain, no matter how long it took. Refilling her glass, he answered, "The reason I haven't told you is that I don't have the slightest idea. Nothing has done as much for unisex as the raincoat. I simply saw a hand thrust forward from the sleeve of a raincoat."

"All right," she said, "we'll come back to that later." How much later? Paul wondered, wincing, but Alice pursued her thought. "In any event, a woman, you've said, was pushed. To you, it is therefore self-evident that she was an intended victim. And yet there are at least three other possibilities, two considerably more likely and one at least no more fanciful."

"Let's have the last first," Paul said perversely.

"Well, if you must find hostility somewhere, isn't it conceivable that the person you saw colliding with Margaret was in turn pushed from behind by the real assailant, and that the walker you've branded a criminal was, in fact, the intended victim? Did you have a good enough view that you can rule that out?"

Paul shrugged in half concession.

Satisfied by the lack of opposition, Alice continued. "Of course not, but in fact I don't think my more complicated version of the murder attempt happened either. Most likely, the person you thought you saw pushing Margaret merely put out a hand to break his or her own fall as the crowd of tourists stumbled against each other. But if you must have an explanation that provides at least a small measure of the melodrama on which you seem to insist, I would suggest to you a third possibility: that the arm you saw thrust in Margaret's direction was intended to push her to safety when the motorcyclist rushed past. In other words, what you saw as hostility might have been an instinctual rescue attempt, just like Agatha Christie's trick with the poisoned coffee cup."

The Pryes declared an armistice while Paul refilled their drinks once again. He had the feeling it was going to be a long night indeed.

It was Alice who was first to return to the offensive. "You know, Paul, I'm beginning to feel that I have not persuaded you in the least."

"You're right."

"Well, there is only one way out of this quarrel. You simply must solve the mystery of the attempted Jack the Ripper walking tour murder." When he waved a hand in a dismissive gesture, she was not deterred. "For once, you're going to do something useful," she insisted. "What have you got to show so far for two decades as a student of crime? You lecture occasionally to a small room sparsely peopled with aggressive and highly competitive book collectors, who don't give a damn about your interests and are licking their chops waiting to tear into you during the question period. And we have a library double-stacked from floor to ceiling with crime books and pamphlets you never seem to have time to read. Believe me, Paul, I'm not going to let you off the hook easily. You blithely tell me you've seen a murder attempt only a hair's breadth away from a fatal conclusion, and you expect me to spend the rest of our married life together wondering which of us was right. You can't think I'll let you waste the rest of your stay here in the bookshops now that you finally found something important to do."

Paul protested. "You can't be serious. I haven't any idea how you go about investigating a crime, and this is certainly not one to cut my teeth on. It wasn't a successful crime in the first place. Nobody has complained. To make matters worse, I don't know the names or relationships of anybody on the scene, except that I think the victim's first name was Margaret. And I haven't the foggiest notion why anybody would have tried to do in such a pleasant and attractive woman."

"The first thing you're going to have to do is to go back to the very beginning. As usual, I've had the impression all evening that you dived into this story somewhere in the middle. For starters, when you first saw Margaret at Tower Hill, was she alone?"

"It's my memory that when I caught sight of her, she was talking to another woman dressed in tweeds from head to toe. The other woman looked English to me, and I would have guessed (without much basis) that she had probably come in from the suburbs. I certainly didn't get the impression that Margaret had come with her or that they had met before. They seemed to be talking in a politely superficial manner."

"Do you think it's possible that Margaret had come with someone else or that she arranged to meet at Tower Hill with a companion who arrived after you first noticed her?"

"Anything is possible, I suppose, but I wouldn't have any reason to think so."

"Well, you've told me that during the walk you noticed her talking vivaciously with a number of the men."

"That's how it seemed to me, but I didn't have the feeling that she had paired off with any of them. She just struck me as a very outgoing person who doesn't take very long to feel at home among strangers."

Alice shook her head. "You're really not being very helpful. I have half a notion to finish my last of many vodkas and go to bed. But let me ask you this: What was her reaction to the accident?"

Paul answered wearily, "I thought I had already told you that at the theater. Her immediate response was to look down the street where the motorcycle had disappeared and curse the 'cyclist. Then she asked the tour leader to find her a taxi and they walked away together. That was the last I saw of her."

"Did she say anything to any of the walkers before she left?"

"Not that I heard."

"Why do you suppose she left so abruptly?"

"That hardly seems to me to rank among the major mysteries of the case. She was obviously shaken by the accident and had lost her enthusiasm for the tour, which was almost over anyway. The weather was lousy, as I've told you. It surprised me that we didn't lose some of the walkers along the way, and for that matter, perhaps we did. I didn't keep count."

He made a final effort to turn her from her purpose. "Alice, you must see by now that this murder investigation of yours is out of the question. I've told you what I saw and you've obviously not impressed. I don't know where to find Margaret, and in any case she thinks she was almost run over by a reckless motorcyclist. I don't know how to contact the other tour members for their views."

"Of course you do," Alice said serenely. "All you have to do is call up the offices of *Time Out* and find out the name of the company that ran the walk. They can put you in touch with Frank Collins."

"Frank Collins; I had almost forgotten."

Paul, who had been slumping more heavily against the back of his armchair, seemed to come to life again. He jumped to his feet. "I took his card before the tour began. It was my plan to call him if I found my notes were confused and I needed more information for my lecture." He looked in his wallet but couldn't find the card, and it wasn't in the secretary he kept in his breast pocket to carry his passport and American Express checks. With both hands he vainly searched, in a kind of regular rotation, all the pockets of his sport coat and trousers.

Even at this late hour Alice could not repress a good-natured smile. Unsummoned, an image from the movies rose before her. Paul reminded her of a pantomime by Jean-Louis Barrault in *Children of Paradise*, portraying a spectator who had just been relieved of a watch by a pickpocket; Barrault's hands, just as Paul's were doing now, fluttered comically and ineffectually from pocket to pocket but could not turn up the vanished possession. Tonight's occasion was not by a long shot the first time that Paul had gone through this performance. He was always losing their claim checks at restaurants. One of his finest hours, Alice thought, was when he successfully reclaimed her fur coat at a New York City restaurant without the cloakroom ticket. It had taken literally an hour.

Once again, Paul was triumphant. He found Collins's card in his shirt pocket, and placed it on the nighttable. He knew that Alice meant business. "I'm not promising anything, you understand," he said to placate her, "but I will call Collins in the morning."

When they had gone to bed and turned out their reading lights, they lay quiet and perfectly still, too still to mean anything but what was in fact the case—that they were both thinking about the Ripper Walk.

"Darling," Alice said at last.

"Yes?"

"I hope the blonde did it." Alice had her spiteful moments.

"I'm sure you do."

"But promise me one thing. If you expect to tell the story of this mystery to your club when we get back home, you mustn't turn out to be the one who pushed Margaret."

"Why?"

"Narrator-murderers are out. Dame Agatha's already done it. *Roger Ackroyd.*"

Paul turned his back and made a determined effort to put the tour out of his mind. But he was resolved to have the last word. Quoting his favorite critic, Edmund Wilson, he murmured to Alice:

"Who cares who killed Roger Ackroyd."

· 3 ·

When Paul Prye awoke the next morning, Alice was gone. A page of hotel stationery on his bed table gave him her parting words: "I've left you for the National Gallery. Call Collins. A. P.S. Wheat Thins and Sanka are in the bathroom." Could it really be that late? Paul looked at his watch in disbelief. Ten-thirty. And yet it was no wonder. The Agatha Christie lecture had gone on into the small hours.

He picked up Collins's card with the same measure of delight he would have accorded a parking ticket pinned under his windshield wiper. Beneath the legend FRANK L. COLLINS, LONDON HISTORY WALKS appeared a residential address in Hammersmith. The place meant nothing more to Paul than a name that flashed by on the road in from Heathrow. No, there was another association, with a detective novel Alice had once pressed on him, David Frome's *The Hammersmith Murders*. Even before he opened the book, the suburb's name seemed to promise the appearance of the traditional blunt instrument.

Given the late hour, Paul decided to ring Collins at the office telephone number that appeared at the bottom of the card. He was surprised when the answering operator announced the name of an accounting firm.

"May I please speak to Frank Collins? This is Professor Paul Prye."

"Will Mr. Collins know the nature of your call?"

"I don't think so; you might mention to him that I met him yesterday afternoon and that he gave me his card." Paul was intentionally vague. He didn't know whether it was generally known at the office that their man Collins was doubling as a Ripper lecturer.

The operator persisted. "Can you tell me your first initial, please?" It appeared either that she feared Collins was about to be deluged with messages from a variety of Pryes, or that she had difficulty spelling "Paul."

"That's P as in Paul."

"Thank you. I won't be a minute."

Soon he heard Collins's voice on the line. He seemed friendly and matter-of-fact, and immediately put Paul at his ease. It did not seem to embarrass Collins at all that one of the walkers had called him at the office. As Paul gave the matter more thought, he realized that his delicacy had been misplaced: if the tour leading were a shameful secret, Collins would not have put the office number on his card.

"It's good to hear from you, Mr. Prye. I won't be a bit surprised if you tell me that your notes of yesterday are soaked through and that you can't read a word."

"It's not as bad as that, but there are a few points that I would like to clarify if you could spare me a little time."

"I'd be happy to give you whatever time you require; there's nothing I'd rather do than rattle on endlessly about Jack the Ripper. Perhaps you'd agree to come over to my office, it's quite near the Blackfriars tube station." Then, as if aware he'd been carried away by the first rush of generosity, he added, "I'd like to invite you over now, but I am expecting some clients to arrive very shortly."

"Actually, I was hoping that you might let me take you to lunch if you're not engaged."

"I wish I could say yes," Collins replied courteously, "but my meeting will take me straight through the lunch hour. However, if you could possibly come to my office at about two, I would be glad to see you. My day has started miserably and it shows no sign of getting better. By afternoon I expect that I will welcome a break.''

Paul put the receiver back on the cradle with a sense of accomplishment. Alice would be much impressed with him; he had put a foot in the door and still had five toes to show for the effort. But the first step into this amorphous inquiry was by far the easiest. How was he going to steer the conversation with Collins from Jack the Ripper to yesterday's murder that had almost, but not quite, taken place?

Paul's late awakening, combined with the early date he arranged with Collins, had left him little time to do anything productive in the morning, either as a tourist or in his newly adopted role of detective. Without knowing why, he hailed a taxi and gave the address of the Spitalfields Market. Paul ordinarily would have found some trivial subject for conversation with the driver, for despite his impression that tempers were shortening noticeably on a worldwide basis, London cabbies still struck him as a good deal friendlier than their counterparts in New York. But today he was preoccupied and rode in silence.

When he left the cab at Commercial Street, the sun was shining. He didn't suppose that under any weather conditions the street would ever be regarded as one of London's great beauty spots, but it certainly looked a lot better than yesterday. He walked to the place where his memory told him the group had left the sidewalk to cross the street. Compulsively, he aligned the tips of his shoes with the edge of the curb and rocked slightly back and forth on the balls of his feet, as if inviting the assault of an unseen assailant at his back. Neither this exercise nor any effort of will could bring him back yesterday's disorientation and loss of equilibrium—the sensations he felt on those rare occasions when his smoothly flowing life unexpectedly bent into a new channel. He did not know whether to blame his failure to recapture his agitation on the sunlight streaming into the street, on his own lack of imagination, or on the impression he had reconfirmed yesterday in Mitre Square that the aura of uncanniness does not remain very long in the scene of a crime, however infamous.

Paul turned into the market entrance where the walkers had taken shelter. To the considerable astonishment of the produce dealers, their morning customers, and the passersby in Commercial Street, he then executed an elaborate pantomime, repeated many times without variation in any detail. Into his pocket would go an invisible notebook; three times he would pat his flank to see that the book was safely stowed; then he would leave the entrance at a rapid pace, his eyes fixed ahead toward the street. As he moved forward, he remembered that he had tried to pick out Collins at the front of the group but that his susceptible eye had fallen instead on the full-bodied silver-gray hair and shapely neck of the woman they were calling Margaret. Then had come the threatening roar and chaos. He recalled now he had been blinded and deafened for a moment until all resolved itself into one distinct gesture of hostility.

At last Paul was content that he had reconstructed his precise movements at the time of the "accident," and turned to walk south along Commercial Street. He nodded vigorously to himself in the eccentric manner his friends had so often noted as a sign that he had stopped listening to them and was sealed away in his own thoughts. His present nods meant to say there was no doubt of it, he could have seen it happen. But the apparent mood of assurance that had been induced by his recent exercises at Spitalfields Market masked a reservation that lay deeper. Was he prepared to assert without qualification a fact that would surely be difficult to maintain in the face of controversy? All his historical training had taught him to weigh probabilities, to give respectful consideration to opposing views, and above all never to stray too far from the comfort of documentation—the protective barricade of his footnotes. And had not his generation, nurtured at classic film festivals and on late-night TV by repeated showings of *Blow-Up* and *Rashomon*, been trained to mistrust eyewitness testimony and to accept as an article of faith the insoluble mystery of things seen?

He nodded once again for the last time and walked on at a faster pace. He was going to give the puzzle a try. Like a member of that more ancient profession who insists "never on Sunday," he saw no reason why he could not give up academic self-doubts while he was on vacation.

It did not take long for Paul Prye to discover that he had greatly overestimated the difficulties of getting Collins to talk about yesterday's events.

When Paul arrived at the address near Blackfriars and gave his name to the receptionist, Frank Collins personally claimed him in the lobby and ushered him into his office. Paul accepted his offer of tea, and while his host excused himself for a moment to bring a tea tray from the lunchroom down the corridor, Paul looked quickly about the room. Neat and completely unstylish, it contained a dark oak desk before which two ladderback chairs were drawn up close. One sidewall was occupied by a built-in bookcase tightly filled with sets of professional-looking tomes. The desk top showed no sign of clutter and gave no clue to the nature of Collins's work. But there was conclusive evidence on the rear wall between two small windows. There, Paul noted on closer inspection, was a certificate proclaiming that Frank Collins, who had only the day before been lecturing to him about the dismemberment of Mary Kelly, was a chartered accountant. Another framed document indicated that he specialized in bankruptcy receiverships.

It seemed to Paul that news of Collins's double life would do wonders for the public image of the accountant. He recalled an article a few years back in the *Wall Street Journal* that had rated accountants as the least glamorous professionals in the public mind and had driven its point home by predicting that the last science fiction movie to be filmed would be entitled *Space Accountant*. At Columbia one of Paul's colleagues had once joked that an actuary is best defined as a child who had dreamed of becoming an accountant but hadn't the personality for the job.

Collins returned and deposited the tea and biscuits on the desk top. After he handed Paul his cup, he closed the office door with what struck Paul as a manner of exaggerated discretion. Then, instead of sitting in the black leather armchair behind the desk, he chose the side chair next to Paul's and turned it toward his guest so as to give their conversation as informal a setting as possible.

"I see that you are a chartered accountant," Paul began.

"That is correct. I have been with this firm for almost a decade."

Paul, though a reasonably polite man, could not prevent his preconceptions about accountants from showing. "Doesn't it strike your colleagues as . . . unusual that you are also occupied in enlightening tourists about Jack the Ripper?"

Collins responded without any hint of discomfiture. "Not at all. They are perfectly delighted that, instead of displaying my hopeless golf in their company, I spend my afternoons off in such a harmless activity. By the way, Professor Prye, I should tell you, for I suspect that you are a true-crime aficionado, that I actually know very little about Jack the Ripper. Until this blessed centennial of his came along, I did lecture walks on the pubs of Charles Dickens, and Dr. Johnson's London. But this summer I've lectured only on the Ripper, and sometimes as often as twice a week. I must say, I've become fascinated with these crimes, and someday I may actually turn into the expert I pretend to be."

Paul was groping for themes of small talk that could fill five or ten minutes until he could find an opening for his awkward inquiry, but he was brought up short when Collins appeared suddenly to change the subject.

"Tell me, Professor Prye, I have never been to America. Is it true that your countrymen are very quick to assert personal injury claims?"

"I'm not sure that I really am in a position to give you any helpful information on that subject. What sort of claims are you thinking of?"

"Well, I suppose primarily it is traffic claims that I have in mind. Friends that have visited New York tell me that if they've had the slightest collision in a taxicab, even though they have not suffered as much as a scratch or a bumped knee, they will find an insurance adjuster waiting for them when they return to their hotel room."

"I've never had an experience like that myself," Paul said. "But I suppose that our society has always been litigious. Is it very different here?"

"I think it is. I think that in many circumstances when you might sue, we would be content to roll down the car window and call the other fellow an idiot."

Paul wondered how it was that they had found themselves in a discussion of comparative law, but Collins, after a detectable hesitation, told him what was on his mind. "I've been thinking quite a lot about this matter since that regrettable incident yesterday on the tour. As I've told you, my colleagues in the office do not begrudge me my avocation, but I don't think they would be highly enthusiastic to find my name in the newspapers as defendant in a lawsuit."

Paul put down his teacup and rubbed an index finger back and forth across his lips. From a completely unexpected quarter, Collins had presented him an opportunity to explore the Commercial Street nightmare without being immediately thrown out of the office as an eccentric or a madman. But Paul wanted to proceed cautiously. The best way to lay the ground was to hear Collins out.

First he put in a word of encouragement:

"Who in the world could make a claim against you based on yesterday's events? It was a close call, but nobody was injured."

"I have no doubt that you are right, Professor Prye, but the person who gives me most concern is that American lady who seemed to have taken quite a hard fall."

"Do you mean the middle-aged woman who asked you to find her a taxi?"

"Precisely."

"It didn't seem to me that she suffered any serious injury. In fact, I am not quite sure why she left the tour as she did. If she had only waited a few minutes, she would have heard the end of the lecture and you would have guided her with the rest of us to Liverpool Street Station. I supposed at the time that she must have been upset by the danger or the shock of her fall." He paused before adding, "Unless something else was bothering her that we don't know about."

Collins seemed to ignore Paul's last words and lapsed into silence. After waiting for him to take up the thread of the conversation, Paul saw that he seemed given over to his private reflections, as if he had lost awareness that he had a guest sitting only a few feet away. He therefore prodded him gently by asking, "Am I wrong? Did you think that the woman had been hurt?"

His words seemed to recall Collins's attention. "Not in the least, so far as I can tell. But I agree with you that she seemed extremely upset. That is actually what bothers me the most. It seems to me I have heard that Americans have successfully sued for negligent infliction of emotional suffering even in the absence of physical injuries."

"I wouldn't know about that, I'm afraid," Paul responded. "But what makes you think that she would blame you for the accident? I remember that she was very emphatic in putting the blame on the motorcyclist. I was standing quite near her when she looked up Commercial Street where he had vanished and said something quite uncomplimentary in his wake."

For the first time since they had begun talking about the accident, Collins smiled. "You heard her then. I was hoping that I was not the only one standing close enough to catch her words. Do you remember what she said?"

Paul thought for a moment. "It was something like, 'That damned idiot nearly hit me.'"

"That's precisely what I understood her to say." Collins showed his pleasure by taking off his metal-rimmed glasses and beginning to polish them vigorously. He really does look like Crippen, Paul thought, recalling his first impression on Tower Hill. But if he was to accomplish his purpose in this interview, he could not afford to fall into daydreams about his favorite poisoner—not when the conversation had taken a favorable turn that, if pursued with caution, might permit him to be far less candid than he had feared he would have to be. He decided that it was time to take the initiative.

"Then am I to understand, Mr. Collins, that her harsh

words for the motorcyclist have failed to convince you that you have nothing to fear from her?"

Collins gave him an openly worried look. "That is the situation, exactly, and there is unfortunately good reason to be worried. If she was hard on the cyclist, she was not much kinder in the observations she made to me when I went with her to find a taxi. She didn't mince her words. She told me that the accident was entirely my fault, in that I had led the group across Commercial Street against the traffic light. I will be frank to tell you, Professor Prye, that I was delighted to receive your call, because I have been hoping you could confirm my very clear memory that the traffic light had turned red and that I followed every proper precaution in crossing the street." Collins had dropped his pretense of sociability and was now hanging on Paul's response with an earnest expression that bordered on the comical. Paul felt sorry for the man and for a moment almost forgot his own mission. He was beginning to say something reassuring, but he moderated his response in midcourse.

"I think I could be of some help to you. I believe that your memory is quite right, and I would be glad to give you a written statement to that effect. But to be honest, I was not in a very good position to see the traffic light, and I was giving my main attention to catching up with you and the rest of the group. I do think, though, that I could make some other suggestions that might be of some value, if you would not regard me as presumptuous."

Collins gave a distracted imitation of an ingratiating smile. "I can assure you that I will listen to any suggestions with great interest. Strange as it may seem to you, I have not been able to get the matter off my mind. You see, there is one other disturbing detail I have inadvertently omitted. Just as I had put the lady in a taxi, said good-bye, and turned back to rejoin the group, she called to me through the cab window. When I returned to hear what she wished to say, I received the most unpleasant shock: she requested one of my business cards, to which she stated emphatically she might have occasion to refer in the future."

Paul, giving his best imitation of a psychiatrist from stage or screen, looked superbly unshocked. He said, "That leads me directly to my first thought. I think that what should be done, to begin with, is to call upon the lady to express your concern as to how she has recovered from her disturbing experience. Indeed, if you would feel awkward calling her right out of the blue, I would be happy to talk to her first to see how the land lies. Would I be correct in assuming that, when she took your card, you obtained her name and address?"

Collins looked embarrassed. "I'm afraid that you will not form a flattering impression of my professional competence, but I must admit to you, Professor Prye, I was so upset by her sudden accusation that the thought of asking her name and residence never crossed my mind."

Paul tried to put him at his ease. "That's no cause for concern. If she seriously means to pursue a claim, I suppose we'll learn her name all too soon. But there's much we can do to protect you in the meantime. I'll send you my statement—for whatever it's worth—and perhaps we can round up some other group members who were in better position to observe the traffic lights."

"How could we do that? I don't know their names either. We don't record advance reservations, but, as you observed, merely sell tickets to all those who turn up at the rallying point."

"I think it would be possible to place a discreet advertisement in the London newspapers."

Remembering his duties as host, Collins proffered a

plate of biscuits. He then remarked, "I don't think that would accomplish much. Most of the walkers with whom I spoke were apparently foreign tourists."

"What about those three young men in blue jeans?"

"They were Dutch. As a matter of fact, I had an interesting conversation with them. They're studying at a police academy back home and were here to gather material for a project on the history of the London police. They had already been to the Bow Street Museum—"

Paul in his impatience cut him off. "Did you notice a tall, slim couple in raincoats who seemed to be rather quarrelsome?"

Collins was patronizing in his answer. "Not everybody who is tall and slim is English. That pair were obviously Swedes, and I suspect that she is rather hard of hearing."

Paul was impressed. Had he met a Sherlock Holmes of accounting? He asked, "How did you figure all that out while you were busy leading the tour?"

"A few years back I spent a summer in Stockholm, and I learned a bit of the language. The woman you mention reacted to almost every paragraph of my lecture by elbowing her husband and hissing, '*Jag kan inte höra ingenting.*' Many people might have occasional trouble hearing me on a noisy street, but she was constantly complaining, and so far as I know, only Swedes would use those words." He beamed at his little triumph.

Now Paul understood why the angry woman's words sounded like muffled English. He'd had the same sensation at Ingmar Bergman films—the feeling that if the actors would only speak a little more distinctly he could ignore the subtitles. Although this minor mystery was cleared up, he regretted the solution. The flare-up between the couple was the only sign of hostility he had observed on the tour before the crucial moment. Now he would have to search for anger or malice in some other direction.

"What about the man with the limp, the woman in tweeds, and your competitor in Ripper lore? Will you tell me that they are also foreigners?"

"No, they are certainly English, but they may not be Londoners and it is far from certain that a newspaper advertisement here would reach them."

Paul tried to look diplomatically vague. "And then there was that attractive young blond woman."

"My lord, Gladys! I had quite forgotten her." Collins struck his forehead with the flat palm of his right hand.

Paul was intrigued by his response. "Gladys? She is a friend of yours, then?"

"No, I couldn't say that, Professor Prye, at least not yet. But the fact is I found her quite attractive and took her name—it's Gladys Hunter—and her telephone number."

"If you don't mind my inquiring, have you called her yet?"

Collins grinned. "From this point on I shall decline precipitously in your estimation. I haven't called her at all. The fact is that I have led a great many tours during the summer season, and there are several young ladies ahead of her."

The double life of the accountant was becoming easier to understand: the man had invented a kind of mobile singles bar. Paul risked a slight barb.

"But Mr. Collins, isn't that sort of thing against the rules of your profession?"

"Absolutely not, I assure you. There is nothing on the point in the accounting rules."

"I meant the rules of the walking-tour profession."

"So far as I know, a code of conduct has not been promulgated."

Having made this mild attempt at locker-room banter, against which his exaggerated sense of privacy naturally rebelled, Paul went back to business. He obtained Gladys's daytime number from Collins. She was a theater-ticket agent stationed in the lobby of a West End hotel. It was arranged that Paul would visit her to find out what she had seen of the accident and whether she could provide leads to other witnesses. They telephoned her together, and she agreed to meet Paul during her lunch break the next day.

As Collins was seeing him out, Paul Prye suddenly paused at the threshold of his office as if struck by an afterthought. "Do you think it possible, Mr. Collins, that the American woman came on your tour with anyone else?"

"What an odd suggestion. The thought has never crossed my mind, frankly."

Paul thought he could detect a trace of suspicion forming in Collins's eyes. The accountant qualified his initial response: "I suppose I wouldn't have any means of establishing that she was alone when we gathered at Tower Hill, but of one thing I have no doubt whatever. She certainly left alone."

"Perhaps it was a ridiculous question as I formulated it. What I should have asked is whether anybody on the tour seemed to know her. Did you see anybody talking to her as we moved along? Obviously, I don't mean while you were lecturing. Then, of course, we were all ears."

"I'm afraid I haven't the slightest idea whether anyone talked to her at all. You may think me too self-absorbed to be cut out for a good tour leader, but I rarely take much note of my walkers."

"You need not apologize to me on that point. I am hardly the most trenchant observer of the passing social scene. But I do seem to recall someone in the crowd—

perhaps it was more than one person—addressing her as Margaret."

Collins shrugged. "I wouldn't be surprised in the least if you were right. You Americans can be astonishingly friendly at the drop of a hat. She had probably introduced herself to the entire group before I spoke my first word."

Paul thanked Collins for his time and hospitality and promised to report the results of his conversation with Gladys Hunter.

•

Alice was furious. Paul was sure of that as soon as he opened the door of their hotel room. Her lips were tightly pursed and she hardly returned his greeting.

"What's the matter, darling?"

She finally seemed to take full notice of his return. "You will not believe what I have had to put up with from some joker at Mainwaring's Gallery."

Mainwaring's was a Bond Street art dealer. Since "joker" was Alice's ultimate term of abuse, Paul settled himself comfortably in an armchair to listen to her grievance. Alice stood before him with her fists clenched and began.

"I had never seen the man before during any of my earlier visits. I thought at first we were going to get along swimmingly. When he found out we were from New York, he told me about the dreadful experience a wealthy English collector had recently at a Madison Avenue gallery. It seems that the collector was quite young and liked to dress informally, to say the least. He asked the dealer to show him some paintings by James Tissot. The dealer complied, but when the collector asked their prices he was told that he really wouldn't want to know; they were completely beyond his reach.

"'Can you imagine the arrogance of that dealer?' the

Mainwaring's man asked me. I shook my head in affected disgust and asked to see his Helleu prints. He looked me straight in the eye (it was only a few moments after he had finished his story) and said, 'It's too late, they're much too high. You should have visited us two decades ago.' "

Paul tried to console her. "I don't think he's half as bad as you make him out. It sounds to me as if he did a pretty good job looking after my bank account."

Alice waved him off. "Wait, I haven't finished; it gets worse. To console me for my poverty, the dealer offered me gratis a catalog of a French realist show he had just mounted in Paris. 'You'll find this interesting,' he said, 'and fortunately it's one of my last copies of the English translation.' Can you imagine the gall of the man? He offers me an English translation, and I've published in the *Gazette des Beaux-Arts!*"

"You really shouldn't be too hard on him. It's your own fault for still looking as if you were in your twenties."

Alice was not charmed. She continued to fume in silence. After a few moments, though, her face brightened as she recalled Paul's quest. "Since I've had such miserable luck today, I expect wonders from you. Did you call Mr. Collins?" She did not add "as my note reminded you to do," but the emphasis on her question made that reference unnecessary.

Nevertheless, Paul completed her thought for her. "Yes, I saw your note, and I did your bidding, from Wheat Thins to Collins." He told her about his meeting with the accountant.

"I can't say that I think much of Mr. Collins," Alice said. "He's even less observant than you are, if that's possible."

"Perhaps Gladys Hunter will have more to tell me."

"What do you mean, 'me'? You don't think that after twenty years of marriage I'm going to let you have lunch alone with a miniskirted blonde?" Although her tone was light, it was one of Alice's most deeply held beliefs that all sorts of bad things began at lunches with unattached women—particularly blondes. "I'll be there spoiling your little tête-à-tête. I've just mentally canceled all my important plans for midday."

That evening, after being unable to agree on a play, they went to a staged performance of Schoenberg's unfinished opera *Moses and Aaron*. It was being presented as part of some obscure music festival Paul had dredged up from the fine print of *Time Out*. Alice was kind in her judgment. It was a little slow, she said, until the Golden Calf scene. As an art historian, she was attracted by the visual aspect of opera and was happy to let Paul puzzle out the tone rows.

They had dinner after the opera, and by the time they returned to the Piccadilly it was well after midnight. But Alice was to have no sleep for a while. Handing her her vodka nightcap, Paul firmly announced that he was claiming his right to equal time.

"Last night belonged to Agatha Christie. Tonight let's play F. Tennyson Jesse."

There was no complaint from Alice. F. Tennyson Jesse, grandniece of Lord Tennyson, was a grand passion that the Pryes shared. It was her masterpiece, *Murder and Its Motives*, that had been the immediate cause of Paul's obsession with crime history. In that book Jesse had written a brilliant introductory essay neatly dividing murder motives into six categories and had appended individual case studies to illustrate each classification.

Paul began. "We seem to know so little about this Commercial Street business and the people involved that perhaps we could make some headway if we were to speculate a bit about possible motives."

"Why not," Alice agreed. In fact, speculation was second nature to her. Even in her college days she had regarded herself as something of a sleuth, having often propounded brilliant theories about the social (and sexual) relations of her classmates.

"Before we begin, though," Paul said, lapsing into the professorial manner that Alice usually tolerated and occasionally subjected to good-natured satire, "we must pose certain fundamental questions that will recur as we examine alternative motives:

"First, did Margaret go on the tour alone? Putting it more precisely, did she arrive alone at Tower Hill, and if she did, had she come there with an appointment to meet one of the other walkers?"

Alice was already anxious to make her own contribution. "I think that your first question is much too narrow. Shouldn't we put it in another way: Did Margaret know one of the other walkers, and if not, did one of the other walkers know Margaret? If we answer either of those questions yes, then a subsidiary question is whether they met accidentally, by appointment, or by the design of only one of them."

"As usual, you've shot way ahead of me. I think you've anticipated at least my next three questions. And since you are bound and determined to outshine me, I've no choice but to move on. The next question that I keep stumbling upon is Margaret's reaction to her close call. At first she was mad at the motorcyclist, and then it was all poor Collins's fault. But why is it that she never had a word to say about the real villain, the person I saw push her?"

"Well, I suppose the most logical explanation is that your murder attempt never happened."

"Look, Alice, you're not playing fair. I let you and Agatha gang up on me last night and you've got to give Fryn Jesse a chance."

"Sorry about that, Paul. It won't happen again."

In a peacemaking gesture, Alice handed him her empty glass for a refill and tried to look attentive.

Paul continued. "And my last question is related to the previous one: Why did Margaret abruptly leave the group alone when the tour was so close to over?"

Alice lost her patience again. "Really, Paul, I'm willing to entertain your other mysteries for the time being, but I see nothing strange at all about Margaret's departure. She was shocked by the accident, perhaps she had been bruised, and in any event, you could hardly blame her if at that point she had lost interest in the fate of Jack the Ripper."

"Perhaps you're right, but only if you have made certain assumptions about how my earlier questions are to be answered. If she was accompanied on the tour by someone else, or even if she had met a friend there by accident, it would be odd for her to stalk off without a word of good-bye."

"Well, I'll withhold judgment for a while. Now are we finally ready to play Murder and Its Motives? Because if you are intending to spend all night bewildering me with all these other interlocking puzzles, I am very likely to call it quits and go to bed."

"It is getting late," Paul admitted, "but perhaps we can make a beginning. Here we go. Motive Number One: 'Murder for Gain.' This is presumably the most straight-forward of all motives for murder, the easiest to under-stand because we are all so greedy."

"Speak for yourself, Paul. I will have you know that I bought absolutely nothing at Mainwaring's."

"Only because, as I understand it, you were intimi-dated into leaving. So expect no credit on that score. I still think you will agree that murder for gain is the least complicated category we can propose. The trouble is, it doesn't seem to fit our crime at all. What could the murderer have hoped for? That in the confusion, as Margaret lay dying or seriously injured, he could filch her purse and walk calmly away from the scene?"

"Paul, one hint from a good friend. Don't start with the assumption that the murderer is a male. I warned you about that last night, if you were really listening. Women are better shoplifters than men, and I also suspect they would be more ingenious about hiding a purse. But that's beside the point, because I agree with you. *Your* murder-for-gain theory is laughable. I can't believe your would-be murderer was a purse snatcher."

"Well then, are you ready to move on to the next motive?"

Alice looked nettled. "Absolutely not. You really disappoint me at times. To think of all the nights you've wasted in your library poring over dusty volumes of *Notable British Trials*, and you can't come up with a more ingenious hypothesis than purse snatching."

Paul's face took on a resigned expression that indicated he was ready to listen to a more elegant theory.

Alice smiled. "Don't be prepared to humor me too soon. There really are other possibilities, you know, and they fit right in with the earlier questions you posed. You've started off with an assumption that this is a 'stranger' crime. The murderer and victim are strangers to each other, the murderer just like one of our muggers from New York and Margaret a victim picked at random from a group. But what if Margaret was marked out in advance for the crime? If she had died, maybe we would have read in the papers that she was a Bostonian heiress and that someone back home, after drying very brief tears, had come into a lot of money."

Paul showed a bit of grudging interest. "Assuming you're right, then who was the person who attempted to kill her?"

Alice gave him another self-satisfied smile. "The nice thing about this theory is that I can sustain it no matter how we answer the question as to whether Margaret knew her assailant. Let's assume first that she didn't know him. And why didn't she know him? Quite simply because he was a professional hit man hired by her heir. I like that possibility, I must confess; it has a modern ring to it—or you might prefer to say a Halloween quality." Alice was trying to placate Paul by referring to a family joke. Many years ago they had been invited to a Halloween costume party (just the kind of regimented socializing that they hated) and had been ordered to appear as famous lovers. After a stream of Antonys and Cleopatras had announced themselves, Paul and Alice appeared in civilian clothes. When challenged by their hosts, they announced that they were a notorious midwestern judge and his mistress who had been accused of hiring an assassin to dispose of the judge's wife.

Alice went on. "But my theory still holds even if Margaret knew her attacker. He might have been nobody else but her heir-to-be. Now don't rush in too soon with your next objection. I'll make it myself: Why then wouldn't Margaret have accused him? I think that in the shock of understanding his designs on her, her first instinct would simply have been to escape. And perhaps their relationship was such that she could not bring herself to incriminate him; there could have been some element of loyalty at work. Besides, nobody would have been likely to believe her anyway. You know, much as I regard you as a basically sensible person, I still don't believe the story of the murder attempt, even though you told it to me as a detached observer and after you had had a chance to recover from the suddenness of the near-catastrophe. Just think how poor Margaret would have felt, screaming murderer as soon as she pulled herself out of the pile of fallen tourists. She would hardly have liked to be branded as a hysteric."

Paul was in a generous mood. "I am going to concede one point for you, Alice. I like your theory much better than the purse-snatching caper."

"As well you should."

"Does that wrap up Murder for Gain?" Paul asked optimistically.

"Not yet," Alice said. "I've a much more brilliant theory. I don't believe in it for a moment but I wish it were true. Let's suppose Margaret was a random victim after all. What would her murderer have to gain? To come up with a different answer, we merely shift the target. The killer's real objective was to destroy the market for Frank Collins's Ripper walking tours. And what was the motive? Isn't it obvious to you? The murderer had been hired by Collins's competition, a rival excursion from the Whitechapel station."

Paul laughed. "What a supremely silly idea. I can't believe there's enough money in walking tours to make it worthwhile to wipe out competitors, though I agree with Liza Doolittle that there are those who would kill for 'a hat pin, let alone a hat.' And besides, the public doesn't know who runs the damn tours anyway. For all I know, Frank Collins and the man you call his competitor may work for the same company. I'm sure that a murder or fatal accident on a walking tour could only have the effect of ruining the business for everyone."

Alice sniffed. "Logic, my dear Paul, has always been a poor substitute for ingenuity. But perhaps I am being too hard. I have found our dialogue positively gripping, and can hardly wait to hear your next revelations. Do you mind if I get undressed?"

"Have I ever minded?"

They were now in their bathrobes. Paul continued.

"Let me group Motives Two, Three, and Four: Murder for Revenge, Murder for Jealousy, Murder for Elimination. Now we're getting into the favorite turf of your beloved detective stories—the 'crime of passion' or the love triangle. A jealous murderer revenges himself on a lucky rival or on a lover or spouse who has forsaken him; or he eliminates an unwanted partner to clear the way for a new romance. He can commit the crime in a moment of rage, or after long deliberation."

Alice kissed him lightly on the forehead. "I'm so glad you've finally come to a crime I can identify with, Paul. Don't worry though, you have nothing to fear at the moment, now that I've disturbed your cozy lunch plans for tomorrow. Still I must confess there's nothing like a crime for love; murder for filthy lucre is so boring. After all, murderers like other men don't live by bread alone. So proceed. How do your new motives bring Margaret and her anonymous brute together on Commercial Street?"

"It could have been a rendezvous. Let's assume Margaret is carrying on a secret affair that has been falling apart. She has told him she's leaving him. He asks for a last interview, and what more discreet place could they choose than a walking tour about the dreadful East End Murders? He tries to persuade her to give him another chance. She refuses. Then, perhaps by plan, or more likely on impulse in a quick reaction to an unforeseen opportunity, he tries to kill her. When it happens, she is shocked and doesn't know what to do. Perhaps she can't believe he meant to harm her. Perhaps she knows he did, but what would be the value of a confrontation before strangers who wouldn't believe her? So she decides to leave without a word to him. She had escaped unharmed and would never see him again. What do you think? Have I convinced you?"

Alice remained a tough antagonist. She gave him a

consoling pat on the shoulder and answered, "With other theories still to come, I reserve judgment. But there's no doubt about it, you've made a lot of progress since your bad beginning with the purse snatching. For the time being, let me just suggest a few variations. First, Margaret didn't agree to a rendezvous, but made the mistake of telling her jilted lover that she was going on the tour. He didn't show up but sent a hired killer."

"Oh, no, your hit man again!"

"I refuse to give him up. But here's another version: Your estranged pair were on the tour as you say, but Margaret's murderous lover was a woman."

Paul gave Alice a look of sheer admiration. It never ceased to impress him how much more sophisticated she was than he.

"Or perhaps you've got the wrong couple in a rendezvous, Paul. Margaret is an abandoned wife and the murderer meets her secretly to plead unsuccessfully for a divorce. Why secretly? Because his new mistress has become even more possessive than his wife had been. Let that be a lesson to you the next time you arrange a tryst with a blonde."

It was clear Paul would never hear the end of Gladys. She would be the theme of cocktail-party conversation for many years to come. He took up the thread of his argument again.

"Just a few words about Murder for Revenge, and I think we've covered these categories for tonight. All these lover's crimes we've hypothesized can obviously be examples of the murder for revenge, but this classification is infinitely broader. How can I possibly come close to imagining all the past slights, real or imagined, that might be nursed by an unknown man in a crowd—yes, you don't have to remind me again: or a woman. You know how those Golden Age whodunits you adore exploit all these ancient grievances. It's a rigid formula—all these suspects we meet around the vicarage dinner table in the early chapters. The future victim is a thoroughly disagreeable character who has done something pretty awful to everyone—he's blocking X's promotion at the office, he's cheated Y in a business deal, and he's surly to a poor relation. And so on with quarrels large and small. And I really shouldn't complain about fiction, for in real life as well the same person who would calculate to the last detail the risks and rewards of a minor crime, will kill for a trifle. My own favorite will always be Mr. Roland Molineux of New York."

"I don't remember him, except that he's one of your people. What did he do?"

"In 1898 he tried to poison his club's athletic director for permitting guests to use bad language at the swimming pool."

After they went to bed Paul said, "You know, I've only been in this detective business for about a day, but after listening to your clever armchair deductions, I already understand how Sherlock Holmes must have felt about his brother Mycroft."

"I hope you mean he loved him," Alice said as she slid over in his direction.

Later, it was Paul who broke the silence. "Alice, now can we go back to discussing the case?"

"You certainly have some nerve," she answered sternly. "It can keep until morning."

Freeze-dried decaffeinated coffee is not a gourmet delight, but it can beat capuccino when you have a wonderful conversation going.

During their meager portable breakfast, Alice stifled her impatience to be off for some early shopping and agreed to talk about Motive Number Five.

"Murder from Political Conviction," Paul announced rather portentously.

Alice furrowed her brow. "Paul, you don't seriously hope to persuade me that your mild Margaret with her librarian's glasses and silver hair is a spy, and that someone's gone and blown her cover? Have I got the terminology right? I've never been clear, it's not my genre. Do spies in real life look like Margaret instead of that glamorous Sidney Reilly on TV? If so, you've brought me my final and bitterest disillusionment."

"I will remind you about my college classmate who we learned to our amazement was an eminent CIA operative." Too eminent for his own good, as it turned out; he had been assassinated in Turkey. The memory sobered both of them. Paul paused for a few moments to let the shadow pass, and then went on.

"What do you think spies should look like, or murderers, for that matter? Is it only Peter Lorre or Mary Astor who can steal a secret or a life? I once attended a murder trial in Philadelphia; it was long before I knew you. In the dock sat a woman who had shot a neighbor's child and hidden her gun in a package of ground round in the deep freeze. There she sat impassive, in screaming fuchsia, while lawyers quarreled over her Rorschach test. It is sweet people like you, Alice, who acquitted Lizzie Borden. Defense counsel said to the jury, 'Look at that respectable young woman there. Can you imagine her wielding an ax?' Of course they couldn't. But no matter who had sat before them, their imagination would have failed. So let's concede that Margaret could have been a spy—or worse."

"She was nothing of the sort," said Alice confidently. "Is that all that can be said for Murder from Conviction?"

"Far from it. I'll yield the point to you: Margaret was as innocuous as you suppose. She could still have been the target of a terrorist."

"And who would have been on the phone claiming responsibility?"

"IRA; Argentinian diehards; Shiites; Libyan or Iranian 'students'; you take your pick. The point is, what an advance they would have made! Before, they have marked out Heathrow or posh restaurants. Now they would have targeted an obscure group of tourists to show that nobody in this entire metropolis is safe."

"Why must the motive be political?" Alice argued. "There are other kinds of 'conviction.' Couldn't there be someone at large who just doesn't like tourists, or at least tourists who are preoccupied with murder?"

"Theorizing is fun, darling, but must your speculations come so close to home? I'm going to close the discussion before you settle on me as the next victim."

Paul pretended to make light of her suggestion, but she had a point. Many people, rightly worried about the rise of street crime, resented academic fanciers of ancient murders. Once, after giving a public lecture on crime literature, he had drawn a spate of poison pen letters. Of course, the newspapers hadn't helped. After his talk, it was pointed out to him that the lecture hall where he spoke had been the site of an early-twentieth-century assassination. He had responded with some show of interest, which had been magnified into a headline reading "MURDER HERE? HOW DELIGHTFUL!"

Paul therefore could readily accept Alice's notion of a murderous enemy of crime buffs. But for the time being, their "motive" game was broken off, and the Pryes prepared for their day in the city. Paul packed his green tennis bag with an antiquarian book guide, Geographia map, and umbrella, while Alice stuffed her purse with fabric samples and shopping articles from *The New York Times*.

While the doorman hailed them a taxi, Alice asked him what he had planned for the morning.

"Book shopping, I guess."

"Out of the question. You haven't unpacked the last lot from Toronto. You can come with me to Hyper Hyper. It's the least thing you can do for a liberated wife who is willing to humor your foolish infatuation with Gladys Hunter."

"Hyper Hyper what?" Paul asked suspiciously. The unashamed superlatives dazzled him.

"You'll see. Here's our cab." She gave the driver an abbreviated address: "Hyper Hyper, Kensington High." It seemed to register.

When they arrived at their destination, Paul was a bit confused. "Wasn't this place the Antique Hypermarket?" He stood before the familiar colonnade of caryatids, but something dreadful had been done to them. They had been painted a deeper shade of pink than they could ever have achieved by the most relentless exposure to the sunshine of their native Attica. Leaning against their pedestals were signs advertising the wonders of the new regime: HYPER HYPER OVER 40 INDIVIDUAL MENS AND WOMANS WEAR DESIGNERS; THE HYPER HYPER ORIGINAL PULLMAN TRAIN RESTAURANT.

"The Antique Hypermarket was nothing much," Alice reminded him. "You'll love what they've done to it." She ushered him inside, her arm firmly surrounding his waist as if he might be tempted to escape. He was soon caught in a maze of boutique stalls, each presumably presided over by its own creative genius. Many of the designers looked to Paul much like Gladys Hunter, and he wouldn't have been in the least surprised if she had bought her clothes here. His jaw began to sag in wonder before the big leather jackets and white baggy pants; earrings of rock and shell; aluminum jewelry; stockings with Chinese characters; draped black satin right out of the movies of the thirties; and phosphorescent dresses in nightmarish colors.

"Just what I need," Paul said when he had recovered his breath. "A wife who glows in the dark."

"I'm not here to buy," Alice said with the emphasis Paul had learned to mistrust. "I'm just looking."

Paul's eyes settled on a booth sign gaudily emblazoned with the name *VESTI LA GIUBBA*. The inventory displayed was limited to loose-sleeved cotton jackets with huge highly colored buttons, and billowing trousers in coordinated patterns. Why was it that people, as the sign suggested, wanted to dress up as clowns? As Paul pondered his own question, looking over the garments that overflowed into the aisle, he summoned up a wonderful idea for a new modern-dress production of *I Pagliacci* at the English National Opera. All the villagers would be dressed as clowns and the audience would be invited to do the same by appearing in clothing purchased at Hyper Hyper. When Canio launched into his famous solo, he would take off his flowing jacket and his voluminous pants and would don a conservative pinstriped business suit.

He began to grumble more and more as Alice paused at a number of the booths to try on earrings and to price sweaters. She finally lost her temper. "This is impossible. I was almost done, and I was going to take you to another place you'd really adore. Portobello Green—it's all the rage. But you've gotten to be a pain before we've been here more than a few minutes. It's best for me to get rid of you. I'll see you at lunch." She gave him a distracted kiss. It was a kind she had perfected, that left the right hand free to continue probing a rack of dresses.

Free at last, Paul returned quickly to his own shopping

paths. His first stop was at the house of a Kensington dealer in true-crime books and ephemera. Whenever they set out on one of their frequent trips to London, he announced pessimistically that he would never find anything in the bookshops to match the trophies of past visits. He was always wrong, and so it turned out again. He bought from the dealer a great souvenir of the Ripper centennial: a newspaper poster that had screamed from a London kiosk in 1891, "POLICE BELIEVE THEY'VE CAUGHT JACK," and then, recovering a sense of balance, had added, "LATEST FOOTBALL RESULTS." Paul completed his purchase, the poster was scrolled up in a tube, and with the treasure under his arm, he strode down Kensington Church Street at a triumphant pace. At his next port of call, a shop specializing in Staffordshire figurines, he repeated his success, acquiring a replica of the house of the mass poisoner William Palmer.

There was no doubt about it. Things were going very well this year. To make it a perfect vacation, all he had to do was clear up that strange business on Commercial Street.

•

When Paul saw Alice again, in the lobby of the hotel where Gladys worked, she was buried under a mountain of packages and shopping bags from Hyper Hyper, Portobello Green, and other morning way stations of which she had failed to warn him. He took many of the encumbrances from her, uncovering her beautiful face beaming with victory: "It was a *fantastic* morning. I hate to say this to you, Paul, but things really picked up after you left."

They walked together into the interior lobby, where they sighted the theater ticket desk positioned near the concierge's station. There sat Gladys Hunter, telephone caught between an ear and a hunched shoulder, while she spread a theater-seating plan before her clients. She was wearing a gray T-shirt and the same black leather miniskirt she had shown to such advantage on the tour. During the Victorian age, all women, no matter how humble their household, owned a black satin outfit for wear on respectable social occasions. Paul wondered whether that venerable fabric had now yielded the place of honor to black leather. When Gladys finished the order, the Pryes introduced themselves.

"Hello, Miss Hunter. I'm Paul Prye and this is my wife, Alice. You probably remember me from the Jack the Ripper tour."

"I can't say that I do."

Alice smiled broadly in her best quasi-maternal manner. Paul felt suitably chastened. As he moved more deeply into his forties, he had come to know that one of the supreme embarrassments about staring at young blondes in miniskirts was that they seldom stared back.

Gladys, however, had softened the terms of her response. "Of course, I was very happy to hear from you and Mr. Collins yesterday, although I've wondered how I could possibly be of help. Did Mr. Collins say something about an insurance claim?"

"Why don't we talk about it at lunch," Paul suggested, "if you're ready to close shop for a while." Gladys agreed. She opened the drawer of her desk and, after fumbling about for a little, located her "out to lunch" sign, which she slid across the desk top. As she rose from her chair, Paul restrained his admiring glance.

In the hotel lounge the Pryes ordered sandwiches of prawn and mayonnaise, which were their standard noonday fare in London, while the slim Gladys opted for a salad of greens. Paul was sure that when the lunch had ended Alice would tell him that Gladys was anorexic.

The Pryes didn't think it was proper to plunge right into the subject of interest and as an opening gambit requested Gladys's professional advice on the theater season.

"Have you seen *The Mousetrap?*" she asked them brightly.

"We've never seen it in London," Alice said, "but we've seen some local productions back home. Paul can never remember who dun it, but as I'm very likely to remind him, we've agreed not to go again."

Gladys had another suggestion. "I find that many Americans are very fond of the new farce *Hanky Hanky Hanky Panky*. It has a wonderfully clever plot. You see, it's about an au pair girl who goes to work in a Mormon household."

The Pryes exchanged a conspiratorial look, but let the theater talk run its course.

When lunch was served, Paul had brought the conversation around to Collins's worries.

It was hard for Gladys to take the subject seriously. "I don't know why he's given the matter a second thought. The woman wasn't injured, except possibly for a bruise or two when she fell."

Paul explained. "I think that he regards us Americans as a quarrelsome lot. She must have spoken to him quite sharply when he put her in the taxi. She seems to have blamed him for crossing against the light. Do you happen to have noticed whether the light was red when he led the group away from the curb?"

Gladys gave him a blank look. "I'm afraid I don't have any memory of that at all. I just followed along with everybody else. But if you'll forgive me for speaking my mind, I wouldn't be at all surprised if the woman was right. I think he was a bit careless about traffic. Do you remember the way he dodged a lorry when he was bringing us across Fenchurch Street?"

Alice was beginning to get the impression that Gladys

Hunter would not be the most favorable witness for Collins. But she suspected that the problem could be easily cured if the accountant would call her for a date. Some men never seem to get the point that it isn't the greatest compliment to women to collect their telephone numbers and to file them away for a rainy night.

"Do you remember anything about the American woman?" Paul continued rather vaguely, as he tried to feel his way.

"One thing I remember very clearly is that she certainly wasn't bashful with the men, which struck me as not exactly proper for a woman of her age."

Gladys thought she saw Alice's eyes narrow a little. She blushed and tried to explain. "What I mean is I would have expected her to have been a little more reserved, since most of the men in the group were a good deal younger. But instead she was busy shaking hands and introducing herself as if she were running for election."

"Do you recall her name?"

"I'm not certain. She never addressed a word to me. But I think her first name was Marjorie or Margot or something like that. She seemed mostly interested in the men. And what foolish questions she asked. Anything to strike up a conversation. Why they were going on the tour. What were their feelings about Jack the Ripper, whether they'd ever been to the Old Bailey, what they supposed the people in the East End thought of these tour groups."

Alice changed the subject. "Do you remember what she was wearing?"

Damn it all, Paul thought. She can't get her mind off her morning shopping. He listened with a perfect lack of comprehension while the two women exchanged fashion terms. In a slightly patronizing tone Alice then translated for him. "Margaret (or Marjorie or Margot; whatever her name was) was dressed in a taupe fisherman's sweater and a brown jersey skirt."

Paul tried to take control again. "Miss Hunter, did the woman seem to be alone on the tour?"

"I didn't take any notice of her at all until the walk began. She certainly didn't lack for companionship once we were on our way. That kind of woman never does."

Paul ignored the obvious hostility. "But among the men you saw her talking to, did she seem to single out anyone in particular?"

Gladys frowned in an effort of recollection. "Now that I come to think of it, I do seem to recall that there was a man she sort of paired off with. They would stand together while Mr. Collins was talking, and I think he once took her elbow to guide her in the right direction when she was about to make the wrong turn."

"What did he look like?" Alice intervened again.

"He didn't make a dazzling impression on me. I think he was rather tall."

Perspective, Paul reflected; one of Alice's favorite lecture themes from Piero della Francesca onward. What were they to make of a "tall man" viewed from the vantage point of Gladys Hunter, who would be lucky to stand five feet two in spike heels?

"And he was dressed like so many of the men, in a raincoat, which is hardly a surprise. It really was a wretched afternoon. I don't know why I didn't go home instead of staying to be drenched to the skin."

When the Pryes by degrees brought Gladys around to her memories of the accident on Commercial Street, she could not have been more disappointing. She had been standing at Collins's side at the time, presumably having recovered from her temporary annoyance over his praise of the brunette Mary Kelly. She had heard the roar but never even seen the motorcycle. Someone had stumbled against her and she had fallen. It was the gallant Mr. Collins who had helped her up. She had not seen the American woman fall and had not heard her say anything after the accident.

Alice asked, "Did she seem to be hurt?"

"I remember her rubbing her hip or thigh a little, but she seemed all right to me. Many of us took a rather hard tumble, but then of course she was quite a lot older." Gladys suddenly thought about what she had said, and blushed again.

Paul then resumed the questioning. "Do you have any idea, Miss Hunter, why she left so hastily?"

The answer was immediate. "Decency, I suppose."

The Pryes looked puzzled. "What do you mean?" Paul asked.

"Well, I don't suppose she would have felt comfortable continuing with the group, when her skirt had been so badly torn. I mentioned before seeing her rub her hip, but I think that what she was mainly trying to do was hold her skirt together where it had ripped during her fall."

Paul then quizzed Gladys about her recollections of the other people in the group. Their memories seemed to match pretty well, except in two respects. There was first the tall man to whom she thought Margaret attached herself. The man was dark, she said, and if she had only added "handsome" she would have completed the cliché. The other figures in raincoats, and the three young men in blue jeans whom Collins had identified as Dutch police cadets, had remained as faceless to her as to Paul. But the second bit of identification she had for him promised a new lead. The bearded expert on Jack the Ripper had given the lovely Gladys his card and taken her telephone number. There were tender emotions in the fierce man after all. His name was James Holloway and he was a solicitor from Birmingham.

After lunch they escorted Gladys back to her desk and

said good-bye. They assured her that Frank Collins would be very grateful for the useful information she had provided.

On the way back to the Piccadilly Hotel in their cab, Alice said to him, "So much for your great mystery of Margaret's sudden departure. What self-respecting woman would want to prance about with strangers in a torn skirt?" She reflected for a moment and added, "One thing's certain. If Gladys Hunter ever tears her skirt, she'll be arrested for indecent exposure."

•

Paul's second choice from the music festival was more to Alice's taste. It was a two-hour ballet fantasy based on Pierrot Lunaire. Throughout the performance the audience heard snatches of Schoenberg's song cycle on a tape recorder activated in some mysterious fashion by the movements of the moonstruck clown who danced the title role. Alice would not have grieved over a short circuit in the recorder, but she adored clowns—not the jolly clodhoppers of the circus but the theatrical clowns, impulsive, sad, demented, or even sinister, who haunted the canvases of modern art. She found the performance absorbing. Things did get a little out of hand at the end, though, when the addled Pierrot began to crash into walls (were they symbols of a padded cell?) and threatened to tumble into the first row center, where Paul and Alice were seated, thanks to the services of their new friend Gladys Hunter.

At dinner and during their customary nightcap, Alice enthusiastically lectured Paul about Pierrot Lunaire, and Picasso, and the distinction between Continental pantomime and the English Punch and Judy Show. It was fascinating, and he hated to interrupt her. Nevertheless, he finally did:

"I'm so glad we've at last picked something we both liked, and that it's a show to which you can bring the whole family—as long as one of them is an art historian. But no more clowns for tonight, please; we haven't disposed of our last 'motive.'"

"You know, I'd completely forgotten. Go ahead, your companion in detection is listening."

"Okay. We've come to Jesse's last category: Murder for Lust of Killing. Jesse calls this 'killing for killing's sake.' With her passion for classification, she subdivides these crimes into murders that themselves satisfy lust, and those that accompany or follow a sexual act."

"Where would you place Jack the Ripper?"

"I'm embarrassed to admit I'm not clear on that. He's not one of my favorites. It's my memory that there's no reason to believe he had either raped his victims or had sex with them. But somehow the impulses to sex and violence had tangled in his psyche, or in his nerves, or wherever we're supposed to locate these dark drives now that there is no soul; and perhaps the fact that the women were prostitutes aroused him in some fatally decisive way. He's not the only serial killer to have specialized in prostitutes. There was Dr. Neill Cream, who fed strychnine to several of them, though he had first perfected his technique on an old paralytic man whose wife he had seduced. But there are moments when I think the prostitute connection is overemphasized. After all, these were crimes of the Victorian age, when a man would find it much easier to be alone with a prostitute than a respectable woman. If he hated the entire sex, what could be more convenient than to mutilate or poison a prostitute in some deserted street?"

Alice shook her head. "None of your feminism, please, it's going to warp your objectivity. I warned you about this when you first brought me the story of the Commercial Street assault. I refuse to believe that Jack the Ripper hated all women. He hated prostitutes—at least that's all we can be sure of."

Paul stuck to his position. "I can't prove you wrong, but I'm not willing to draw so narrow a compass for our murderer. We know from our own time that lust-killers don't stalk only prostitutes; nobody is safe. And therefore don't expect me to devise all sorts of lubricious fantasies about Margaret's private life. She looked to me like a perfectly proper middle-class woman and so she will remain, unless proven otherwise. I hope you haven't been taken in by Gladys's innuendos. Margaret was very friendly, but let's remember that it was Gladys who collected two telephone numbers. No, I'm not being quite fair. Margaret did collect a telephone number herself—from Frank Collins, you'll recall, but it was only for reference in case she decided to make a personal injury claim. What could be more solidly middle class than that?"

"Will you fear that you've lost your audience if I ask for another vodka?" Alice slid her cup across the low table at which they sat in the Klondike-barroom gesture that Paul always found endearing. "I'm not prepared to quarrel with you about Margaret. You seem to have been in a particularly impressionable mood that afternoon. What old Frank Sinatra records do to some people a Jack the Ripper lecture does for you. I do hope, though, that your criminal doesn't turn out to be a lust-killer. I'm still rooting for a hired assassin; that breed has the classical detachment I always admire. Remember too how hard you've tried to dream up some personal motive for the attack on Margaret; don't give up too easily. Speaking for myself, I would far rather be done in by a vengeful lover or even an edgy heir than by some faceless loony who doesn't know me from Eve. I take it I'm right there, Paul: your lust-killers don't generally know their victims, do they?"

Paul put his two forefingers together and his voice took on a lecture-room tone.

"I'm afraid that's an issue that we cannot generalize

about. For instance, Neill Cream, the poisoner I mentioned a few moments ago, seems to have struck up some kind of friendship with Matilda Clover about ten days before he murdered her. And there've been all sorts of wild theories that Jack the Ripper may have known one or more of his victims. So if you're determined to hang on to the hypothesis that Margaret knew her killer, there's no reason to despair just because we make him a lust-murderer. My quarrel with this category is quite a different one, simply that it doesn't adequately deal with many of the crimes F. Tennyson Jesse would have us believe it fully explains."

"You mean there are species of lust yet undiscovered—like exotic butterflies?" If he insisted on the professorial role, she would play the wisecracking student, secure in an A average.

Paul answered soberly without acknowledging her satire. "It isn't the phenomenon that is so hard to identify, it's the theory that's inadequate. I can't help but think of Jesse, much as she might have thrown up her hands in horror to hear it, as an amateur Freudian. To her, pleasure in killing had to be either bad sex or a sex substitute. Whenever she couldn't find one of your whodunit explanations—the stolen atomic secrets, the jealous wife, or the hidden codicil—and was thrown back on what appeared to her to be a 'motiveless' crime, she always found the same convenient explanation: sex gone bad. But there are many other pleasures murderers have derived from killing that are subtler and harder to bring to light.

"In fact, Alice, perhaps we start on a false trail when we assume that the enjoyment must arise from the act of killing itself. There is something old-fashioned in the notion that a direct, personal involvement in a murder is a prerequisite to its enjoyment. We may be misled here by outworn notions of sadism—that the direct experiencing of the victim's agony is necessary to arouse the offender's jaded senses. Maybe lust-killers once belonged to this type, but as early as the eighteenth century the Marquis de Sade saw a change coming. The only fault he found with the mass killings of the French Revolution was that the horrors had become so widespread and impersonal that nobody could enjoy them any longer. I don't think that the modern sadist requires deep involvement in the act of murder. He may be motivated instead by a generalized hostility, a hatred of mankind or classes of mankind that is satisfied by the fact of death wholly apart from its agonies. So our Jack the Rippers tend to be snipers who spray a campus with bullets, too far away to read the looks of terror on their victims' faces."

Alice interposed a mild protest. "I never expected to hear such a eulogy of the eighteenth-century brand of sadism. But in any event, Paul, it's hard to accuse the Commercial Street attacker of remoteness. You say he used his own hand in an attempt to kill Margaret, and if he was a lust-murderer, he might have hoped to see her lie dying."

He nodded. "I'll score another point for you, but I won't surrender completely without pointing out other defects in Jesse's concept of lust killing. If I've not persuaded you that there is a kind of generalized hostility that is more than a sex substitute, what will you say of the other pleasures a 'motiveless' murderer may feel? I would call one of them an exaggerated drive to self-aggrandizement or self-glorification. How many murders have been committed, not so much because the killer had anything against his unfortunate victim, but because he hoped to see his crime in the newspapers—or on late-night TV? This isn't really a newfangled concept at all. One of the reasons Henry Fielding opposed public hanging when he was a police magistrate is that it tended to make heroes out of criminals and to inspire imitators."

"Well, to have the pleasure of hero worship, wouldn't the murderer have to be caught?"

"Not anymore, it seems. The Tylenol murderer hasn't been caught, but I suspect he is mightily pleased with the news coverage of his crimes and that his sense of pleasure has been magnified by his having baffled the police and saved his skin in the process. But in many cases, I suspect, you're right. The pleasure does turn on being found out and being publicly celebrated as a cunning monster. It is in this kind of murderer that we often detect a related but distinct motive for which Jesse wholly fails to account: the desire of the murderer to be caught and punished. What a wonderful way to satiate twin desires for glory and for the expiation of some secret guilt that has who knows what origin—perhaps having cheated a baby brother at marbles."

Alice made a diplomatic attempt to bring the harangue to a close. It was hard to stop Paul when he got into these crime history tirades.

"Well, now that you have demonstrated that F. Tennyson Jesse should go into still another edition, where has our motive game left us? Are you about to lock all the doors and announce the murderer's name? No, I suppose you couldn't do that since there's no one here but you and me, and I really have an iron-clad alibi for the day— or perhaps I should say silk-clad."

Paul, who had seemed while he was talking to have gathered a second wind, now appeared properly weary. "I don't suppose we've really gotten any closer at all to understanding what I saw or why it happened. But perhaps I've at least gained a little sympathy now that you realize what a tough job of detection you saddled me with."

"We'll sleep on it," Alice said airily. "And it certainly is high time for sleep. Remember, we're taking an early train."

Before the theater Paul had called James Holloway in Birmingham. They were to meet the next day (which was Sunday) at the Birmingham Art Museum. Alice was thrilled to come along, because she had always wanted to see the museum's Pre-Raphaelite collection.

When they were in bed Alice had an afterthought. "Paul, are you still awake?"

"If I said no, would you believe me?"

"I've never found you completely trustworthy—particularly in bed. But I'll let that pass, because I have a new worry about tomorrow."

Paul turned his head slightly toward her to show that he was willing to listen at least for a little.

Alice said, "I'm beginning to be troubled by all these interviews. You seem ready to quiz the whole damn tour group one by one as they may happen to turn up, in the apparent belief that everybody will be an innocent bystander except the last person you stumble upon. I was willing to concede you Frank Collins, who seems to me much too ineffectual even to pull off a bungled murder attempt, and I don't think Gladys Hunter, had she pushed with all her eighty pounds, would have budged Margaret an inch. But shouldn't we draw the line somewhere? How do you know that when you come to see this man Holloway, who sounds aggressive enough from your account, we won't be face to face with Margaret's enemy?"

Paul laughed and took a decisive roll back to his side of the bed.

"If that's all that's on your mind, you can sleep easy. Wait till you meet Holloway. The man must stand six foot nine and weigh over three hundred pounds. If the criminal assault to be successful was to be committed unobtrusively in a crowd, I just don't happen to think that the most likely suspect is an overfed giant with a fiery beard."

"Well, I suppose you may be right," she conceded. "In any event, I'll be charitable. If he kills us both, I won't remind you of my warning."

Over breakfast, Alice suddenly knew that Paul had stopped listening. He had opened the morning newspaper that had been slipped under their door, but the first page had not distracted him from nodding or even making an occasional remark. It was when he had turned the page that she became aware that his attention was riveted in disbelief on what he was reading. Before she could ask what had engrossed him or crane forward to find out for herself, he handed her the paper as if he had just remembered he was not alone.

"My God, Alice," he stammered, searching for words that would make sense, "we've found Margaret, but she's dead."

"Margaret?" Alice asked, and then began to focus better. "You mean your Margaret from the walking tour?"

He showed her a photograph on page 3. "That's her. I'm absolutely sure of it."

Alice noted the fine features, almond eyes, and unrimmed glasses and read the accompanying column:

MARGARET AMES SANDERS, FAMED AMERICAN DIRECTOR, DIES IN LONDON

Margaret Ames Sanders, world-renowned American theatre director, was found dead last night in her London hotel room. She was 45.

Sanders had arrived here recently to begin work on a West End revival of Edwin Justus Mayer's Newgate prison tragicomedy *Children of Darkness*. The director, who has been active at the Yale Theatre, Harvard's Loeb Theatre and in New York and Los Angeles, is particularly noted for her successful productions of classic crime melodramas, including *The Petrified Forest*, *Angel Street* and *Night Must Fall*. According to Sanders's professional colleagues, rehearsals of her London play were not scheduled to begin for several weeks. Anthony Johnson, the producer of the play, said that "little has been seen of her since her arrival." He added, however, that "she was notorious for immersing herself in history and background before embarking on a new project, and we would not be surprised if she had spent a good deal of time at the Old Bailey and on the streets associated with London's crime history." Among the characters of *Children of Darkness*, he explained, is the real-life eighteenth-century archgangster of London, Jonathan Wild.

The cause of death has not been determined. Representatives of the hotel where Sanders was staying have disclosed that she was confined to her room for the last two days, apparently suffering from a fever. She refused all offers of medical attention. Friends report that Sanders, a native of Boston, was an ardent Christian Scientist.

Alice bent low over the newspaper and planted her elbows on the open pages as if to stake a proprietary claim. At last she looked up to Paul.

"What do you make of it?" he asked.

She could find no better way out of her bewilderment than to ward off the strange issue that faced them. "How do you know it's the same woman? In the overexcited state you've worked yourself into in the last two days, you would have sworn that any Margaret who had the good or bad fortune to appear in print was the mysterious woman of Commercial Street."

Paul had no immediate remedy for her disbelief. Perhaps he even found some comfort in the formidable hurdle of persuasion that faced him, because if they were to agree that the article reported the death of the right Margaret, he would be more at a loss than ever. With all the difficulty he had had convincing himself that he had witnessed a murder attempt (he doubted whether he had ever brought Alice around to his vision), how could he reconcile himself to having all his scrupulous speculations rendered irrelevant by a death of fever in a lonely hotel room?

Paul's reflections were shattered by the ring of the telephone. He extended his long arm to the receiver, slightly heading off Alice, who had sprung from her chair as soon as the phone sounded. She had to be content to paste her ear to Paul's.

Collins was on the line. He had seen the obituary and was having as much trouble finding his bearings as they were.

"I've no doubt she's the woman," Collins was saying. "And yet how can it be? Is it possible that we can live such a prey to coincidence as to meet a woman for the very first time and see her spared a violent death, only to read that she has died in her bed two days later. Is Shakespeare right? Are the gods wanton boys who kill us for their sport?"

Paul murmured something noncommittal. What a wonderful country this was, he thought, where accountants quote the Bard.

Collins had not really expected an answer to his question, because it was only the prelude to a restatement of his unwavering concern. "You don't think it possible, do you, that people can literally die of fright? And if they could, would you not expect them to go into instantaneous shock instead of returning to their hotel to die at leisure in bed?"

"Come now, Mr. Collins," Paul interjected. "You must get this insurance business out of your mind. We simply can't pick convenient times to die. We can be carried away after our greatest triumph and we can die in our sleep after surviving an accident or an air raid."

"I hope you're right." But Collins's voice broke perceptibly, showing that his hope was not strong. "You don't suppose, do you," he added, "that she'd had the time to show my card to her friends?"

Collins's egocentricity would have been shocking had it not appealed so strongly to Paul's sense of the incongruous. He actually found himself impelled to comfort the accountant. He told him that he had nothing to worry about, that whatever cause for worry he might have had ended with Margaret Sanders's death. He appended a judiciously edited summary of the meeting Alice and he had had with Gladys Hunter, reporting that for good measure they had arranged to go to Birmingham that morning to talk to the bearded Ripper expert. He supposed that the meeting would be pointless now, but they both felt that it would be courteous to keep their appointment and Alice had always wanted to visit the museum. Collins thanked him for his interest and hung up.

Paul flashed a self-satisfied smile. "Well, Alice, what do you have to say for yourself now?"

"Just because two grown men indulge the same fantasy I don't concede you're right. It's probably just another case of *folie à deux*. But as I've done from the start, I will continue to constrain myself to believe in you, however tentatively. What do we do now? Are we still on our way to Birmingham? Because if we are, we don't have much time to catch the train."

"Of course we're going. Whose turn is it to wash the dishes?" He gave a wry look at the plastic coffee cups that were the only remnant of their breakfast.

For the first few minutes of their train ride they sat in silence. Alice was glancing through a catalog of the Birmingham Museum, and Paul looked vaguely out of the window at the vanishing suburbs of London. He finally turned to Alice. "You know, you've managed successfully to come through the entire morning without venturing an opinion. How do you account for Margaret's death?"

Her response was serene and she gave it without looking up from her pages. "Of course it's a coincidence, and not such a strange one at that. The death of someone we know, however slightly, always comes as a shock to us, whether they drop dead while jogging or die of a ripe old age. Is it any odder when someone dies shortly after your first meeting than if a dear friend of twenty years passes away in his sleep after you have just seen him, healthy and expansive, at a Saturday-night party? You'll remember several years ago when we met your beloved Lord Snow quite by accident at a London theater. We would never have encountered him except that we had changed our tickets at the last moment. Shortly after our return to America you read that he had died. Did his death lend any greater significance to your meeting? Did you conclude that when you had shaken hands you had given him some communicable disease?"

Paul rejected the suggested parallel out of hand. "Alice, one of your greatest talents is your almost irresistible power to prove me wrong. I feel its force on me again, but you're trying to sweep under the rug what I've told you and believe with all the conviction I am capable of. Someone tried to kill Margaret on a London street, and two days later she dies in her bed. I don't know whether I can put this quite right. It isn't so much the coincidence that I reject, it is that I cannot accept the irrelevance of what I saw on Commercial Street."

When they reached the outskirts of Birmingham, Alice still seemed to be studying the catalog. Her mind, though, had found its way back to their mystery.

"Paul, do you want to know how Agatha Christie would have dealt with this morning's revelation?"

"I'm sure I'm fated to know."

Alice ignored the sarcasm. "She would demonstrate that you've been looking for the wrong kind of link between Commercial Street and Margaret's death. It's the old logical fallacy: *post hoc propter hoc.* Just because one event follows another, it doesn't mean that it is the result of what has already happened. Of course, you can cudgel your brain forever if you are determined to prove that a miraculous escape from a pedestrian accident causes a woman to die in bed two days later."

"She might have had a heart condition," Paul ventured.

"Nonsense. You don't believe that. Give up your primitive notion of direct cause and effect. Agatha wouldn't put up with anything so obvious. No, she would show you that you are half right, which means that you are also half wrong. There could be a tie between the two events, but it must be a much subtler one than you have in mind. The significance of Commercial Street, if you saw things right, is that someone wanted Margaret dead and came close to getting their wish. Margaret survived, but *so did the hostility that had almost claimed her as a victim.* In a Christie whodunit, the 'secret adversary' of Margaret would have followed her to her hotel room and murdered her there by some means that the hotel physician wasn't clever enough to detect."

Paul was about to interrupt but was warned off by Alice's emphatic frown. "No, you must let me finish. The beauty of the theory is that it leaves all the options open as to the murder motive. The killer who stalked her to her hotel could be the terrorist, the secret agent, the lust-murderer, or even the jilted lover. I'm glad to welcome the lover back as a suspect. If he's our man, we revert to the proposition that Margaret didn't know she had been pushed, and left the scene abruptly without a good-bye because she was upset, or—as Gladys Hunter would have it—simply because she had a torn skirt. Therefore, she wasn't afraid of her friend the murderer. When he visited her at her hotel to inquire how she was doing, she welcomed him without reservations. Who knows? Perhaps he fed her poison pills, like Dr. Cream. Now I'm ready for your questions."

Paul treated her to mock applause. "Bravo. Just the kind of solution that strikes us as iron-clad when we finish reading a thriller at two in the morning; and fortunately, by breakfast we've forgotten the obvious flaws. Let me be sure I've got it straight: Margaret meekly swallows poison dispensed to her by the murderer, and when she feels its effects, doesn't take the trouble to ask the hotel staff to summon aid. I don't think her Christian Science would carry her that far."

But before Paul could continue to muster his objections, he was deterred by the expression on Alice's face. She had broken into a broad grin. Paul receded into a discouraged silence. She was pulling his leg. She didn't believe a word that she had said, but was just playing one of her endless virtuoso variations on the themes of her favorite author. She was definitively persuaded that his imagined murder attempt had been refuted once and for all by Margaret's surprising but nonetheless natural death.

•

Paul was pleased to learn that in this age of mass media it was still possible, for half a day at least, to retain one's innocence in Birmingham. James Holloway had not yet heard of the death of Margaret Sanders. Looking a bit less piratical as his jaw slackened in amazement at the article that Paul showed him, he read in silence, darting a staccato forefinger at certain words or phrases that he seemed to find significant. It was a professional quirk, Paul guessed; he knew lawyers who could not read even a sports report without wielding a yellow highlighting pen over its columns.

There was no need to ask whether Holloway had recognized the photograph; his immediate absorption in the obituary had dispelled any remnant of doubt on that score to which Alice might still have clung during their train journey. At last the solicitor neatly folded the newspaper page and returned it to Paul.

"Would it be callous to say, 'It's an ill wind that blows no good'? This unexpected development should dispose of our honored tour leader's concern about an accident claim.'"

Paul caught an expressive look from Alice that he wished she had taken more trouble to encode. Lawyers are the same worldwide, she would tell him later. Even personal tragedy did not deflect them from their single-minded devotion to the relevant.

"Then I assume you've concluded there's no connection?" As a delaying action, Paul decided to belabor the point, for he was actually pretty much at sea, not knowing why he had come or what he could hope to gain from exploring riddles that only the night before had intrigued him. "What I mean to say is, have you ever in your experience encountered a case of a traumatic aftershock of some sort, for example, a person with a heart condition, perhaps undiagnosed, who overcomes a traffic accident with no visible ill effect only to succumb to an attack a few days later? Or possibly a head injury suffered in a fall, which results in a subdural hemorrhage that takes some time to run its fatal course?" He hoped he was conveying a stronger sense of suspended judgment than he actually felt.

"I'm afraid such questions are not in my line. My practice is limited to construction contracts. Our clients have had some wind-shattered glass, but good fortune has always spared the pedestrians below. Nevertheless, I would venture the guess that phenomena such as you suggest would manifest themselves rather soon after the accident, perhaps in a matter of hours at most."

Paul lapsed into silence for a moment. He was not likely to be making much of an impression on Alice with his skill as an interrogator, but she would not hold his failings against him. To her practical mind the short-lived lure of the Commercial Street affair had faded with Margaret's death, and she would not expect him to do more than go through the motions of pursuing the interview whose purposes he had outlined to Holloway the previous evening.

As Paul continued to tread water, talking about Margaret Sanders's career in the theater and summoning a half recollection that he had seen her production of *Night Must Fall*, Holloway came to his rescue. Despite the passage of a few days, and the surprising news of the death of one of the walkers, the solicitor was still assiduously nursing his grievances against Frank Collins.

"The man's a perfect incompetent, and I can say no better of the company that employs him. That is, if anyone is foolish enough to employ him. Would you happen to know whether he does work for a touring agency? I saw you take his card. I have more than a half a mind to write to the management."

He did not wait for Paul's answer.

"But it would probably be a waste of time. I have only myself to blame. The man knows nothing about Jack the

Ripper; he dragged out one tired old canard after another. I should have brought a map and done the walk alone. To make matters worse, of course, the weather was miserable and I caught a cold that is determined to hang on."

"What bothered you about his lecture?" Paul asked. "It struck me as completely 'canned.' I think he's got it memorized to the last word, but so far as I could tell— I'm no expert as you obviously are—the facts seemed accurate."

It was a dangerous question if the Pryes hoped to visit the Museum galleries before they closed. Holloway ranted on with no end soon in sight. With the vehemence of a pedant, he seized on minor imprecisions of time and place, none of which seemed to Paul to detract in the slightest from the main line of Collins's narrative.

Holloway continued his indictment.

"It's needless for me to repeat that the whole plan of the tour was a hopeless jumble. I fear that you heard enough from me on that theme during the walk. Still, it does seem to me to border on fraud to advertise a tour on the East End murders and to leave out Whitechapel entirely. And the route we took may have saved some steps, I grant you that, but the chronology was all wrong and must have left everyone in a fog—unless they knew the history quite well beforehand."

For some reason Paul felt obliged to put in another good word for Collins. After all, the man had served him tea. "I don't think it's completely fair to blame the route on Collins. I've already mentioned my impression that he had his script memorized, but isn't it likely that his words as well as his itinerary were dictated to him by his employer?"

Holloway made no concession but clawed his beard reflectively, as if he were pondering other charges that would be harder to rebut.

"That may be, but you can't blame the agency for the fact that the fellow simply was unable to keep the group under proper control. When you told me, during our telephone conversation, of his concern about an injury claim, I was not surprised in the slightest. I didn't notice the traffic lights but if, in fact, he led us across the street against the lights, it would have been in keeping with the slack management he showed from the start. At times the group was strung out an enormous distance behind him; he would stop and start without warning, and much of the time one couldn't hear a word he said because of the loud complaints from others who said they couldn't hear. You tell me he's an accountant. I would only hope that he is more meticulous about figures, for as a tour leader he's an unmitigated disaster."

Paul persisted in his defense of Collins, hoping to draw out more particulars of Holloway's observations. "I didn't think the tour was as chaotic as you make it out."

"I suspect that may be because you had a special interest in the subject. Had you looked round, you would have seen as I did that within the first twenty minutes he had lost the attention of most of the walkers. For example, the woman who's died, Margaret—what was her last name, Saunders?—she seemed to have set up in business as a rival tour leader, gathering about her her private contingent, particularly among the men."

"I did observe that she was very friendly. It's strange, Mr. Holloway, but apart from Collins, she was perhaps the only person in the group whose name—at least her first name—I recalled after the tour was over. She must have introduced herself quite freely. And I think that her informality struck a responsive chord, because I have the distinct memory of hearing people in what you call her 'contingent' addressing her as Margaret."

"You may be right," Holloway said, "but I have no recollection of that."

Paul pursued the question. "It didn't seem to me that Collins was responsible for the formation of Margaret's coterie. If you place a person with charisma in a small group, it doesn't take long for the influence to make itself felt. In any case, I think that my memory may be a little different from yours. I do recall Margaret Sanders shining brightly among the men—and I think there were some women too—who were crowded about her in their raincoats and slickers, but I believe that by the time we took refuge in the Spitalfields Market, she had detached herself from her followers and paired off with one of the men." Paul remembered nothing of the kind, but he was trying out Gladys Hunter's possibly malicious story.

The response was immediate. "You are absolutely right. I made the same observation myself. I thought at the time that she had fished in well-stocked waters and come up with rather a poor catch."

"Why did you think that?"

"It was not a charitable thought, I know, but he really was a puny little fellow." To this behemoth of a man, Margaret's Commercial Street companion was "puny." Could he have been the same person whom the diminutive Gladys Hunter described as tall? How could the police deal with the illusions of perspective and prejudice? They would need wanted posters with accordion pleats.

"I wonder, Mr. Holloway, whether you and I are talking about the same fellow. What did he look like?"

"I suppose we all looked pretty much alike that day, wearing our rain gear as you have mentioned. All I can recall is that he was an emaciated man with prominent cheekbones and slit eyes that almost disappeared when he talked."

Paul took the word *emaciated* with a grain of salt. James

Holloway had not missed a dessert, let alone a meal, for many long years.

"Did you hear the man's voice at all?"

Holloway, lost to the present in his recriminations about the tour, did not seem to notice that their conversation was beginning to wander far afield.

"I don't know that I took any particular notice of anything they were saying, but it was obvious that the man was a foreigner."

"We seem to have had quite a miniature UN out there," Paul commented breezily, to disguise his growing interest. "There was a Swedish couple, and I believe some young men from Holland. Could you tell from his accent what the man's nationality was?"

Holloway did not try to hide his boredom. "I am not blessed with a great ear for accents. I suppose I divide Continental accents into two categories, French and everything else. This man fell into the second class. But it doesn't really matter who the man was or where he was from, for you've actually helped me make my point. If the tour had been properly led, would the group have broken down into mating games?" His vehemence was on the rise again. "Our leader hardly set us the best example in that regard. He was flirting in the most outrageous manner with Gladys Hunter, and, if I can trust my eyes, had the effrontery to ask for her address. I have never seen such unprofessional conduct in my life."

In his indignation, Holloway had quite forgotten that he too had obtained Gladys's name and number and that the Pryes were well aware of that fact, since it had been Gladys who put them in touch with him. It was this very oblivion that convinced Paul that they had sounded at last the very foundation of Holloway's rage against Collins. Granted, his annoyance had been aroused at the start by the tour plan, but he would probably have gotten over that grievance. Instead, this mountainous man, with a social diffidence that was all too apparent beneath his aggressive exterior, had taken a fancy to a pretty girl. Accustomed to rejection, he had probably had the dizzying success of exchanging names and addresses with her during the wait on Tower Hill. Then what had happened? He had suffered the humiliation of watching her attach herself to Collins and grant him the same favor of her telephone number. Inured to failure as he was, the ungainly giant did not expect to find a rival in his tour leader. Surely this was what his law books would call unfair competition.

Paul brought the conversation to a conclusion as soon as politeness would permit. When he was about to say good-bye, he was startled to notice that Alice, who had sat quietly during the conversation, must have despaired of its ending and had slipped away unobtrusively to the galleries.

•

Alice was waiting for him at the entrance of a visiting exhibition of Victorian paintings, which they had agreed would be their first port of call.

"I suppose you didn't even notice I had gone," Alice said. "I gave you all our patented signals: stare at watch, shake watch, swing head like pendulum. Nothing seemed to work, so I tried 'the lady vanishes.' Success at last. I'm glad to see you. By the way, the man was an incredible bore. Did you learn anything we should add to the Commercial Street dossier before we file it away forever?"

"Lots. The tall man Gladys saw with Margaret is a 'puny little fellow' according to our elephantine solicitor. He's got bony cheeks and a non-French accent."

"The last part of the description fits you pretty well. Promise me it wasn't you that pushed Margaret on some obscure impulse. You've been shoving me around for years." The whole business had become a joke for her again. "Are you ready to give up murder for the other fine arts?"

"Just about. But I was hoping that you might tell me what you thought of Holloway—that is, if you had time to form any impression before you sneaked away."

"Well, I don't think he would have dazzled me had I sat there with you all day, as it was beginning to appear would be my destiny. He is a clumsy man, as you told me he would be, and of course you were right all along: he couldn't pull off a crime that required him to move unnoticed in a crowd. So if we're to play our game to the last inning—and it's beginning to strike me as disrespectful of Margaret if we do so—then I would agree to scratch Holloway from the list of suspects. It's not that he lacks the hostility, God knows, but it seemed to be all directed toward the tour leader. Collins is really the lucky one to have come back from Commercial Street alive. Now that I've shared all my wisdom with you, can we see the exhibition?"

They bought the catalog and Alice read as they moved along. Usually he liked nothing better than to listen to her witty mixture of catalog excerpts and personal commentary on art styles, iconography, and the clumsiness of wall-label prose; it was a personal audiovisual aid that he would not have bartered for any headset. Today, however, the usual magic was not working. Where he should be seeing beauty illuminated by Alice's expertise, he saw only reminders of crime and violence.

Here, for example, was a group of works by the delightful fairy painter Richard Dadd—his *Oberon and Titania*, lent by a private collector, and *The Fairy-Feller's Master Stroke*, a masterpiece that they knew from the Tate. *The Fairy-Feller* had always looked to him like a landscape in a dream or, better still, a trance. Hedged and partly obscured by a bold diagonal of weeds were a profusion of fairy folk. The first faces that caught the viewer's eye were human and even idealized, as if in an illustration from a children's edition of Hans Christian Andersen. But look again, and encounter a small white-bearded figure, sitting with knees hunched together, his head an absurdly swollen bald dome that weighed down and concentrated a stare of pure insanity. To the left there was a grotesque red-turbaned dwarf gesturing palm upward toward the central figure, the Feller (woodcutter), who was flanked on the other side by another watcher, hands clasping bent knees, with a profile distorted by his close attention. The Feller, who is viewed from the back, raises a stone ax to split a nut to make a new chariot for Queen Mab.

When he had seen this canvas before, Paul had always associated the scene with fairy tales and with Mercutio's praise of Queen Mab. But now he saw a crowd of figures chaotically grouped—as the walkers must have looked as they scrambled to avoid the motorcycle—and most of all a central symbol of aggression, the upraised ax.

Was his reaction hopelessly subjective? Perhaps not, he thought as he listened to Alice's summary of the catalog entry. She quoted from Dadd's commentary on the painting: "Splitting is either good or bad." The annotator had commented that it was impossible not to read in these lines "some reference to the artist's personal tragedy." On a summer night in 1843 Dadd had murdered his father with a knife and razor he had recently bought. A year later he was admitted to the Criminal Lunatic Department of Bethlehem Hospital (Bedlam). The murder site was not far from Gad's Hill; Charles Dickens never tired of showing the spot to his visitors.

Alice had moved several paces ahead and was admir-

ing a ballroom scene of Frith. She was about to look for
the catalog entry when she observed that she had lost her
audience. Turning back to Paul, she scolded him mildly.
"I should have known I'd have to drag you away from
the Dadds. He's one of your people, isn't he? It's just the
kind of paradox you love—the whimsical fairy painter
who in real life turns out to be a disciple of Sweeney
Todd and Lizzie Borden. We really should do an article
on him together. I'll deal with his brush and you with the
razor. But enough of your daydreaming. We have at least
a dozen other rooms to cover if we're to finish the exhibition and see the nineteenth-century galleries in time to
catch our train."

It was with a sense of relief that Paul passed on to the
work of other artists, but time and again even the most
familiar pictures took on the lineaments of Commercial
Street and the subsequent death of Margaret Sanders.
The Victorian preoccupation with death, suicide, and the
dead body made the fixation of his thoughts on these recent events even stronger. On the left wall of the next
room they entered was another familiar painting, Henry
Wallis's portrait of the poet Thomas Chatterton lying
dead on a garret cot, having taken arsenic in despair over
his poverty and the failure of his prospects. Wallis had
meticulously rendered the details of reports of the suicide, showing the livid body convulsed—as it would
have been from the workings of the poison—and an arm
dangling over the side of the cot. The half-empty phial of
poison, though, for dramatic emphasis appeared on the
floor rather than grasped in his hand as it was found by
the police.

It was not remarkable that the Chatterton painting had
reminded him of the morning's obituary, but other more
arbitrary associations made him wonder whether he was
losing his—what was the word he had applied critically

to the recollections of Gladys Hunter and James Holloway? Yes, his perspective. For now he had come to an
image of death as serene as could be imagined, the
drowned Ophelia of John Everett Millais. There she lay
supine in the stream, a human flower among dozens of
plants that Millais had portrayed with botanical fidelity in
the work. Near her right hand were daisies, pansies
floated on her dress as symbols of "love in vain," and the
artist had encircled her neck with violets that spoke of
faithfulness. But when Paul looked on this icon of peace,
he changed it involuntarily: on the young face of
Ophelia, her chestnut hair trailing in the water, he super-
imposed the features of Margaret Sanders, her finely
molded head, firm chin, and—ludicrous as it seemed—
even her rimless glasses. Strange to see this vivacious
woman lying so still.

Alice looked over his shoulder to see what it was that
kept him standing so long. She smiled and said, "You're
quite right, she is perfectly lovely. You always have had
impeccable taste." It was a frequent joke of hers, in
which there was more than a grain of truth, that he
lacked her wonderful eye and was easily distracted by
subject matter—the cool green of a summer woodland,
or a woman's face.

She at last wrenched him free from his brooding.
"Look, Paul, there it is, right ahead. Could you ever have
believed it would be that beautiful."

They found themselves arrived at the final goal of the
Birmingham pilgrimage, as far as Alice was concerned.
They stood before one of the jewels of Birmingham's own
Pre-Raphaelite collection, the great *tondo* of Ford Madox
Brown, *The Last of England*. Madox Brown was one of Al-
ice's passions and, ostentatiously closing the catalog, she
swung confidently into her own appraisal.

"It's *The Last of England*. You must remember it from

the Tate show of a few years ago. It was inspired by the emigration of the Pre-Raphaelite sculptor Woolner to Australia. We're not sure that Brown saw him off but he was deeply moved by his friend's departure; Brown and his wife Emma appear in the painting as grief-stricken emigrants.

"This catalog entry is a complete shambles," she continued. "All biography and no formal analysis. Have you ever seen a more wonderful composition than this, circles within circles, echoing the shape of the *tondo?* Look at all the curved lines. In the foreground the ship's railing, and near the top left a white arc—I've never quite made out what it is exactly, something nautical no doubt—rises behind the fist a cursing reprobate shakes at his homeland. Then there's the circle of the woman's bouquet, and even a curving string holding the man's hat to his coat button.

"Now look more closely at the interlocking principal figures, the emigrant couple. She holds his hand in her right and with her left she grasps the tiny hand of their baby, whom she carries in her cloak, hidden from the sea spray. The design is incredibly unified without losing a jot of realism. Note how the crook in his right arm is paralleled by the broken arcs of her cloak and how these shapes are repeated in the umbrella he holds above her as a shelter."

Dutifully Paul followed her instructions, and his eyes settled in the end on the umbrella. They settled there for quite a while—and perceptibly widened.

The umbrella! How could he have forgotten it?

· 6 ·

The conversation on the ride back to London was much livelier than it had been on the morning train. It had not been difficult for Paul to remind Alice of the mysterious 1978 murder. They had been in London at the time and Paul, whose mania for slang and strange words rivaled his love of crime history, saw on every newspaper kiosk the indecipherable headline "POLICE SEEK BROLLY MAN". The next morning they read in the *Times* of the murder of the dissident Bulgarian broadcaster, Georgi Markov, by a poison-tipped umbrella. They had thought little more of the case until their memories were jogged by programs on the murder that they saw on "60 Minutes" after they returned to New York.

Alice's first reaction to Paul's brainstorm was of shock that left no room for appraisal. He had literally dragged her without explanation from the museum, promising an explanation when they were alone. They collapsed on the first unoccupied bench they could find and without prelude he told her what he had learned from *The Last of England*. When she had recovered her poise and, even more important, her breath, she told him she hoped and half believed he was right. As she said this she wondered at her own words, for his new idea, though claiming the stamp of history, was more bizarre than anything they had conceived in all their elaborations of Agatha Christie and F. Tennyson Jesse. Perhaps her enthusiasm for his theory was partly due to her wanting to believe in the truth of the "revelation" of the Madox Brown painting. If he were proved right, what wonderful homilies she would draw for her students about life, and even death, "being illuminated by art."

The rush of her enthusiasm, however, did not spare Paul from a skeptical, almost carping, question as soon as they were comfortably seated on the train: "How is it that you never thought of the umbrella before? I don't recall that in all your accounts of the walking tour I ever heard you mention an umbrella."

"You're probably right about that," Paul admitted. "May I take a leaf from your own book, and summon a mystery writer to explain for me? You remember the Father Brown story of the 'Invisible Man.' That's the one where a crime is committed in a household and the residents, in listing the persons who had access, overlook the very person who committed the crime—the postman. He is the invisible man whom people don't see because he just doesn't count for them. He comes and goes but doesn't exist as an individual.

"I think that the same phenomenon occurs in our perceptions of things as well as people. Of course, all of the walkers or most of us, certainly, were carrying umbrellas—I had one myself—but I didn't think of mentioning the fact. Umbrellas are just what you carry in bad weather, and in London, if you're wise, you carry them all the time.

"And yet now that my mind has been jarred by Madox Brown, I realize how indispensable the umbrella must have been to my belief in what I thought I'd seen happen on Commercial Street. You remember how I described my sensation as dreamlike, as surrealistic. And so it was. Certain details detached themselves from the mass of impressions that suddenly forced themselves upon me. I'll never forget the garish decoration of the motorcycle—its ground the color of blood being drawn for a test, and radiating black stripes like those on the Spiderman's costume—just as I have an indelible picture of the outward thrust of the murderer's arm.

"But dream visions—at least it's true of mine—don't only heighten certain details, they suppress others, and perhaps some that are more crucial. I had omitted all the umbrellas, but most important, I had censored the *murderer's* umbrella. And in doing so, I'd failed to recall the very fact that made me focus, in the midst of all the confusion, on a single act of hostility."

"You simply said you saw the murderer push Margaret into the motorcycle's path," Alice said.

"You're right in reminding me; that is what I thought I'd seen. But I was wrong. You'll remember the alternative interpretation you dredged up out of Agatha Christie: that the man had put out his arm to break his own fall. I told you that you were wrong, but I couldn't prove it. And why? Simply because of what my memory had edited out. When a person stumbles against another in an effort to break a fall, he's likely to do so with hands outspread, to gain a better hold and (if he's instinctively considerate) to soften the collision. But what I'd instantaneously seen—and just as quickly forgotten—was that this man's thrusting hand was not spread, it was tightly clenched—as it would be if it were clasping the handle of an umbrella."

Alice continued to probe his revised memory. "Are you saying now that you actually saw him jab her with the umbrella?"

"No, I can't claim that. But I'm sure about the clenched fist. I don't know why it ever escaped my mind; it must have been that I was so positive he'd pushed her I just shunted aside anything that was inconsistent. My mistake seems easy enough to understand looking back. It was the motorcycle that had grabbed my attention; small wonder. When I saw that arm shoot out, it just had to have something to do with the motorcycle, someone was trying to have that woman run over. Any other possibility, any evidence of danger that pointed elsewhere, was obliterated.

"Of course, I was wrong. It was the motorcycle that played a secondary role. Among us in the crowd was the murderer, armed to strike at a convenient moment. And then that fool on the motorcycle gave him an ideal opportunity, when nobody could take any notice of the murderer's actions."

Alice put in a fond qualification. "Nobody, that is, except my eccentric husband who just happened to finish his daydreaming at precisely the right moment. Well, that proves again, if proof is still needed, that there is no such phenomenon as a perfect crime. Every group is bound to have at least one eccentric. Come to think of it, your tour seems to have had more than the usual quota. Nevertheless, so far as we know, it was only you among all the bystanders who saw the jab of the 'invisible' umbrella. Have I got my lesson from Father Brown right?"

Alice brightened with an additional thought. "But was it really invisible? You don't recall seeing it in the murderer's hand when he lunged at Margaret, but another witness observed the effect of its impact. It must have been the umbrella that tore Margaret's dress. Bless the sharp eyes of Gladys Hunter."

"I know Gladys thinks her dress was torn," Paul said. "But I never saw that myself."

"Really, Paul, you're too much. Here I sit listening, with willing belief, to a man speculating about clenched fists, and you now want me to doubt Gladys Hunter. Men may be experts on clenched fists, but women are unlikely to be wrong about a torn skirt. Especially if another woman's wearing it; that's when it particularly delights the soul. Tell me, you can confess it to me in this empty carriage. You believed Gladys, didn't you? But you thought it was strange that Margaret would have torn the skirt in her fall in the street—muddied it, yes, in the downpour, but why torn? Gladys had presented us with another minor mystery among many of greater consequence, so we put it aside. Now you come up with your umbrella theory, it seems to fit with what you saw, and it is confirmed by a woman's eye. I couldn't be prouder of you."

"The trouble is," Paul said after their late dinner at the hotel, "I'm not clear about what we can do. The police probably won't listen to us, and if they do, they're likely to bundle us off to some quiet place. Is Dadd's Bethlehem Hospital still in business?"

Alice didn't share his concern. "Not to worry. If we've learned anything at all from our trips to this blessed isle (other than always to carry an umbrella—sorry about that, it just slipped out), it's that you must have an introduction. What about your journalist friend, what's his name, Donaldson?"

Paul had known Bill Donaldson for many years. He was on the editorial staff of one of the Fleet Street newspapers. They had met at one of the monthly dinners of the Crime Writers' Association to which the Pryes had been invited as guests by an author with whom they had spent a pleasant evening in New York. An amateur among the mighty champions of crime writing, Paul had been delighted to come upon Donaldson at the bar. Bill was not a member, but was a great favorite of the crime writers because he managed to make room in the columns of his newspaper's literary supplement for reviews (generally favorable) of their works. He was a square-jawed man with heavy black hair that curled halfway down the back of his collar; the creases in his face and a perennial suntan, always faded to the point of respectability, suggested boating or some other health-giving recreation that was foreign to Paul. The journalist was a fastidious dresser; his favored tones were dark, and just the right amount of his cuffs showed. Paul could never envision him in a pressroom, short-sleeved, feet on the desk, cigar planted between his teeth. Perhaps this archetype had died out or never lived at all anywhere, only to surface from time to time in revivals of *The Front Page*.

Alice's suggestion that Paul talk to Donaldson about the death of Margaret Sanders was a good one, but had its embarrassing side. "You're probably right. He must have some contacts at Scotland Yard. But I'm a little squeamish about asking his help. We've been in London almost two weeks and haven't called him yet."

"He'll forgive you. He knows by now that you're a compulsive shopper and culture vulture, and will be delighted to hear that you've found something more productive to do—solving the crimes of the city."

Paul reflected for only a moment. "I'll call him in the morning. It's too late now."

In a while, he returned to the subject. "I hope he can get me an interview without too much delay." A wistful tone crept into his voice. "I hate to think of it, but a week from Wednesday we're going to be on our way back to New York. I'd hate to leave with this business still unresolved."

During a trip to London many years ago he had paid a visit to Criminal Courtroom No. 1 at the Old Bailey, where an unlicensed foreign doctor stood trial for an abortion homicide. He arrived at the high point of the drama, the cross-examination of the defendant by a bewigged female barrister who put great warmth and verbal skill into her task. The following day they left England with the jury still out. From New York he wrote to the court clerk inquiring about the verdict, and promptly received a typed official card reading: "Guilty. Ten years." Though he would have loved to hear or read the closing arguments, perhaps that was all he needed to know about the matter. But in the case of Margaret Sanders, would it be enough for him to scour the newspapers for weeks or months hoping for word of the outcome? There were so many things he wanted to know apart from the name of the killer, and besides, though it was odd for him to admit it, he, the inveterate reader of other people's detections, wanted to be in on the hunt.

Alice interrupted the train of his thoughts. "You don't have as much time as that. I hope you haven't forgotten that this Wednesday we're going up to Glasgow for the conference." Paul had quite forgotten. The Glasgow art museum had scheduled a symposium in connection with its important current exhibition on French Realism. The curator of the show, an American scholar who was a great friend of the Pryes, had invited Alice to speak on Courbet.

Paul looked so disappointed by her reminder that Alice took pity on him. "Don't worry. If you're making headway on the case by then, you don't have to come with me. But I really expect results. You're not simply going to use Margaret Sanders as an excuse to escape from the art historians. And I have one further requirement."

Paul gave her a look of grateful obedience, ready for her command.

"I don't expect to hear on my return that you've been to Raymond's Revuebar." Paul had been trying to get her to go for years, but Alice objected: they saw plenty of tourists in the hotel lobby without seeking them out on Brewer Street.

•

Bill Donaldson had been glad to hear from Paul. His pleasure didn't lessen when Paul told him that there was something worrying him, and that he thought Donaldson could help. He listened without comment as Paul went on to specify his request: could Donaldson meet with him today to refresh his memory on the details of the Markov poisoning? Donaldson agreed to do so, and to bring along his clipping file. They had arranged to meet at the Cheshire Cheese, but even on a dreary Monday afternoon at 2:00 they found that it was still swarming with tourists and no standing room remained. Bill hunted out an obscure pub nearby where they ordered lager (pretty good) and chicken sandwiches (very dry).

After the usual amenities were exchanged between friends who had not seen each other for a year, Paul wasted little time in turning to the subject that was on his mind. "Tell me, what do you know about ricin?"

Donaldson opened a manila file and spilled out some clippings and handwritten notes, which he consulted occasionally as he spoke. "You're referring, of course, to the poison used in the Georgi Markov case. Let's see what I can tell you. Ricin was the poison found to have been shot into Markov's thigh in a pellet ejected from the tip of an umbrella. It is some kind of extract from the castor-oil bean and an incredibly powerful poison, quite worthy of the James Bond books. One of the articles published in our newspaper says that an ounce of the stuff in a pure state would be quite sufficient to carry off 90,000 souls.

"We had not heard anything of ricin here in England before the Markov case. However, the chief pathologist of the British chemical and germ warfare establishment reported at the time that much work had been done on it lately in the laboratories of Czechoslovakia and Hungary. We later learned from *The New York Times* that the poison had been well known to your CIA for many years. For all we know, it's been the subject of experiments there, as well as electric stun guns, calibrated blackjacks, marshmallow barrages, and whatever else will be part of the 'next generation' of your espionage weapons."

Donaldson was somewhat surprised to observe that Paul Prye had taken out a rain-warped notebook and was scribbling in it as he spoke. Paul's pencil stopped as he turned a page and asked, "What about the pellet? How did it work?"

"To me that was the most ingenious part of the whole business. The pellet was no bigger than a pinhead. It was made ninety percent of platinum, and the balance of iridium. The pellet was about one-fifteenth of an inch in diameter and had two holes drilled into it to hold the poison. Each was about sixteen one-thousandths of an inch deep, and they were placed at right angles. It is thought that there was some kind of filling in the holes that gradually came away or dissolved after the pellet was imbedded in the flesh, permitting a delayed release of the poison into the bloodstream."

"At what range was the pellet shot from the umbrella?"

"That seems to have varied, so far as can be ascertained. In the case of Markov it appears that the umbrella tip was actually jabbed into his thigh. As he was walking by a bus queue a man in a raincoat stabbed him with the umbrella and apologized as if it were an accident. Some of these poison umbrellas, though, seem capable of firing a pellet at least a moderate distance. After Markov's death, you may recall, one of his compatriots, named Kostov, reported a similar assault. He was going up an escalator in a Paris metro when he heard the sound of a crack behind him. It was later discovered by electronic scanner that he had been shot with a pellet identical to the one that killed Markov. In Kostov's case, then, it seems that the pellet must have been fired through the air and that the crack was the sound of its ejection from the umbrella. If we only have these two cases as a basis to form a judgment, the contraption doesn't seem to be as effective from a distance. Still, I must tell you, Paul, I find it hard to believe that this weapon exists in the real world. Didn't it first appear in your Batman comic strip as the lethal instrument of—what was the name of the villain with the sword-umbrella?"

"The Penguin," Paul contributed.

"Precisely. And now the Czechs or Hungarians or Bulgarians, whoever they may be, have produced a real-life Penguin. And why? Because men like Markov and Kostov had the honesty to write and broadcast about corruption in Sofia."

"Remind me, Bill: how long did the ricin take to work?"

"Well, of course in the case of Kostov it didn't work— at least not as it was supposed to work. The man became ill but lived to tell the tale. Markov, as I recall, lingered for about four days. Yes, that's about right. He was admitted to St. James's Hospital about a day after the attack and died there three days later."

Paul was adding to his notes. "Alice and I saw something about the case on American TV, but I don't recall the details after all these years. How does ricin poisoning kill, and what are its symptoms?"

"It may not be possible to generalize about the symptomology, but we do have at least the two cases to go on. Both Markov and Kostov had high fevers, and I think that Markov also vomited blood. There was another suspicious death of a woman in her Munich flat a few months before Markov died. In her case the initial postmortem indicated a heart attack, but subsequent examinations disclosed traces of a toxic substance in her body. If it was ricin, perhaps her death had followed a somewhat different course.

"The workings of the poison, of course, can be traced best in the Markov case. After he was brought to the hospital, his claim that he'd been attacked by a man with a poisoned umbrella was understandably greeted with skepticism, but the doctor who admitted him was puzzled by a skin puncture he discovered on the back of Markov's right thigh. It was much too big to be either an insect bite or the track of a hypodermic needle. It was many months later, as I recall, that the full results of the postmortem were first disclosed at the coroner's court in Battersea. The medical testimony indicated that after Markov's admission to St. James's he was suffering from severe blood poisoning, which developed into septicemic shock; his white blood cells had multiplied to triple the normal number."

Paul closed his notebook. "I'm quite impressed by the ease with which you can summon all these facts back to mind. You've hardly looked at your file. I suspect you must have total recall."

Bill dismissed the compliment. "It's not surprising that the case is clear in my mind. I took a special interest in our news gathering at the time because the police were not very generous in regard to their public statements. I even took a hand in a long leader we ran, complaining that the authorities were holding back more information than was warranted by considerations of national security. Nevertheless, I'm gratified to have been able to answer your questions, and I seem to have done a fair job since I observe you've put your notebook away. Would it be rude for me to inquire at this point what has brought about your sudden new interest in Markov?"

"Take a look at this," Paul replied. "Do you think that this report would be consistent with a ricin poisoning?" He handed a newspaper clipping across the table to Donaldson; it was the notice of the death of Margaret Sanders.

Donaldson read it quickly and returned it with a noncommittal grunt. "I don't see much ground for any opinion. The cause of death is not determined, and the only symptom mentioned is a fever. It has been the sad lot of mankind to die of assorted fevers long before Eastern Europe discovered ricin."

Paul was not discouraged. "Of course you're right. But suppose I added to the equation the fact that Margaret Sanders was, for no good reason, struck from the back with an umbrella tip about two days before her death; that at the time of the attack she seemed in good health and high spirits; and, finally, that the attack was personally witnessed by your reliable friend who has asked you all these questions about ricin. What would you say about the matter then? What I am hoping you will say is that it should be brought to the attention of Scotland Yard and that you will help me do exactly that before the body goes back to America and it's too late for a postmortem."

"The first thing I would say, Paul, is that you have interested me and I would like to hear the particulars."

And hear them he did as Paul recounted his experiences on the walking tour, culminating in the nightmare of Commercial Street. It was an edited version he gave, reflecting the corrections he had made to his original vision as a result of the trip to Birmingham. Perhaps, in so doing, he had exaggerated the clarity of his evidence, but he saw no point in reliving with Bill Donaldson all the doubts of the past few days. Bill was a good friend, likely to give him the benefit of the doubt in any event, but Paul desperately wanted the ear of the police and he was in no mood to jeopardize his best hope for an introduction.

Donaldson heard him out without interruption. When Paul had finished his story, the editor, with what seemed to be calculatedly leisurely motions, lighted a cigarette and took a few reflective draughts. At last he broke Paul's suspense. "You could have seen it all correctly and still got the conclusion wrong. Suppose he did jab her with the umbrella. He might have fallen forward and never have thought to throw the umbrella aside or to prevent its striking the woman in front of him."

Paul sighed heavily. "It is my fate to live surrounded by skeptics. You're going to be a worthy rival of Alice in that department, I see that already. The only answer I can give you is the same I think has finally satisfied Alice: there is a difference between an accidental and an intentional thrust of the arm; there was no mistaking the jab for what it was."

Donaldson paraded a number of other objections and reservations, but in the end he agreed to help. He couldn't afford to be wrong, he said, if there was even a small chance that the umbrella man or another of his ilk had returned. He would rather leave to Scotland Yard the onus of rejecting Paul's evidence. Could he obtain an introduction? He thought so; he was on very good terms with one of the Deputy Assistant Commissioners, they had done many favors for each other in times past, and Bill thought there were still a few that stood to his credit. He would call Paul later that afternoon to let him know whether he had made any progress.

Delighted with Donaldson's promise to help, although well aware that he was far from having convinced him that there was anything of substance in his story, Paul took a taxi across town to meet Alice at Justin de Blank, a cafeteria in Duke Street. It was one of Alice's favorite lunch places in London, and Paul had always suspected that her fondness for its cuisine was sharpened by the anticipation of visiting a fabric shop that was only a few doors away. She was waiting for him when he arrived and, finding her half-buried in parcels, he deduced correctly that she had reversed her usual order of proceeding. "You won't believe what I found today," she said by way of greeting, and began an enthusiastic narrative of mohairs, mill remnants, and discounts. After expressing admiration for her conquests and laying claim to a table by depositing her bundles on it, he went directly to the end of the cafeteria line to order the dessert to which they were both addicted, fruit brûlé. With the caramel clogging his teeth deliciously, Paul told her about his meeting with Donaldson, Donaldson's summary of the Markov case, and his willingness to help Paul get a hearing at Scotland Yard.

Alice was pleased with what she heard, with one exception. "One thing still doesn't make sense to me and that's the problem we started with, the motive. Markov and Kostov were dissidents whom the Bulgarian regime had found to be a nuisance. What could they possibly have against Margaret Sanders? You will never convince me that she was some sort of secret agent. But from what you tell me this is shaping up to be some kind of political crime. Is there any other possible explanation?"

"I don't know," Paul said. "It's too early to say."

•

At the hotel desk, a message from Bill Donaldson was waiting: "Road is clear. Meet you at the Yard 7:30 P.M."

"I knew we could count on Bill," Alice said. "He's such a competent man. And don't be fooled by the big show of disbelief. He obviously smells a story. I hope you've noticed that he's counted himself in on the interview."

After dinner in their room, Paul took a taxi to Scotland Yard. He had only been to the new building once, when he had visited the Black Museum. He still couldn't suppress an antiquarian regret that this venerable police force had moved its home to such a flavorless modern setting. He only had to wait a few minutes for Bill Donaldson to arrive, and felt proud of the fact. Perhaps he was finally beginning to overcome his early-arrival complex. Alice would be thrilled.

Donaldson and he gave their names at the reception desk and were announced by telephone. Soon a young man in a dark business suit called for them. Above the lapels of his suitcoat sparkled a heavily starched rounded shirt collar; his tie seemed remarkably florid for his profession. He mumbled his name (which sounded like Goss) and took them in the lift to an upper floor, where he abandoned them in a room past a second or third bend of the corridor. Paul was glad that the young man was not so insincere as to request that they make themselves at home, for the room was hardly inviting. It was furnished only with a battered oval wooden table (which must have been a survivor of the earlier Yard), around which four chairs of doubtful solidity were arranged. Another lone chair was placed near the entrance. The walls were bare except for the framed portrait of a former Commissioner, Sir Robert Mark. He stared out at the viewer, rectitude in every trait, his attachment to the uniformed services made plain in his braided cap with its checkered band.

"Let's compare paranoias," Paul said to Donaldson after they took seats at the table. "Do you suppose we're being watched?"

"Of course not. They're just not quite ready for us."

"You must be right; I suppose things are ordered differently in England. You see before you, Bill, a man badly shaken by the experience of applying for a job with the CIA. I was ordered to appear at a disreputable-looking house in northwest Washington. I was ushered into a room much like this one, and there I was left alone for at least a half hour. I think that the table at which I sat was of much the same vintage and perhaps the same make as this one, but it was covered with dog-earred popular magazines. I waited in the silence of the room and in time found myself pondering and embroidering all the myths I had heard about the CIA. In very little time I had convinced myself that I was being viewed on some hidden TV screen, and that the whole point of the exercise was to see whether I would reach first for the *Playboy* or *Field & Stream.*"

"Did you get the job?"

"No, I didn't, as a matter of fact, and the sad thing for me has always been that I can't recall which magazine I have to blame. I'm glad to see that Scotland Yard, however devious it may be, is at least not inclined to spy on our reading habits. But assuming they are listening, let's make it worth their while. What have you been able to find out today about Margaret Sanders?"

Bill referred to some notes. "She was forty-five years old, I believe that was mentioned in the newspapers. Never been married. Several discreet affairs, and she generally had the good sense to pick her men friends from outside the theater world. It's nice to know when you read a bad review that it's your work they hate."

"Did she have any romance going currently?"

"Nothing's cropped up of interest on that front. She seems to have come to England alone and she hasn't surfaced much since she's been here. We did confirm the news reports that her rehearsals were still two or three weeks off."

"What were you able to find out about her family?"

"Shabby genteel, in the words of our immortal Thackeray. Not much money there, but two great New

England names. She was living modestly in an apartment she rented in an unfashionable neighborhood of Cambridge with a spinster sister, Emily Sanders, her only close relative. Regular habits, regular hours, a Christian Scientist, as I believe you will recall. The only odd thing about her at all, so it seems, was her strong interest in crime and stage thrillers."

"I don't see anything odd about that at all," Paul said somewhat defensively, "and judging by the run of *The Mousetrap*, I would guess that the same could be said for just about any Englishman."

Bill leaned across the table, exaggerating a confidential manner. "I'll let you into a secret on that subject: since opening night, there hasn't been an Englishman in the house."

"You may be right," Paul acknowledged. "Did you learn anything about her other interests? For example, is there any indication that she'd ever worked for the government or was politically active?"

"Absolutely none. She seems to have lived for her art."

"You mean, like Anthony Blunt?"

Donaldson let the question fade unanswered. Paul had never thought his friend had much of a sense of humor, or perhaps it was his own fault that he did not recall whether the journalist was a Cambridge man.

Before they could renew their conversation, the door opened and the man who had brought them to the room reappeared, followed by a middle-aged man, who introduced himself simply as Warren. He was Detective-Inspector Daniel Warren, Donaldson later explained, but Paul would never have figured that out from his appearance. Warren was a stark contrast to the portrait of Sir Robert Mark, in his distinctly non-military bearing and his unpressed business suit of an indefinable muddy color. A comfortable bulge of his midsection severely tested the strength of his suit-jacket button, suggesting that, if he had ever been a member of the Flying Squad, he had long since come to roost behind a desk at Scotland Yard. Paul, who had perhaps nourished the unrealistic hope that he would be escorted directly to the office of the Deputy Assistant Commissioner his friend had mentioned, shot an inquiring look in the direction of Donaldson, who slightly shrugged his shoulders as if to answer, "One can only do his best."

Inspector Warren extended his arm toward his younger colleague. "I expect you've already met Detective-Constable Garson." In Warren's clearer speech, the young man's name had taken on a second syllable. The inspector sat down heavily at the table, and Garson, notebook and pencil now in evidence, took the chair at the door. Paul could not help succumbing to a wave of disappointment. Not only was he received by this most unimpressive man, but the Yard seemed to be taking pains to make him understand that they regarded his visit as an inconvenience to be disposed of with as little ceremony as possible. They hadn't even dignified his call to the point of receiving him in a room that belonged to anybody; Bill and he sat in what must have served as a waiting room for informants or witnesses of little consequence. From under his braided peak Sir Robert Mark appeared to say commandingly, "Speak, you fool, and get the hell out of here."

Donaldson, who had apparently sketched the nature of Paul Prye's business when he arranged the appointment, tried to smooth the way for the interview. Professor Prye, he told Warren, was one of the greatest living admirers of Scotland Yard. The inspector would positively blush, he assured him, if he had had the pleasure to hear any of Professor Prye's lectures on the Yard's famous triumphs.

While Bill was talking, Paul took a closer look at the

detective. Warren had the fleshy, unlined face of a child who had never aged; an unruly shock of curly hair fell over his brow. His nearsighted eyes, slanting downward at the outer corners, were diminished by the thick lenses of his glasses, but perhaps not even this was a sign of advancing years; Paul could imagine him as a myopic schoolboy squinting at the blackboard. A faint smile constantly played on the inspector's lips. At first it could be taken as a sign of warmth or at least sociability, but as the man listened, expression unchanging, to Donaldson's bantering introduction, Paul soon saw the smile as a reflection of amusement at all the incongruous human conduct to which he had been exposed, and perhaps his anticipation of a wonderful joke at the expense of his superiors for foisting yet another eccentric on him.

Inspector Warren did not acknowledge Donaldson's words but, when he had finished, turned to face Paul Prye.

"Tell me, Professor Prye, have you ever been to Scotland Yard before?"

"Oh, yes, in fact twice, on visits to the Black Museum. Once in this building and earlier at the old location."

"Have you ever had occasion before to assist a police inquiry?"

"No."

"Have you ever sworn out a criminal complaint?"

"Never," Paul answered, but trying to achieve a lighter tone, he added, "I've often been tempted, though, to set the dogcatcher on my neighbor's Doberman."

Warren's smile of slight amusement did not register any change. "Have you ever testified in a court of law?"

"Only once, in a traffic case, and I must admit that I didn't make much of a witness. I couldn't remember the location of the lights at a street corner only a block or two from my home. Worse than that, I forgot to wear my glasses and staggered into the witness box like a blind man. I never could see where the jury was sitting. Are you supposed to look at the jury while you are testifying?"

Paul didn't receive an answer and hadn't expected one. He found himself in one of his characteristic postures, which he always found uncomfortable, trying to please someone who looked like he was going to be difficult to win over.

Warren pursued his questions, his smile unflagging.

"I understand from Mr. Donaldson that you think you've witnessed a ricin poisoning."

Paul hedged his response. "That may be overstating my position. I wish to report my observation of a woman being stabbed by an umbrella, a woman who died suddenly about two days later."

Warren ignored the qualification. "Is it fair to assume that you are familiar with the notorious Markov case?"

"Not all that familiar. Of course, the case received a good deal of attention in America, as it must have throughout the entire Western world. But I never made a close study of the case and I'd long since forgotten most of what I'd read or seen on television. It was Bill Donaldson who reminded me today of the technical details."

"When you saw the umbrella attack, did the possibility of a ricin murder occur to you immediately?"

Paul became wary, but was reluctant to claim instant enlightenment. "No, I can't say that. It still strikes me as incredible that I could have been a chance observer of such a bizarre crime. And furthermore, there was no reason for me to fear anything so lethal when I saw the woman pick herself up off the street without showing any sign of harm. It was only after her death that I started thinking about the ricin possibility." Paul could not bring himself to confess his moment of epiphany before the Madox Brown painting. He was having enough trouble establishing any credibility as it was.

"Then it would be right to say that your ricin theory came to you as an afterthought?"

Somewhat resentfully, Paul nodded. His resentment was directed against his own acquiescence. Why must he always be so anxious to ingratiate himself with perfect strangers? He was beginning to despair of his mission. This man Warren obviously was treating him like some kind of loony who loved to run to the police with tall tales or, even worse, some British-crime buff who wanted to tell the friends back home that he had been to Scotland Yard not for another museum visit, but on official business.

Well, perhaps the detective was right, but if he was and if Paul was in fact to lecture some evening to his book club about his adventure at Scotland Yard, he was damned if he was going to come out looking like a coward. He mustered as firm and direct a look as was in his arsenal, and said, "Inspector Warren, I know that you are a busy man, and I am grateful that you have been willing to see me, particularly on such short notice. But I must assure you at the outset that I am not an eccentric or a publicity seeker. My wife and I have been enjoying our trip to London, as we always do, and the last thing either of us wanted was to get mixed up in a crime. A lot of people in our city, if they happen to witness a mugging, walk as fast as they can in another direction. I don't admire them, but I understand the instinct. I'm here because I'm convinced I saw a murder done, by a means that is astonishing to me but not impossible, if I guess right. I would only request earnestly that you give me a fair hearing before you show me the door."

For the first time Warren's smile disappeared, replaced by a quizzical look. "Professor Prye, I don't want to begin with a misunderstanding, and so I propose a pact I hope you will find acceptable: I won't treat you like a bungling amateur, and in return, you won't treat me like Inspector Lestrade."

Paul nodded in ready agreement. Perhaps he had misjudged the man.

"Let's begin with the deceased," Warren said. "Had you ever seen Margaret Sanders before you met on the walking tour?"

"I'd never seen her and as far as I know I'd never seen her picture. When I saw her name in the newspaper, it seemed to ring a bell. I'm quite sure my wife and I went to one of her productions. *Night Must Fall*."

"How interesting. In any event, I understand that yesterday you saw her photograph in the newspaper."

"That's correct."

"And this is the photograph you saw?" Paul had not noticed that one of Warren's elbows rested on a brown envelope, from which he now withdrew a number of newspaper clippings. They all seemed to contain the same photograph he had seen, some better focused, others blurred. "And you're quite sure that this is the woman who was with you on the walking tour?"

"I'm quite sure."

"And what would you say about the photograph I shall now show you, is it the same woman?" He now took out of the envelope a glossy 8 × 10 photograph. It must have been a recent publicity portrait. There Margaret sat, her back to bookshelves lined with plays. She looked down through her rimless glasses at what seemed to be a typescript of a play. From her critical frown it appeared that she was not favorably impressed with what she was reading.

"That is the woman," Paul said with assurance. "She's captured there very well, and I would say it is a much more recent photograph than the one the newspapers used. She was wearing these very glasses, and her hair has gone much grayer since she sat for the other portrait."

Paul answered as unemotionally as he could, but it was hard to stifle his first stirrings of encouragement since the interview had begun. It did not seem after all that Warren had dismissed Donaldson's call out of hand; he had obviously gone to the trouble of picking up the publicity photo in the short time available before their appointment.

"That's good, very good," Warren resumed. "Now suppose you tell me your story from the beginning. Don't be disconcerted if Constable Garson slows you down from time to time. He's a promising young man, but not the fastest stenographer in the department."

As he began his narrative, Paul suffered for a while a feeling of loss of reality, as if he had dreamt himself on center stage of a thriller. Could he really be talking to a Scotland Yard inspector while a subordinate dutifully recorded his words? The differences between make-believe and reality only sharpened his memories of the theater conventions. This evening, at the hub of the Metropolitan Police, he had hardly caught sight of a blue uniform except at the reception desk. And of course, a dramatist could have done little with a volunteer witness, preferring to have the inspector make an ominous sudden appearance announcing his belief that the leading man could be of assistance in connection with the police inquiries.

When he got over these qualms, Paul sailed through his story with surprising poise. In part, his ease was built on lack of candor, for he presented as seamless an account that he had stitched from the several halting versions he had told to Alice, supplemented by corrective insights from Collins, Hunter, and Holloway. Perhaps it was his self-confidence that spared him the probing questions he had expected from the detective. Really, this man made a poor show after the skeptical barbs Alice had thrown with unerring accuracy at the weak points in his evidence.

The few interruptions Warren made were courteous and almost perfunctory. Had the woman been accompanied on the tour? Paul thought not. Could he describe her assailant? On this point Paul felt constrained to be modest, citing the descriptions of Gladys and the solicitor, but disclaiming any personal observation of the man's features.

Only one of Warren's questions set him thinking afresh. "Professor Prye, let us grant that you are right in your statement that the man struck her with an umbrella. How do you know he did not do this by accident as he fell?"

Before he replied, Paul reflected on the point for what seemed to him an embarrassingly long time. When he answered, he was surprised by his own words. "Quite simply because the man did not fall; I am certain of that. In fact, as I tried to see who lay sprawled in the street, my view was partially obstructed; I had to move my head to look over the man's shoulder."

"I wonder, Professor Prye, whether you have recalled that detail from the beginning or whether it is a memory that has just occurred to you now?"

Paul did not take offense. "I can only say that I have never had the feeling of certainty about the point that I had when I considered your question. Frankly, it is a matter that has given me considerable difficulty."

Warren's face did not reflect any appraisal of Paul's answer. Instead, he turned and said to his assistant, "Garson, would you be good enough to ask Superintendent

Higgins to join us? I think that he would like to meet Professor Prye—and Mr. Donaldson."

When Garson had gone, the three men at the table waited without exchanging an additional word. While Paul, who had a dread of gaps in conversation, racked his brains for a time-killing subject, he was startled to feel Donaldson thrust a wadded paper into his hand under the table. Paul bent down in a clumsy pretense of retying his shoelace, certain that he was not deceiving Warren. He opened the paper and read: "You're on to something. I think Higgins is Special Branch." Looking across to Warren, Paul thought that his faint smile had become a shade more intense. Struggling even harder for a way out of the silence, Paul mustered an inoffensive question. "What do you think of the Broadway headquarters compared to the old building? I'm probably a typical tourist, but it does seem to me that New Scotland Yard has taken its 'newness' a little bit too seriously."

The detective did not find the topic engaging. "The difference in environment is lost on me. I never worked much at the old place. I was transferred here directly from one of our district offices." Having delivered himself of this brief response, Warren was content to have the silence descend again. Either the man had no small talk or he was reluctant to resume the interview until his colleagues reappeared. Mercifully, they did not have to wait much longer. Garson opened the door and stood deferentially at the threshold. With a moment's delay, as if for dramatic effect, in strode a tall man in a navy blue pinstripe suit.

Paul's eyes were immediately drawn to the man's bald head, which rose in a dizzyingly high parabola. His narrow fringe of iron-gray hair, closely shorn at the temples, and his pencil-thin mustache put Paul more in mind of a civil servant than of a detective on the track of foreign

agents or IRA bombers. He could best visualize Superintendent Higgins, attired in his Sunday best, as the un-
flappable guest on a BBC news interview. He would be
just the man to be assuring the panel of reporters that the
Special Branch was not the action wing of MI5, but was
as directly responsible to the British public as the policeman on his beat. Looking into Higgins's unblinking
eyes, Paul, for one, would think long and hard before he
believed him.

As the introductions were made all around, Higgins
barely acknowledged the presence of the two visitors. He
sat at the table by Warren's side and seemed to stare over
Prye's head at the portrait of Sir Robert Mark, as if the
former leader were the only man in the room worthy of
his attention. Paul was struck by the strong contrast between the newcomer and Inspector Warren. If Warren
resembled a slightly mocking schoolchild, Higgins was
an eternally disapproving parent.

Without further ceremony, Inspector Warren sum-
marized for his colleague the information that Paul Prye
had given. It was a virtuosic display of memory and
exposition, beginning with the walking tour and re-
capitulating the results of the meetings that Paul had had
with the three tour members with whom he had been
able to communicate. Warren spoke without notes, and
he never paused to search for a word or a thought or to
reconsider the sequence of his presentation. Paul, who
did not feel comfortable delivering a talk without a detailed outline before him on the lectern, listened with
growing admiration and envy, but these reactions were
swept aside by a new surge of optimism that was inspired by the very comprehensiveness of Warren's report. The detective was not omitting or discounting any
detail—indeed, any speculation—that Paul regarded as
significant. Was it possible that, despite the skeptical
smile, Warren was inclined to share his suspicion?

Superintendent Higgins heard the report out without interruption or comment. When Warren had finished, Higgins thanked him, rose from his seat, and, with a minimally polite good-bye, left the room.

His emotions on a seesaw, Paul wondered, What now?

Warren's answer was not long in coming. "Was my summary accurate, Professor Prye? I'm happy, in any event, that we shall both have an opportunity to review Constable Garson's notes when they have been transcribed. I have only one more request to make of you this evening, Professor Prye. I would be very grateful if you would be willing to identify the body."

Before Paul was able to overcome an involuntary shudder of revulsion, Warren went on, "I hope, Mr. Donaldson, you will not take offense if we excuse you from accompanying us. Constable Garson will see you safely out."

· **7** ·

Garson drove them to the suburban mortuary to which Margaret's body had been brought at the request of her sister, who was expected to arrive soon from Boston to make arrangements for transportation home.

Once they were alone in the back seat of the police car, it did not take long for Warren to put off his official manner and assume an informal, almost confiding tone.

"I very much regret what may have struck you as a hasty parting with Mr. Donaldson. I know he is a good friend of yours, and we are grateful that he brought you to us. We have found him to be helpful in the past and have the utmost confidence in his good judgment, but there are reasons for us to proceed with caution. Some of those reasons I am not at liberty to disclose to you; two points, however, I can clarify, and it is important for me to do so. First, you may not be aware of the fact that the police have had what we might call a problem of press relations over the past several years. There was controversy over the handling of public announcements in the Yorkshire Ripper case; it was feared that premature identification of the suspect had jeopardized the prosecution. I think personally that the criticism was overblown, but we have proceeded with circumspection—perhaps I should say greater circumspection—ever since. Therefore, I ask you to be understanding of the delicacy of our relations with Mr. Donaldson and the press corps generally. I don't ask that you shun him completely, but I do suggest that you use discretion in communicating to him any insights you may gain, or may think you have gained, with respect to our investigation of the matter you have called to our attention.

"There is a special reason for exercising a high degree of care in this case. If there is a chance your surmise is right, there is a dangerous man in our midst, armed with an insidious and highly lethal weapon. We do not want him to learn the names or whereabouts of any of the witnesses of his crime. We should not, for example, want him to learn through a thoughtless disclosure your name—or the name of Mrs. Prye."

The mention of a possible risk to Alice struck Paul as gratuitous and marred what he otherwise would have taken as a gracious request for confidentiality. He stifled his resentment and said that he fully accepted Warren's advice. He would be very careful about what he told Bill Donaldson.

The conversation had effectively distracted Paul's attention from the rather tortuous route they had taken, and he had no idea where they were when they stopped before a large gray stone house on a tree-lined street that led up a steep incline to a small square. The neighborhood reminded Paul of Highgate, which he often visited in his never-ending quest for books.

They were expected. The manager of the funeral home received them wordlessly and led them to a small room illuminated only weakly by a table lamp. In the center of the room was an open coffin, which Paul approached gingerly, thankful for the semidarkness. He had always been ashamed of his squeamishness at funerals. His shame was not due to his sense of a lack of manliness; instead, he was distressed that his preoccupation with his own bodily reactions to the sight and presence of death impaired his consciousness of loss and his sympathy for the dead and the survivors.

Through partly closed eyelids, he looked down into the casket. There she lay, looking much as he had remembered her. She was a fair woman, and her face did not seem paler in death; perhaps her cheekbones were more pronounced, bringing into stronger relief the contours that Paul had found so striking.

He identified her without hesitation. But then he surprised himself. He did not walk quickly away as he had done at the funerals of relatives and friends who meant so much more to him. He felt swept by a new emotion, as if for the first time he had looked upon death without thinking of himself. Forcing his eyes to widen, he gazed at her beautiful face. Painstakingly, he imprinted her features on his mind as if he were again in the painting gallery, standing before a drowned Ophelia whom he could not see again for the price of an admission ticket. But try as he did, he could not understand the feeling that kept him standing there as the moments passed. What was Margaret to him, that he should grieve for her?

Warren did not hurry him away. At last, they returned

to the car. As Paul closed the door, he happened to look down a side street. A van was parked near the corner; it was marked with the crest of the Metropolitan Police. Paul did not think he had seen it there when they arrived.

They drove back to London in silence, as if the case no longer held any interest for either of them. But Paul realized that this was only an illusion of his weariness; more likely, the inspector recognized that his spirits were flagging and had considerately decided not to intrude on his private thoughts. Then again, Paul reflected, perhaps he was giving the man too much credit. Warren didn't seem much given to irrelevant conversation. Paul remembered the long silence that had descended while they sat waiting for Higgins to join them during his visit to the Yard.

But the inspector was easy to misread. When the car pulled up at the hotel, Warren unexpectedly reached across the back seat and shook Paul's hand warmly. "You have been very helpful indeed. I cannot tell you how much, but you must believe me for the moment. You'll recall my having questioned you about your 'afterthoughts.' Keep having them, by all means. No good detective could dispense with them. I have the feeling that we will be talking again before you leave London next week."

When he returned to the hotel room, Alice greeted him eagerly at the door. "Before we go to dinner, you must tell me everything that's happened. Leave absolutely nothing out."

Suddenly feeling exhausted, Paul lay down on the bed. Closing his eyes, he did his best to run through the evening's events, but he knew that, in his haste to be done, his narrative was confused and that on many points he was not satisfying Alice's great appetite for detail. When he came to the scene in the mortuary, he simply said that he had identified the body, and then fell into a long silence. Alice tried for a while to get him to continue, but then gave up in knowing exasperation.

"Paul," she said, "I've always known you were a susceptible man; it's one of your charms. But this time you've gone a little far, don't you think? I really believe you've fallen in love with a dead woman."

•

Tuesday was a day for backsliding. What more was there for Paul to do, since he'd put the matter in the hands of the police? He considered himself a success as far as he had gone. He felt confident that Warren believed his story, and if Donaldson had correctly identified Higgins, the Special Branch had taken an interest too. Unless he had fallen prey to an overheated imagination, it was likely that the van he had seen parked outside the funeral home had taken Margaret's body to a forensic lab for a postmortem. The police must have had a hell of a time getting Margaret's sister to agree. He wondered whether she was a Christian Scientist too.

He had not brought himself to ask Warren about the postmortem, and he had no idea whether the detective would let him know the results. After having been the secret owner of a murder case for the past few days, it was a strange feeling for him to be firmly relegated to the role of an uninformed outsider. Yet he clutched at a straw of comfort; after all, Warren must have meant something more than politeness in suggesting, as he said good night, that they were likely to talk again.

There was another personal reason to take some time off from the case. Alice was leaving on the next afternoon for Glasgow and he had promised to provide what she liked to call "escort service." They spent the morning in the boutiques of Covent Garden. It was a comfort to Paul to pack up the Commercial Street riddle and to delve again into the ephemera of past crimes. When the fellow members of his book club asked him why he persisted in studying only antique cases, he liked to quote what Harvard Professor Kittredge had written of witchcraft: "It is easy to be wise after the fact—especially when the fact is two hundred years old." The justness of the observation had never been so clear to him. From his new experience he had also learned another lesson: it is far easier to enjoy crime in fact or fiction when you don't have to think of the victims as real people who lived, died, and suffered.

In spite of what he'd been taught by his direct confrontation with murder, Paul slipped back with remarkable ease into his fascination with crime trivia. At Pollock's Toy Theatre Shop he made quite a haul to start the day: the cardboard characters and scenes from *Blackbeard the Pirate;* an early nineteenth-century actor's print featuring Captain Macheath, the highwayman from *The Beggar's Opera;* and, as the pièce de résistance, a book of paper dolls called *Infamous Women.* The paper figures included a young woman dressed in muslin while waiting to don her cutout court dress; she was none other than Madame de Brinvilliers, the mass arsenic poisoner of seventeenth-century Paris. At a record shop specializing in theater music, Paul was delighted to come upon the reissue of the original London-cast recording of Wolf Mankowitz's musical comedy based on the Crippen poisoning, *Belle, or The Ballad of Dr. Crippen.* He had always enjoyed the jingoistic sentiment of the last chorus:

> *The year was 1910,*
> *And we showed the world again,*
> *That you can't beat a British crime.*

The secret joke that Paul particularly treasured was the fact that Crippen, who was probably the second most famous "British" murderer of the past hundred years, after Jack the Ripper, was in fact an American who received his medical (and presumably toxicological) education in Cleveland, Ohio. If Queen Victoria was right, Jack the Ripper may have been foreign too. None of her subjects, she thought, could have been so unkind to women.

Paul rendezvoused with Alice at the western end of the market. She absolutely refused to admire his purchases as she could often be persuaded to do when the day's schedule was more relaxed. However, next on the agenda was one of the high points of her visits to London, a ride out to Camden Passage for antique shopping and a mid-afternoon feast at one of the local restaurants. They had resumed their customary London routine so fully that Paul supposed that Alice had quite forgotten about the death of Margaret Sanders. In fact, though, it was Alice who brought the subject up again when they reached the triumphant finale of a countless series of courses at the restaurant, something French with raspberries.

As was his custom, Paul was looking greedily across at her half-filled plate, and after ignoring him unsuccessfully, she finally extended a fork more heavily laden with disapproval than raspberries. She said, "I'm not at all sure that you've fulfilled the terms of our agreement. I said I would leave you behind in London if you seemed to be making progress on the case. So far you've managed to get a foot inside Scotland Yard, due to the contacts of Bill Donaldson. It's true that you've identified Margaret Sanders, but I never had any doubt she was the woman in your group. Still, we haven't heard a peep from the police to suggest that they've decided to examine the body or, if they did, that they found anything out of the ordinary. Nevertheless," she added, stretching out the word, "all the shopping and eating has put me in a generous mood, so off I go alone to astonish the Scots."

Paul was very pleased with her. "You're turning out to be a perfect detective's wife. It's nice of you to let me stay, really. We'll talk on Wednesday and Thursday night and you can give me a firsthand report on how everything went. Anyway, you don't leave until tomorrow afternoon and we'll have a lot of time together before then. *Midsummer Night's Dream* tonight." They were going to the Barbican, and Paul was glad that they had chosen something very unlikely to remind him of death or murder.

Paul observed with regret that Alice had finished her raspberries without any further assistance from him. Waiting for the coffee to arrive, she came back again to the subject of Margaret Sanders.

"There's one point on which I deserve your current opinion before I leave—we've debated it long enough, it seems to me. Do you think Margaret was into some kind of undercover business? If so, I certainly hope she was on our side. Our generation has had quite enough disenchantment."

Paul was glad he hadn't told her of his feeble joke about Anthony Blunt at Scotland Yard. He said, "If it turns out that Margaret was some kind of female Sidney Reilly, it will take me a while to get used to the idea. But would it really be all that more surprising than the whole damn business, or than the fact that I happened to witness it? There is a new thought, though, that's beginning to stir in me. Perhaps it's only a foolish rebelliousness on my part. You see, when I met that man Higgins who Donaldson says is Special Branch, I didn't like him much. He isn't the most appealing person at first meeting. He struck me as cold, uncommunicative, and not terribly interested in what I had to report. Whatever the reason, I started thinking: This guy's got his mind made up. He's already decided that if, against all odds, I turn out to be right and they have another ricin case on their hands, it must be part of some deep-laid political plot that's miles beyond the comprehension of the man in the street— even of a man like me who was in the very street where the crime was committed.

"And so I've started thinking. Suppose it does turn out to be ricin; Higgins may be starting down a blind alley. The fact that it's the same weapon that was used against Markov doesn't mean that the victim is another Markov."

He warmed to his theme. "I don't know how many James Bond movies you and I have seen by now where some villain, for his own private purposes—generally blackmail—gets ahold of an atomic bomb and threatens to blow the world up. Thank God that's never happened, but maybe we're conditioned to worrying about such possibilities after seeing all this science fiction trash. And besides, if you can visualize the day when atomic weapons might fall into the hands of a Qaddafi, how much more responsible is he than the typical James Bond villain?"

"I'm not sure I know where all this leads you," Alice said.

"Quite simply to this point: If it is at least conceivable that an atomic weapon could fall into private hands, is it not more likely and more worrisome that the smaller, the more portable, the even microscopic weapons of modern political terror could be diverted and used for nonpolitical crimes? Maybe that's what has happened here; I may have witnessed one of the first examples of a horrible new genre of modern murder—committed with a secret service weapon gone astray."

"All right, if it isn't the KGB and their Bulgarian friends this time, who is it?"

Paul shrugged. "I wish I knew. I'm beginning to see the shadow of a possibility, but it's too vague for me to work out yet, and I could be wildly wrong."

"Don't tell me. I love a surprise. Your brilliant solution can be my welcome-home gift when I come back from Scotland."

All in all, it was a wonderful day. They had seen a beautiful (though acrobatic) performance of *Midsummer Night's Dream* and were getting ready for bed when the telephone rang. It was Bill Donaldson calling for Paul: "I hope your new chums at the Yard haven't convinced you I have herpes. You needn't reassure me, I'm not all that sensitive. To show you we're still friends, I am calling to suggest you give the morning newspaper a particularly close look before you plunge back into our wonderful shops."

"And if I follow your advice, what will I read there?" Paul asked.

"There will be two points that I think you'll find of interest. First, that Margaret Sanders, as you suspected, was the victim of a ricin poisoning. Second, that she was not the first. Good night."

Paul tried vainly to hold him, but Bill had hung up.

At an indecently early hour the next morning, Paul brought Alice a newspaper and a lukewarm cup of decaf. Under a tall headline they read:

TWO NEW UMBRELLA MURDERS

Scotland Yard announced last night that it has confirmed the commission of two new poisoned-umbrella murders that appear to follow precisely the pattern of the assassination of dissident Bulgarian broadcaster Georgi Markov in 1978. The victims, Policewoman Janet Sterling, 27, and American director, Margaret Ames Sanders, 45, died only a day apart, on Friday and Saturday. The death of Miss Sanders, previously reported in articles that were widely published in Sunday's newspapers, had been attributed to an "undetermined" cause. For some reason that is not yet apparent, news of WPC Sterling's death had been withheld until the present announcement.

Policewoman Sterling was stabbed from behind as she walked in a rush-hour crowd near Victoria Station last Wednesday afternoon. She was assigned to T Disctrict (Hounslow), and it has not been disclosed what had brought her to Victoria at the time of the attack. Admitted to hospital late Wednesday night complaining of a high fever, she stated that she had been struck by an umbrella wielded by a man in a tan raincoat. She chased him into the station, where he eluded her.

The details given out by the police about the fatal assault on Margaret Sanders are stranger still. She died in her hotel room on Saturday evening, having refused medical attention for symptoms similar to those of Policewoman Sterling. Only after her death did the Yard learn, through an unidentified source, that she had been stabbed with an umbrella during an East End walking tour on Thursday. One informant adds the ironic footnote that the tour is thought to have been devoted to the murders of Jack the Ripper, whose centennial is marked this year.

Forensic laboratory tests, not yet complete, indicate that metal pellets found imbedded in the right thigh of each victim closely resemble that found in Markov's body, and it is believed that the same poisonous agent, ricin, a deadly extract of the castor bean, was again employed.

The police decline to comment on the direction of their investigations. There is some indication that principal responsibility for the inquiry has been assumed by the Special Branch. A spokesman for the Yard who declined to be named, stated: "We are driven to conclude that the hand of Eastern European secret services has struck these cruel blows, but are thus far unable to identify any link between the two unfortunate women." There is also a report of plans to convene a meeting of COBRA, the special contingency unit that has been set up to deal with serious terrorist incidents.

They finished the article at about the same time, but Alice was the first to speak.

"Of course, I knew you were right all along. I was questioning your theories only to sharpen your thinking." Alice was nothing if not flexible-minded. Nodding to Paul to turn the page, as if she were performing at the piano, she read on. There was a long leader on the police revelations in an inner page. When she had scanned it quickly, she burst out laughing and handed the paper to Paul.

"You won't believe the last paragraph. It's a scream." The leader ended:

It is inexcusable that government and police deferred announcement of the ricin murder of WPC Sterling for almost twenty-four hours. In the interim their silence made it impossible for the public to take suitable precautions for their safety.

"What are the public to do 'for their safety'?" Alice mocked. "Are they to ban the use of umbrellas here, in the rain capital of the West?"

"Probably not," Paul replied, "but without hesitation I predict that operation of cloakrooms at public facilities will be the next growth industry." He was glad that Alice had set this light tone, because he would otherwise have had difficulty in restraining what struck him as an unseemly sense of vindication, of triumph, in the revelation of the ricin murders.

"Alice, I know I promised to spend the morning with

you. Would you be terribly disappointed if I called Inspector Warren to find out if he'll see me? I have some thoughts I'd like to try out on him, but first I'll have to squeeze a few details out of him on the other murder. Is that all right? You don't need any help with a taxi, do you?"

Alice was deep in thought. She stood before the open closet, making the difficult selection of her travel wardrobe. She answered without looking around at him. "Don't worry about me; you go right ahead. I think you're finally making the progress you promised me. I can find my way to Glasgow. It's north of here, isn't it?"

•

There was no question about it, he was making progress at Scotland Yard. This morning he was received in a room that belonged to someone. It had to be Inspector Warren's own office, for on a credenza behind his desk were the family photographs: two chubby schoolboys with rebellious locks hanging over their foreheads, reproductions of the very pattern on which Warren had been designed in such a ludicrously grand scale. By the side of the boys was a haunted sylphlike sister, as lovely no doubt as their mother, who, alas, was nowhere to be seen. The void was eloquent of divorce.

"It is good of you to see me again," Paul began, finding with embarrassment that he was involuntarily adopting Warren's perpetual smile, "but then again, you predicted it, didn't you? You suspected all along, knowing about the policewoman, that I was right. What can you tell me about her and what she was doing when she was attacked?"

Warren held up his right hand, index finger pointing diagonally, in what Paul was to recognize as a characteristic cautionary gesture. "Forgive me if I slow you down for a moment while we establish some ground rules. I am frank to tell you that you interest me, Professor Prye, because you are given to speculation. If you were not, the body of Margaret Sanders would now be back in the United States being readied for fitting burial, and we would have heard no more of her. We would have been left with the solitary mystery of the murder of Policewoman Sterling, no notion stirring that her death might be part of a pattern. I have the hope that you can help us work out the shapes of that pattern."

"I'm flattered."

"Not beyond your merit, based on your performance to date. That is what makes it so difficult for me to lay down the rules I'm constrained to set for our collaboration. But so be it. The fact is that I can't tell you everything we know."

Paul was emboldened by the detective's obvious discomfort. "Is that your own decision or Superintendent Higgins's?"

"So it is intramural gossip you are after; how very disappointing. But I will oblige you to a certain extent. I suppose Higgins made it perfectly obvious Monday. He doesn't share my hope in you; he's convinced we have another Markov case."

"If you'll pardon the observation of an unqualified foreigner, I don't think he did such a spectacular job on the first one."

Warren quickly came to the defense of the Branch. "I don't think I can agree with you. We had a pretty good idea who was responsible there, but the politicians have a nasty habit of getting in the way. You'll remember what happened a few years ago in St. James's Square. But to return to our rules for the present investigation. I'm bound to evade your requests for private information, understandable as your curiosity doubtless is. Instead, I shall ask you to accept, without challenge for the moment, a set of assumptions:

"One. Emily Sanders, with whom we have spoken during her visit to claim her sister's body, knows of no person who might have had violent designs on Margaret or would gain by her death.

"Two. There is no apparent link between Margaret Sanders and WPC Sterling.

"Three. Sterling had no secret assignments in the interest of the Branch.

"Four. We are advised that Sanders, to the knowledge of the CIA, was not engaged in covert activity on behalf of the United States or any other government."

"You may also assume that, at least in this instance, we believe the CIA," Warren added, attempting to relieve his bureaucratic tone.

Paul shook his head emphatically. "That won't do. You're being too stingy, even with your assumptions. What am I to assume that a Hounslow policewoman was doing in Victoria Street?"

Warren was silent for a moment, evidently undecided as to whether he should answer. Paul wouldn't wait for his decision.

"All right, let's approach it a different way. I've got a wild idea that I must test before I consign it to the garbage heap with many other great inspirations of the past week. Let me state an assumption and you simply tell me whether it's reasonable. Okay?"

Warren said nothing, but did not discourage him from proceeding.

"It is my recollection that several years ago Scotland Yard moved the Black Museum to a separate building in Victoria Street. I further understand that the principal use of the Museum these days is for the training and education of the police. Is it fair for me to assume that shortly before she was attacked near Victoria Station, Policewoman Sterling had been visiting the Black Museum?"

Warren's smile vanished, replaced by ill-disguised astonishment, quickly suppressed. "You may make that assumption," he said.

It was Paul's turn to smile, very broadly. "Then I ask only one favor at present: an introduction to the curator for a brief afternoon visit to the Museum. I haven't been there for years. It will be a pleasure to see its treasures again, and while I'm there you might also ask that I be given access to the visitors' book. If you'll do that for me, I am willing to try out this idea I have, at the risk of making a complete fool of myself. Oh, I suppose there is another favor I should ask, namely, that if there's anything left to my theory by the end of the day, I might be able to see you again tomorrow morning."

"All conditions are accepted," Warren said, reaching for his telephone.

A half hour later, Paul Prye, living a crime connoisseur's headiest dream, was being privately escorted through the Black Museum by its curator. In honor of the centennial, a special exhibition of the museum's Jack the Ripper memorabilia was on display. Paul viewed again the police poster he had for years lusted to add to his collection. It reproduced the letter of September 27, 1888, purportedly written by the murderer to "The Boss, Central News Office, London City," and marked the first public appearance of the Ripper's nickname. The letter concluded merrily:

The next job I do I shall clip the lady's ears off and send to the police officers just for jolly wouldnt you. Keep the letter back till I do a bit more work, then give it out straight. My knife's nice and sharp I want to get to work right away if I get a chance. Good luck.

yours truly,
Jack the Ripper

Don't mind me giving the trade name wasn't good enough to post this before I got all the red ink off my hands curse it. No luck yet. They say I'm a doctor now <u>ha ha.</u>

Sir Melville Macnaghten, who became head of the CID in 1903, had always thought the letter was a journalist's hoax. If he was right, it was funny how history repeated itself. The provincial police investigating the Yorkshire Ripper case had been led up the garden path by a similar prankster's letter.

There were several other objects in the Ripper exhibition Paul had not seen before: a police notice of the murder of Elizabeth Stride, another Ripper victim; a surgeon's knife once thought to have been the Ripper's weapon; and a surgeon's drawing of the mutilated body of Catherine Eddowes that looked like the work of a demented child.

It was with difficulty that Paul reminded himself that on this occasion he had not come as a tourist.

Turning to the curator, he said, "I know that Inspector Warren told you that I would be wanting to ask some questions about a Museum tour of last Wednesday afternoon. I know that one of the guests was Policewoman Sterling. Do you recall whether there were any members of the public included in the group?"

The curator, a small bald man with a heavy black mustache, replied in a monotone, "I wouldn't know without consulting our visitors' book. I didn't lead that particular tour. During recent years most of our visitors have been police officers and those on training and instruction courses. Of course, we would like to accommodate the enormous demand for visits by all interested members of the public, but restrictions have been necessary in the interest of operational efficiency. We cannot place ourselves in the position of creating a demand we could not possibly fulfill."

Paul did not think that it was a time for sincerity. "Perfectly understandable, I am sure," he said. "Would you be able to take a moment to consult the visitors' book for that tour?"

"No trouble at all. It is our duty, of course, to serve our operating branches. Come this way, please."

The curator led the way to a record office, where he soon located the current volume of the visitors' books. He turned to the page for the afternoon in question and scanned the list of visitors. "Yes, we have the list here. Almost all police officers and cadets, as I told you."

"Were there any public visitors at all?"

The curator looked at the page again. "Yes, there seems to have been one gentleman we had with us on that occasion."

"Can you tell me his name?"

"I'm happy to do so. The name is J. L. Ventra." He slowly spelled out the last name, which Paul took down in his notebook.

"Would it be possible for me to see the person who escorted that group? It would be helpful if I could find out what this man looked like."

"I'm afraid I can't help you in that regard. I'm quite certain that the tours that day were led by the assistant curator, who happens to be on holiday in Europe at the moment. He should return in about two weeks."

Paul cursed his luck, but then took another tack. "When I was at the Museum several years ago (it was still at Scotland Yard at that time), it was necessary for public visitors to obtain a personal recommendation before we're admitted. Is that still the practice?"

The curator gave a grudging response, as if he were taking pains to ward off a horde of American tourists. "I'm afraid we are not in a position to be as generous in our admission policy as we were at the Yard. Nevertheless, it is still possible to make exceptions for people with appropriate credentials and a genuine interest in police operations. In these cases, as you say, it is still necessary to obtain an appropriate sponsorship."

"Would you be able to determine from your records who sponsored Mr. Ventra's visit?"

"I believe so, if you will give me half a moment." The curator referred to another file. "Yes, here is the notation. Mr. Ventra was recommended to us by Lord Whitman."

"Can you tell me when and how the introduction was made?"

"It is indicated in our record that the recommendation was received on the previous Monday, 15 August, in a telephone conversation from an assistant of Lord Whitman named James Clark."

"Thank you very much," Paul said. "You've been very helpful."

It was Paul's firm belief that the third favorite sport in England, after soccer and cricket, was locking people out. Again and again he had encountered this trait, at first with irritation and gradually with a more neutral feeling. In many different scenes he had come face to face with the national passion for exclusion, whether at the members' pavilion at Lords, in which Alice and he had vainly sought shelter when it started to rain at a poorly attended off-season match; at Cambridge University, where a patch of burnt grass with no more attractions than Trinity Gardens at Tower Hill was fenced off for the sole use of the senior tutors; and most recently in the courtyard of what had been Thackeray's beloved Charterhouse School, where Paul had been threatened with a charge of criminal trespass for intruding a moment to invoke the spirit of one of his favorite Victorians. Now at last, he hoped, the pervasive custom of exclusion might be about to do him some good.

After Paul left the Museum, he went to a nearby telephone booth and called Bill Donaldson.

"Bill, if you wanted an MP's recommendation to Scotland Yard, would there be any particular reason to pick out Lord Whitman?"

Bill answered without hesitation. "His would be the first name to come to mind. He's a notorious police buff, almost a figure of fun for his persistent attendance at police ceremonies. He's our equivalent of your mayors who used to be photographed chasing fires."

Paul was intrigued. "Cast your mind back for a moment. Has Lord Whitman been recently featured in the press in any connection with the police?"

"As a matter of fact, he has been. It can't have been more than a week or two ago that I saw his benevolently smiling face in our own paper; he was the guest of honor on the occasion of the renovation of the River Police Museum."

"And did the event get broad coverage in the media?"

"Reasonably so, as I recall."

Paul spelled out his thought. "So that if a traveler had arrived in London about that time and had given even casual attention to the newspaper or TV, it would not have taken him long to learn of Lord Whitman's attachment to the police."

"Not if he came upon this story. But tell me, Paul, has it already become self-evident to you that our murderer is a tourist?"

"I haven't the vaguest idea, but at least on Commercial

Street I had the impression that most of us were tourists. Bill, do you think you could help me arrange to see Lord Whitman's assistant, a man named Clark?"

Bill thought he could, and as usual he turned out to be effective at opening doors. Later that day, Paul sat across the desk of James Clark, a cordial young man who identified himself as Lord Whitman's appointments secretary. Paul had introduced himself (somewhat inaccurately, but he thought he could now count on Warren's support) as an American criminologist assisting Scotland Yard in a murder inquiry.

"It is believed that a man who might be of assistance to the investigation was recently in communication with your office," Paul said. He told Clark about the visit of J. L. Ventra to the Black Museum. "The curator's records indicate that Mr. Ventra was admitted to the Museum on the recommendation of Lord Whitman, and that the recommendation was transmitted in a telephone call from you a week ago Monday."

"If you'll give me a moment to look at my journal, I can confirm whether that is the fact." He turned the pages of a loose-leaf notebook he kept on his telephone table, and then ran his index finger down the margin of the right-hand page where the book lay open. He looked up and nodded. "Your information is quite accurate. Mr. Ventra called me at two-forty-five P.M. that day and at three P.M. I passed along Lord Whitman's recommendation to the Museum."

"Had you previously had occasion to speak to Mr. Ventra?"

"No, sir."

"Did you know his name?"

"It was completely unfamiliar to me. He introduced himself as a person very much interested in the history of Scotland Yard. He was hoping that Lord Whitman would support his admission to the Black Museum, about which he had read so much."

Always worried about the niceties of bureaucracy, Paul advanced with some trepidation to the next question. "Between Ventra's call at two-forty-five and your call at three to the Black Museum, were you able to talk to Lord Whitman and secure his recommendation of Mr. Ventra?"

Clark was unruffled. "It was unnecessary for me to discuss the matter with Lord Whitman. The entire staff have standing instructions to approve any such requests without qualification. Lord Whitman believes very strongly that the Black Museum should be open to the general public, just as the FBI Museum is in Washington. He once said to me, 'What is the Yard concerned about—that some dishonest visitor will run off with Charley Peace's violin or with G. J. Smith's bathtub?'"

"I quite agree with you," Paul said with genuine enthusiasm. "I have only one more question, which may be something of a long shot after the time that has passed. Can you recall anything about Mr. Ventra's voice?"

"I'm not certain that I know what you mean."

"Well, did he have an English accent?" Paul would have recalled his words if he could, knowing how foolish they must have sounded. It was too late.

Mr. Clark's answer was understandably icy. "I would remind you, Mr. Prye, that we do not speak in this country with English accents. *You* speak with an American accent. Having made that point, I must confess that nothing about the man's speech struck me as peculiar. As I recall, he sounded like an Englishman, and if my recollection is not playing tricks, I would guess that he was a Londoner of middling education at best. However, there was no mistaking his enthusiasm for the Yard, and that is all that matters to Lord Whitman."

"Did he say why he wanted to visit the Museum?"

"I don't believe he stated any particular reason. But judging by the number of requests we've had this summer, it isn't difficult to guess. I expect you've heard, Mr. Prye, that we're observing the centennial of the Ripper murders. The Museum boasts a unique collection of Ripper items. And now, if you'll forgive me, there is correspondence that I must attend to."

Mr. Clark left no doubt that the interview had ended.

When Paul reached the hotel, there were two points on his agenda: a scotch, and a call to Warren. Drink in hand, he dialed Scotland Yard and was put through to the inspector. He began their conversation with what appeared to be a kindergarten riddle.

"Precisely how long is the long arm of the law?"

"Whom would you have us reach?" Warren asked, correctly reading the question as a request for action.

"Are you so feared by your Museum staff that you can summon home a globe-trotting assistant curator?"

"Why would you want us to do that?"

Paul told him what he had learned from the Museum curator and James Clark.

"I'll have to report Lord Whitman to our boss," Warren remarked. "He's playing fast and loose with the rules. Of course, I don't mean to criticize his choice on this particular occasion. For all I know, this man Ventra may be a VIP."

"But it's Ventra we're after. He's the man who killed the policewoman and Margaret Sanders."

There was a pause on the line; Paul could almost see Warren's smile at the other end. Then the detective spoke. "Aren't you rushing things a little? I know I've asked you to find a pattern, some sense to this strange business. But you've leapt far ahead of the facts. What have you to show for the day's sleuthing? I started you off with a fact that seemed to stimulate your thought processes. Splendid; that's what I wanted to do. And what was that fact—that on Wednesday afternoon Policewoman Sterling took part in a tour of the Black Museum. What did that fact mean to me? Quite plainly, that there was nothing mysterious about Sterling's presence near Victoria Station at the time of the attack. She was not there at the request of the Branch to track spies or to establish contact with foreign agents or dissidents. No, nothing as exotic as all that, she was doing the most commonplace thing in the police world, what we'd expect our young officers and even raw recruits to do quite early in their careers: visit the instructive exhibits of the Yard's Museum.

"Now, once she was there, whom did Sterling meet? Very largely other people much like her, other police. But there was one exception—this was your discovery—a single civilian. It's not uncommon to have visitors from outside the police forces, although we don't have the staff or facilities to accommodate the public at large.

"And what do you make of all this? Let me recapitulate the unspoken syllogism. Sterling visits the police museum. She meets a single civilian there. Shortly after she leaves the building she is attacked by the ricin murderer. Therefore, the civilian she met must have been the murderer. It's neat, I admit, but the logic escapes me. The fact that event B follows event A does not mean that B was caused by A."

Post hoc propter hoc. The detective was beginning to remind him of Alice.

"Furthermore," Warren added slyly, "how do you know the murderer was not a policeman? You must not read many thrillers."

Paul refused to be intimidated. "You wanted a pattern, and I'll give you one, because I see a pattern emerging. I'd like to defer tomorrow's appointment until the afternoon, though. I want to do some research on patterns."

"May I suggest the textile department of the V. and A.?" Warren suggested. He agreed to the delay of their meeting.

Paul went out to Wheeler's for a lonely dinner; Alice's plane had left in midafternoon. On his way back he picked up a newspaper in Piccadilly Circus. The headline on the kiosk seemed to turn the clock back a decade. "POLICE BAFFLED BY RETURN OF BROLLY MAN."

When he was about to enter the revolving door of the hotel, a man brushed against him and squeezed in ahead of him. What was the old ethnic joke about the man who could pass you in a revolving door? The stranger was wearing a raincoat, but it was a mild night and he was not carrying an umbrella. Emerging into the lobby, Paul was struck by a momentary panic. He patted down his flanks searching for tender spots and probed the rear of his trouser leg where he thought the man had bumped him.

This was ridiculous. The case was really getting to him.

About 11:00 P.M., Paul called Alice in Glasgow. She filled him in on the results of the first session of the Realism seminar.

"If you haven't solved the mystery yet, I've found a flock of new suspects for you, and all of them art historians. There's more than enough malice floating around up here to account for your murders and many others besides. The Revisionists claim that the Conservatives are defending their outdated textbooks; and they are charged in return with covert assistance to art dealers in promoting slow-moving inventory. Thank God that, when my turn comes tomorrow morning, I'm talking on Courbet. Everybody's afraid to attack *him!* What's new in London?"

Paul gave her a summary of recent developments. He began by reading her a brief article that had appeared in the evening newspaper: Scotland Yard was requesting all persons who had participated in the Jack the Ripper walking tour of last Thursday, 18 August, to communicate with Inspector Warren. Paul was encouraged by this evidence that Warren remained in control of the investigation of the death of Margaret Sanders. He also couldn't help wondering—perhaps his competitive instinct had been piqued—whether any of the other walkers who responded would recall any significant details that had escaped him.

Then he told Alice about his visit to the Black Museum and of his quest for the shadowy Mr. Ventra. When he finished his account, he patiently awaited her praise, but none was immediately forthcoming. Alice was certainly hard to please; for some reason she seemed hung up on what struck him as a completely trivial point. Had she gotten the man's name right? He had to spell it out for her. She was keeping him in suspense, he was sure of it now. Alice had something up her sleeve in addition to a rounded slim arm.

When she was satisfied that she had teased him long enough, she said:

"Your Mr. Ventra's quite a joker, isn't he?"

"He doesn't seem so to me. He's killed two women."

Alice said she would ignore the high-and-mighty tone. She reminded him that he always got that way when he was out of his depth.

"Of course he has killed them, dear," she said. "There's nothing amusing about that, I quite agree. It's his name that's supposed to be a big joke. I'm sure you and your new friends at Scotland Yard immediately figured out the pun."

Paul was puzzled. "Ventra? What's odd about that? I think I once had a graduate student by that name."

Alice sighed intolerantly. "You're not saying his full name, that's why you've missed the point. Repeat after me: J. L. Ventra. Paul, what do the French call Jack the Ripper?"

"Jacques L'Éventreur—" He'd hardly finished the last syllable when he pulled the receiver from his ear, looking down at it in disbelief. He could picture Alice at the other end, her victorious smile now full-blown. She had always been better at French than Paul, but seldom had it bothered him as much as now.

. And yet was she right? It was not uncommon for unknown murderers to taunt the public with pseudonyms or nicknames. Had not Jack the Ripper done the same, if the letters were authentic? Yet sometimes the decoding could be a tricky business. When New York City's psychotic killer Son of Sam attested to his bloody work, everyone had his own theory as to the meaning of the strange sobriquet. Many believed that the murderer was proclaiming himself the dissident child of Uncle Sam. Then Paul came up with his own theory, absolutely certain he was right: who was the "Son of Sam" but "Samson," a man so powerful that he would not be overcome by the puny forces of law and order? When the murderer was caught, the true explanation of the name was much murkier.

So who could tell whether it would not turn out the murderer knew no French; that J. L. Ventra was the man's real name or the name of another, man or woman, whom he loved or hated?

Yet Paul suspected that Alice had unriddled the name, and grumpily, he told her so.

•

Thursday morning, Paul arose rather late because he was confused about the British Library's opening hour. Over coffee, he placed a call to Alice. She had just checked her slide carousel for the last time and was about to go to the lecture hall to present her paper. She sounded confident but preoccupied, and was clearly in no mood to talk about his program for the day's investigation. He did not press the subject, but promised to give her a great dinner on her return in the late afternoon.

No sooner had he hung up than the telephone rang. It was Bill Donaldson on the line.

"I have been trying to reach you for the past half hour. You seem to have a busy social life when your wife's away; in fact, I've heard people link your name with the inspector's." Failing to excite any response, Bill cut short the preliminaries. "However, I haven't called to gossip. The fact is that I am once again returning good for evil. You have neglected me shamefully because you live in terror of the inspector, and instead of taking offense, I am prepared to do you a great favor."

"And what is that?"

"One of your pals from the walking tour has answered the Yard's advertisement."

"How do you know that?"

Donaldson simulated a laugh that ended in a kind of snort. "The gentlemen of the press, like the police, have their methods."

"Who is it that's shown up?"

"I can't tell you his name," Donaldson said. "To that extent, I'm willing to play according to Warren's rules. He seems to worry that if we start identifying witnesses, the lunatic we're dealing with will start picking them off one by one. I can tell you, though, that he's the gentleman whom you so picturesquely described in your account as the Limping Man."

"I'd very much like to see him if it's possible—and also not too gross a violation of the rules."

"I rather thought you'd want to see him, and he seems to feel the same way. All of you walkers appear to have a capacity for instant nostalgia. In any event, I'm happy to oblige. I've arranged that he will be in my office this evening."

"Would it be a terrible inconvenience if I arrived around nine-thirty? Alice is returning from Glasgow this afternoon and I've promised her dinner."

"That's the least thing she deserves after all these mysterious morning telephone calls you've been making behind her back. Nine-thirty it is, then." He rang off.

Finding a taxi in the rank outside the hotel, Paul asked the driver to take him to the British Museum. When he arrived, he was greeted by a scene that had been familiar to him for many years. At a barrier that had been set up on the steps, parcels and briefcases of visitors were being examined. When Paul had first run this gauntlet in the 1970s, the public concern was over IRA bombs. The enemies of civil peace had varied over the years, but the disruption of the older urban life-style—the feeling of security and mutual trust—now seemed permanent. The guards searched Paul's battered dispatch case with rigorous thoroughness and then waved him ahead with the direction to deposit his umbrella in the cloakroom. He believed there was nothing new in the instruction, but thought that it had been given with a new emphasis.

After disencumbering himself of the umbrella, he presented himself at the Ticket Room, where it was necessary to reactivate his reader's ticket. He had not used it for close to a decade, and he was pleasantly surprised to find that it was not only still on file but brought current in a moment by the magical application of an official stamp. To Paul's mind, one of the marvelous things about England was its refusal to dispose of any records. It was a miracle that the island had not sunk long ago under the weight of its archives. However, to the devoted visitor, the compulsive and faithful document retention often proved a blessing. On many occasions Paul had been advised by a London bookstore that one of his "want" orders of ancient date had at last been filled; and now, in a twinkling, his obsolete reader's privileges had been restored.

Holding his ticket before him like a magical amulet, Paul was given safe passage into the holy of holies, the Reading Room. It was a romantic place to him, partly so because he had first seen it in an Alfred Hitchcock movie where the fleeing criminal was pursued through its precincts.

Paul, with the self-assurance of homecoming, approached the circular shelves of bound index volumes that hedged about the station of the Reading Room staff. He selected two volumes and noted on call cards a number of books he wanted to consult. He had decided to order several works on the Ripper; from past experience, he knew that an alarming percentage of the Library's books were lost or misplaced and, in this year of celebration, he did not exclude the possibility that unscrupulous Ripper fanciers might have spirited away some of the books on the murders. Most of the publications listed in the index were old, but that didn't bother him. He wouldn't be helped by any of the revisionist theories of the case that had been spouted incessantly in recent years; crime journalists were becoming as addicted to rewriting history as the art critics who were squabbling at Alice's seminar. No, it was not theories he needed, but certain of the undisputed facts of the crimes that he didn't seem able to keep straight in his mind, facts that would have helped him sort out Frank Collins's somewhat disordered presentation.

After listing about six Ripper items, he closed the index volume from which he had been copying entries and turned to the other volume he had taken from the index shelves. Yes, they had it; he knew they would. He noted the author, title, and call number on another card.

He turned his cards in at the order desk and waited. In about an hour he was delivered two books; only one of the Ripper studies, and the work he had listed from the second index volume. He was told by an attendant that two of the other Ripper books were currently being used in the Reading Room and that the balance were lost. Paul was right: the centennial was making itself felt within these hallowed walls.

His rain-damaged notebook at his left hand, Paul examined the history of the Ripper's crimes. It was one of the first that had been written on the case, and was much the worse for wear. Turning pages rapidly back and forth, he found what he wanted and made a brief entry in the notebook. It was a list that read:

3 April	Emma Smith?
7 August	Martha Tabram?
31 August	Mary Ann Nicholls
8 September	Annie Chapman
30 September	Liz Stride
30 September	Catherine Eddowes
9 November	Mary Kelly

At the bottom of the list Paul scrawled two short questions: "Where are we now? Why so fast?" After the second question he added parenthetically: "Maybe Queen Victoria was right."

The second book had an exotic title: *Thug, or A Million Murders.* It was written by Col. James L. Sleeman to celebrate the accomplishments of his grandfather, who had suppressed the hereditary murder cult of Thuggee in nineteenth-century India, putting an end to a three-hundred-year reign of terror by the Kali-worshiping stranglers. Paul had not looked at the book for many years, and he tended to confuse the Thugs with the equally baleful Assassins of Syria and Persia. A few moments of reading, though, convinced him that he was not mistaken. He nodded to himself. That was the word he was looking for: *beles.* He copied out a short passage from the introductory chapter, called "A Religion of Murder":

> The bodies were . . . carefully buried at *beles* (permanent murder places) selected beforehand. These murders were planned with such forethought that often these graves were prepared many days ahead.

To this passage he appended a comment for his reference during the afternoon meeting with Warren: "Murder places *selected beforehand.* Victims pass by."

As he left the Reading Room, he muttered a sentiment that, more audibly spoken, would have stunned the scholars who sat glumly waiting for their orders to be filled: "God save the British Library!"

•

When Garson ushered him to Inspector Warren's room, Paul was surprised to find him in conversation with Superintendent Higgins, and even more surprised when Higgins greeted him a degree less frostily than at their first meeting. Warren remained the spokes-man.

"Very good to see you again, Professor Prye. I've told Superintendent Higgins of your speculations about the Sterling murder, and about your promise to weave the two crimes into a pattern. We're extremely interested in what you have to tell us. Let your mind run free. We will not interrupt you."

Paul looked at Superintendent Higgins's unblinking eyes as Warren ran through these diplomatic preliminaries, and was struck by another difference in his bearing. Damn it, the man was interested! When they had first met, Higgins had hardly looked at him and made no effort to hide his boredom. Now he was staring at the visitor expectantly. Paul could not explain the alteration in his manner but of one thing he felt certain: *something had happened that made them more curious about Mr. J. L. Ventra.*

Warren raised his brows and bent forward, as if encouraging Paul to begin and promising him full attention. For Paul it was the fulfillment of a dream that he had never dared to dream: he was being invited, almost commanded, to lecture on crime to two detectives of Scotland Yard. He took up the challenge.

"The theme you've set me, Inspector Warren, is to find a pattern in these murders. Yet none of us surely has the slightest doubt that there must be a pattern. At the risk of your branding me an American chauvinist, let me begin by citing a chapter from the crime annals of my own State of New York. Around the turn of the century a strange series of events occurred at a New York City athletic club that bore a strong resemblance to the Tylenol poisonings of recent memory. Within a short space of time, two members of the club received anonymous mailings of patent medicines adulterated with cyanide of mercury. The first recipient died as a result of the poisoning. The second became seriously ill when he tasted the medicine, and an elderly relative who swallowed a larger dose succumbed to its lethal effect. At the trial for the second murder, the prosecution attempted to establish a murder pattern by introducing evidence of the earlier poisoning, but the conviction was overturned by our Court of Appeals. The court clung hard and fast to the old common-law rule excluding evidence of prior crimes. Now the dissenters on the court believed, and I think quite rightly, that the majority had been foolish. How could the defendant be prejudiced by proof of the earlier crime when the common poison, cyanide of mercury, had so rarely been used by murderers and was so difficult to obtain?

"Now I am certain that none of us for a moment would imitate the error of the New York Court of Appeals in this case. We're dealing here with a poison far more exotic and much more difficult of access. The fact is, of course, that I haven't the vaguest idea how the murderer could have gotten his hands on the poison, the microscopic pellets, or the mechanism for ejecting them."

Paul thought he saw an echo of this admission in a shrug of Superintendent Higgins's shoulders.

"Therefore one strand in the pattern we are seeking is the weapon. It seems inconceivable that two murderers are wandering around London armed with ricin-ejecting umbrellas and just happened to claim victims with the use of these almost inconceivable weapons on two successive days. So we begin with the linkage of the two murders by the common weapon.

"What direction would I turn in next to flesh out the criminal design? Ordinarily, I would look to find some tie between the victims, either through acquaintance, common activity, or similar station in life. When I've tried to explore this dimension of the puzzle, I obviously labor under the tight restraints you've put upon me, no doubt properly: you can't tell me what your own inquiries have revealed about the two victims. Since ricin is known to have been used as a political murder weapon by the Eastern Bloc, it was a perfectly reasonable first guess that both women, in their own ways, had found themselves in confrontation with the secret service of some Iron Curtain country. But at our last meeting, Inspector Warren, you asked me to make certain assumptions, and based on the assumptions you propounded, even though you were not notably generous with details, I must conclude that neither victim was a likely target for political assassination, let alone political assassination at the hands of the same killer. Then why did the killer use ricin, and more to the point, how did he get his hands on it? My frank answer to both these questions is that I don't know, but I'll try to deal with these difficulties again later on, if you'll bear with me.

"One further word about the stipulations you've asked me to accept. Just as your assumptions have forced me to conclude that neither Sterling nor Sanders was engaged in any activity that would draw upon her the enmity of a foreign agent, so I must speculate that you have not uncovered any facts indicating that they knew each other or had any common acquaintance or that their lives intersected in any fashion that might suggest the possibility that they would be selected with deliberation as victims of the same criminal. Certainly they had no physical resemblance, and their ages were far apart. Even if we were to hypothesize that the murderer carries in his mind some image—let us say a female image—that he hates, it would be hard to reproduce one that would encompass the young policewoman and the gray-haired director.

"To recapitulate the pattern, so far as I have been able to establish it: we have two murders linked by common weapon, but not by related or similar victims.

"It was at this point in my thinking that, with Inspector Warren's kind assistance, I paid my visit to the Black Museum. And as a result of what I learned there, I began to wonder whether there was not an additional link between the cases—a link of place and time."

If Paul had hoped to read in the detectives' faces the dramatic effect of this new turn in his discourse, he was sorely disappointed. They remained attentive but gave no indication of surprise. He continued.

"These would certainly not be the first sequential murders bound in this fashion. In fact, this kind of pattern is centuries old. I paid a visit to the British Library this morning to review my memories of a similar phenomenon encountered by Major-General Sir William Sleeman in nineteenth-century India. I don't know whether you are both familiar with Sleeman's spectacular success in suppressing the murder cult that has given the word *thug* to our language. The Indian Thugs worshiped a bloodthirsty goddess named Bhowani or Kali. To her they sacrificed travelers whom they strangled, robbed, and secretly buried. One of the strangest features of the Thugs' murders is that they had certain permanent murder places associated with the worship of their goddess that they selected beforehand." Paul took out his notebook and consulted an entry he had made at the Library. "These murder places were called *beles*, and on their grounds graves were prepared for the future victims long before they appeared on the scene.

"I began to wonder whether our murderer had not proceeded in precisely the manner of the Thugs. He appeared to have chosen the sites of the crime in advance and then fastened on victims who had the misfortune to appear at precisely the moment that he was primed to strike.

"It was remarkable that, in contrast with the victims,

who seemed to have no trait in common except that they were both women, the sites of the two crimes were very similar—too similar, in my mind, to be the result of chance. I am sure you see that similarity yourselves, and that is why perhaps you are listening to me with politeness but growing impatience. Let me, though, identify the pattern we must all have seen—that the two crimes were committed in places associated with the memory of Jack the Ripper and occurred in this centennial year of the Ripper murders."

Warren was the first to break his self-imposed rule of silence. "And is it your theory, Professor Prye, that Jack the Ripper is the ricin murderer's god, to whom he offers up victims rash enough to visit places identified with his cult?"

Paul shook his head. "Perhaps what I've said does lend itself to parody, and if that's your point I acknowledge the risk of carrying the analogy too far. That was not my intention, certainly. I wanted only to note the suggestive possibility that the murderer's plan has been to associate his crimes with those of the Ripper, and that the most graphic method that occurred to him to carry out that design was to attack his victims at scenes somehow presided over by the Ripper's ghost, whether they be the East End murder locales or the Ripper collection of the Black Museum."

Warren pressed him further. "And what, in your view, would inspire a murderer to undertake a scheme involving such elaborate calculation?"

Having asked himself the same question many times, Paul was quick to respond. "Not being a psychologist, I'll probably not fully satisfy either you or myself on that point. However, I think we see at work here the phenomenon that has become an unlovely feature of present-day crime: the copycat syndrome. Our murderer is a copycat with a vengeance. He's chosen a unique weapon associated with a sensational murder of the last decade, and at the same time is inviting us to compare him to a more famous murderer of a century ago. To my mind, there is no doubt that, despite his modern weapon, our murderer's principal preoccupation is with the crimes of Jack the Ripper. Why is this so? I suppose if we could answer that question we'd come close to explaining the copycat madness. A part of the picture I think we can make out. Isn't there more than a little megalomania in a plan to emulate Jack the Ripper, to bring his crude weapons up to date, and to steal the show from him in London during the centennial of the East End horrors?"

Paul looked to both policemen as if expecting another question. "May I proceed?" he asked.

"Please do," Warren answered.

"Well then, it's my working hypothesis that the murderer is not only acting under a compulsion to copy Jack the Ripper, he seems bent on competing with him and outdoing him. What I have begun to worry about is just how far he is prepared to play out his deadly game. It was with that problem on my mind that I paid a visit this morning to the Reading Room of the British Library to refresh my memory on the Ripper's crimes. I don't know to what extent you gentlemen are interested in the nineteenth-century history of Scotland Yard. For all I know, you may know the Ripper murders like the backs of your hands. As for myself, even though I think I've read all the books that have been written on the case, I still have trouble keeping the chronology of the murders straight. So this morning at the Library I made a list of the crimes."

Warren was no stranger to the East End murders. "As I recall, there were five murders in all. Am I right, Professor Prye?"

Paul nodded. "That became the accepted wisdom at Scotland Yard, but many people at the time felt otherwise. Before the series of undisputed Ripper murders began on August 31 with the killing of Mary Ann Nicholls and ended on November 9 with the dismemberment of Mary Kelly, two other crimes were committed that bore some similarity to the Ripper's bloody work. On August 3, an aging prostitute named Emma Smith was killed in Osborn Street. Her face and ear were cut and she was sexually violated with some blunt instrument. On August 7, the body of Martha Tabram was found in Commercial Street; she had been stabbed dozens of times in the throat and stomach with something like a bayonet.

"In my list of Ripper crimes I've placed question marks after the names of Emma Smith and Martha Tabram. It seems to me that the time gap between the Smith murder and the later crimes makes the attribution to the Ripper doubtful. The Tabram murder appears to present a closer question, but as an admirer of your institution, I have no reason to doubt that Scotland Yard's refusal to classify it as a Ripper crime must have been justified.

"With this list in hand, I then asked myself a number of questions. First, does our murderer have a detailed knowledge of the facts of the Jack the Ripper case? I have answered that with a tentative yes, though of course I can't prove I'm right. Next I asked: Does the murderer intend to parallel the whole sequence of Ripper crimes? To this I had no firm answer to give but, gentlemen, given the commission of his two crimes in such rapid succession, I am fearful that there may be more to come. And then I posed the question: If he is determined to match the Ripper's murders one by one, where would he begin, or, as I put it in my notes, 'Where are we now?' Well, I suppose that this issue, ironically, turns on whether the murderer has as high a regard for Scotland Yard as I do.

"Let me show you what I mean. So far we have un-covered two crimes committed on separate days. Let's take a look for a moment at the list I have compiled of Jack the Ripper's crimes. We find that whether or not we begin the canon of the Ripper murders with Smith, Tab-ram, or Nicholls, the Ripper on each occasion claimed only one victim on a single day, until he came to Sep-tember 30. This, you may recall, was the night of the so-called 'double event,' when he dispatched Liz Stride and Catherine Eddowes within the space of an hour. Some-where along the line, if our murderer is determined to follow the Ripper's schedule, he is bound to try the hur-dle of a 'double event.' It was a risky venture even for the Ripper, for he narrowly escaped a run-in with the po-liceman on the beat when he killed Liz Stride.

"Now if the murderer we seek is a purist, the double event would be the next crime to anticipate, since he has already claimed on separate days single victims to match Nicholls and Chapman. If he believes that the Ripper's crimes began with Smith or with Tabram, he might still plot one or two more murders before attempting a double killing.

"My own assumption is that he ruled out Smith and Tabram (most people do) and therefore faces the double event as his next challenge.

"Having come this far in my speculations at the Library this morning, I raised another question: Why is the mod-ern murderer proceeding so much more quickly than Jack the Ripper? You'll note, gentlemen, that Mary Ann Nicholls was murdered on August 31 and more than a week passed before the Ripper attacked his second vic-tim, Annie Chapman, on September 8. The double event did not occur for another three weeks, and more than a month passed after those murders before final butchery of Mary Kelly on November 9. I suppose one superficial explanation might be (and I certainly do not intend to be facetious) that everything is faster in our era (perhaps even the rate of commission of serial murders). But I've rejected that explanation and instead I wrote in my notebook this morning: 'Maybe Queen Victoria was right.'"

The reference to the Queen seemed to pique even Higgins's interest. "I didn't recall that the Queen took an interest in the case," he said.

"She most certainly did, even to the point of making suggestions to the Yard on the directions of its inquiries. What I am referring to was her questioning the Home Secretary as to whether the cattle boats and passenger boats had been examined. The reason for the question is, of course, quite plain: the Queen was convinced that the person who was capable of such brutal crimes against women could not possibly be British. Since then we've learned that no nation, however civilized, is immune to the plague of mass murder, so I fear I cannot share Queen Victoria's patriotic sentiment. Nevertheless, I found her hypothesis to be useful to us in this case. Perhaps the modern Ripper is working so quickly because he is on a visit to London of short duration and is determined to complete the series of his crimes before he must leave."

Higgins intervened for a second time.

"Your thesis is truly remarkable, Professor Prye, and I congratulate you on your ingenuity. But let me pose a point that must have struck your hypothetical murderer as troublesome. If he was planning a sequence of crimes that he intended to be compared with the Ripper murders, why would he choose, of all weapons, a poison like ricin, which is incredibly difficult to detect? We are, of course, extremely grateful for the insight and indeed courage that enabled you to identify the Commercial

Street business as a murder and to bring it to our attention, but could the killer have at all reasonably counted on such a remote chance?"

Warren, his perpetual smile broadening, suggested, "Perhaps in this centennial year he was counting on an influx of brilliant criminologists, Professor Prye among them." If he expected any response from his colleague, he was disappointed, for Higgins continued to await a comment from Paul Prye.

Paul replied, "That is a problem, I can't deny it. Strangely, of course, the same question, according to Bill Donaldson, was raised at the time of the Markov case. I understand that it was widely assumed that one of the purposes of the murder was to terrorize other emigrés who might be inclined to criticize their home regimes. Yet the terror effect would have been completely lacking if Markov's death had been attributed, as it well might have been had he not been so insistent, to natural causes. In the present case, however, if the murderer runs true to the form of his model, he won't leave us long in doubt about his plans. Somewhere along the way he'll announce himself and expressly invoke the comparison with Jack the Ripper, a comparison that is, if I'm right, what the whole murder scheme is about.

"In fact, if my wife, Alice, is correct, he may already have planted the first clue for Scotland Yard to see." He told them about her decodification of the name J. L. Ventra.

Somewhat to his surprise, they didn't laugh at Alice's discovery. Instead, Warren said, "What do you make of this, Professor Prye?" He handed him a photostatic copy of a letter, dated the day before. Paul read it so rapidly that he had to go back to the beginning to make sure that he had not skipped over anything in his haste.

*   *   *

The Commissioner,
Metropolitan Police

Dear Sir,

You dont make much progress on my case so it seems I must help you. I am down on women and shant quit stabbing them till I run out of ricin. Jack the Ripper was nothing compared to me. Just a primitive with a knife. My "double event" is the next. Catch me when you can.

Yours truly,
Umbrella Jack

"Well, what do you make of it?" Warren asked.

"Well, one thing is obvious. It was written by someone who knows the Jack the Ripper correspondence. It has phrases taken from the letter posted to the Central News Office on September 27, 1888, a few days before the double murder. The closing taunt comes word for word from a short letter received in October by the Chairman of the Whitechapel Vigilance Committee. Perhaps you'll recall that this letter came in a cardboard box that purported to contain half a kidney from the body of one of the victims. The words 'catch me when you can' ended that letter.

"The second point I'd make is also self-evident. If the letter is bogus, its sender is no fool. Perhaps it's only conceit that makes me say that, because he seems to have come up with pretty much the same theory you've patiently let me expound to you. Do you think it's authentic?"

Warren was unexpectedly frank in his reply. "To tell you the truth, we haven't made up our mind, and the damn letter scares us half to death. As you may recall, the police in the Yorkshire Ripper inquiries made complete fools of themselves going down the false trail of bogus correspondence. If this letter is a fake, I am not at all prepared to admit that the correspondent is as clever as you. He'd have no reason to associate the Sterling case with the Black Museum; we haven't publicized her visit, as you probably noticed. The letter could well be a pure exercise in black humor, inspired by the undue attention the Ripper centennial has been getting over here."

Paul was not convinced. "I hope that the letter does turn out to be a fraud, but you'll forgive me if I keep on worrying until a good deal more time goes by. Of course, I have no idea what channels your investigation is pursuing, and you wouldn't tell me if I asked. I'm therefore left with the maddening thought, I hope unfounded, that there's nothing much that can be done to prevent the next attack."

Neither detective disagreed with him. Instead, Higgins changed the subject. "Before we adjourn, Professor Prye, you will recall your promise to favor us with your views on how a political weapon such as ricin could fall into private hands."

Paul was glad to be reminded. He had almost lost track of the point in his fascination with the Ripper letter. "First of all," he said to Higgins, "I'd have to concede the possibility that 'Umbrella Jack' might be pursuing his crimes with the blessing of his government. Inspector Warren (and perhaps I should not exclude you, Superintendent Higgins; you may well be a Jack the Ripper expert in your own right), you'll remember that a similar theory was advanced concerning the East End murders. It was suggested (I forget by which of the countless writers on the case) that the Ripper was a czarist secret agent who had been directed to commit the atrocities to demonstrate the ineffectiveness of the British police. Now I, for one, have never believed in the incompetence of the British police, either now or in the nineteenth century, so this possibility has never had any appeal to me. Therefore, I acknowledge that you have correctly interpreted my theory to assert that Umbrella Jack is a 'private' murderer. How did he get the ricin? There are a number of possibilities, none clear, but some at least less likely than others. I suppose there is a physical possibility that the killer works in a laboratory where ricin pellets and weapons are manufactured, but I find it hard to believe that his bosses would allow someone with such a delicate assignment to be traveling freely in the West. Another possibility, of course, is that he formerly held such a position and has absconded with a supply of the dreadful stuff. It is understood that, properly stored, ricin could retain its deadly potency for a considerable period of time. Nevertheless, I am inclined to a third explanation, which is perhaps the most unsettling of all: namely, corruption. What if this murderer has access to an employee in a ricin lab who has been willing to supply the poison and the related equipment to him for a substantial bribe? Sometimes I think that we in the West are so obsessed with our own political and financial scandals that we don't appreciate the enormous scale of corruption in the Eastern Bloc. After all, it was against corruption in Bulgaria that Markov inveighed at the price of his life. In the Soviet Union business corruption is punished capitally, perhaps in large part because of a cruelty of which England ridded itself in the nineteenth century but also, I suspect, because of the sheer enormity of their problem with bribery and fraud. So, Superintendent Higgins, I propose to you, until you come up with a better theory, that Umbrella Jack simply purchased the ricin from a government employee. It is the possibility that I find to be the single most horrifying dimension of the case."

The two detectives rose from their chairs almost simultaneously and thanked Paul for his help. Warren showed him out with what was becoming his regular curtain line: "I expect that we will talk again."

•

Alice was more easily placated than Paul had anticipated. Her lecture had been a smashing success, for which she was willing, no doubt with justice, to claim the lion's share of credit, while at the same time conceding that after a day of wrangling, the contending parties of scholars were relieved to be able to rally around the tried and true banner of Courbet. In her hours of professional glory she tended to look upon Paul's pursuit of the hidden facts of crime as trivial or, even worse, unacademic. To this general predisposition her two days' absence from London lent its weight; her store of curiosity, which had gradually accumulated as Paul continued to propound new mysteries about the Commercial Street murderer, was now, if not wholly dissipated, sadly depleted.

It was therefore no sacrifice for her to release Paul for his evening meeting with Bill Donaldson. He had, of course, offered her a bribe—dinner at Le Relais at the Café Royale. Their visits to London after all these years remained "sentimental journeys" to the shrines of their favorite artists and writers, and both of them were unreasonably devoted to Oscar Wilde, who had favored the Café Royale as the site for the disastrously expensive banquets he gave for his worthless friends. The Pryes had been grief-stricken when the Relais had been temporarily closed a few years back, and had exulted in its reopening.

After negotiating the hazardous pedestrian crossings between Regent Street and Piccadilly, Paul left Alice in the hotel lobby and took a cab for Fleet Street. Bill Donaldson met him in front of the newspaper building, which Paul had not previously visited, and took him directly to his office. There, in a chair drawn up before

Bill's desk, sat the "Limping Man," his look as commanding as Paul Prye remembered it but perhaps a bit less fierce now that his irritation over Holloway's antics had been swallowed up by a baffling tragedy in which he found himself, to his own amazement, playing a part.

Bill made the introductions, if that is what his opening words could be called.

"I assume you gentlemen will remember each other as participants in the Ripper walking tour that has now earned notoriety in such an unfortunate manner. Nevertheless, I have an unusual request to make of you both. I know you've both spoken to Inspector Warren, so perhaps what I am going to ask will not come as a surprise. Please do not mention your names to each other. You are to remain, for the time being, as anonymous one to the other as you were during the tour. Warren is terribly concerned about the names of witnesses appearing in the press or becoming known in some other fashion to an apparently deranged murderer who may still be on the loose in London. I think that it is an extreme position, but it is, of course, our policy to cooperate with the Yard."

Paul and the other visitor agreed to the condition, but Paul couldn't understand what Donaldson hoped to accomplish by a journalistic investigation conducted under such tight restraint. Donaldson explained that during the police inquiries the paper had no intention of running any stories based on privately gathered information, but that once the criminal was caught (which he had no doubt would happen soon) they wanted to be ready with a special feature, perhaps for the Sunday supplement.

Paul was impressed by this display of self-discipline, but it was very much what he would have expected from Bill Donaldson. His entire office desk breathed order and control. Donaldson sat at a large leather-topped desk whose surface was protected by a shining glass slab on which Paul could not detect a scratch. The desk top was clear except for two red files tied close and identified by typed, color-coded tabs. On the back wall were framed awards and several distinct galaxies of photographs. Among the pictures was no sign of family, but then Bill had never mentioned any in all the time the Pryes had known him and he did not invite an exchange of personal confidences. Instead of family groups, the photographs showed a smiling Donaldson standing at the side of the great and the once-great, including the Pope, a succession of prime ministers, and Geraldine Ferraro. On a side wall was a group of portraits of Donaldson alone or among friends on the deck of a sailboat; Paul was happy to see this proof of the authenticity of the journalist's permanent suntan.

Although Donaldson had barred an exchange of names, he had allowed his guests to describe their backgrounds. Paul learned that the man he had been invited to meet was a retired schoolmaster who had taught Classics at a boys' school north of London. Bill explained why he thought the two men would be interested in comparing impressions of the walking tour: one of them had witnessed what proved to be a murderous attack, while the other had more closely observed the murderer.

The schoolmaster demurred somewhat from the appraisal of his recollections. He could not say much about the man's appearance, he said, for his eyesight had become greatly impaired in recent years. Paul was surprised to hear this because the man had seemed to walk with complete assurance and to follow Frank Collins's sometimes wavering lead without hesitation. However, Paul suspected that, just as the teacher had adopted his assertive stride to compensate for a limp, he had dispensed with glasses out of vanity or fear that the authority that flashed from his eyes might have diminished impact on his schoolboys if filtered through thick lenses.

The teacher's disclaimer was only partial. He thanked the Lord that the dimming of his sight was remedied by the soundness of his hearing and by the special aptitude he had always had for nuances of voice and accent. He was confident that if he were ever to hear the murderer speak, he would recognize him in an instant.

"How do you know we're talking about the same person?" Paul asked.

"Mr. Donaldson has told me something about your impressions of the attack and its antecedents, and one circumstance you have cited matches my own recollection precisely. That is the fact that the victim began the walk as the central figure of a small admiring group and at some point seemed to pair off with a single member of the group—a man. They were certainly walking as a couple by the time we arrived at the Spitalfields Market, and I think it likely that he was in the best position to stab her when the motorcycle threw us all into a panic."

"How is it that you would remember the man's voice?" Paul asked. "I can't say that I ever paid any particular attention to their conversation."

The teacher replied, "I probably would not have taken any notice either, except that I may have had the dubious privilege of standing close at hand when the man first spoke to her. You see, I was for a time walking with Miss Sanders's admirers. The talk had somehow turned to theater and opera and their comparative merits in London and New York. Since reading Miss Sanders's obituary I have wondered less at the subject of our conversation, since she worked in the theater world and struck me as possessing a personality strong enough to impose her interests on a circle of new acquaintances. However that may be, I am certain that she spoke with great warmth of recent productions at the Public Theater. Her words drew an enthusiastic response from a man in the group whom I had overlooked before. And how could I have done otherwise? He was wearing a tan raincoat, as were many others, and carried an umbrella, which he kept furled even when the worst of the downpour began.

"Well, when she praised the Public Theater to the skies, this man suddenly emerged from the ranks, as it were, and surpassed her tributes with his own. He often traveled to New York, he asserted, and while there spent almost every free night at the Metropolitan, or the New York City Opera, or on Broadway. Miss Sanders seemed delighted with his enthusiasm, and I think it was at that point they drifted into private conversation. I must say I didn't receive the impression that either of them took any strong interest in what the tour leader was saying about Jack the Ripper. I can't say that I blame them, though. It was a mediocre job."

Paul didn't agree but was not prepared to enter a distracting debate. "What do you remember about the man's voice that would enable you to identify it if you heard it again?"

"There was first of all the accent. He was, I feel certain, from one of the Central European, perhaps Balkan, countries. It is not an accent I encounter often around my home in Hertfordshire. Then too, the quality of the voice was quite distinctive. He spoke in a high-pitched voice that rose even higher when he attempted to emphasize a point he was making. His speech was very rapid, but there would sometimes be long pauses between sentences or paragraphs, as if he had halted for breath."

"Or perhaps to grope for a word?" Paul suggested.

"Possibly, but it seemed to me that he was extremely proficient in English, and that neither its vocabulary nor syntax held any terrors for him."

The schoolmaster had finished his story. At a signal from Donaldson, Paul then gave an abbreviated version of his own observations of the tour and the attack. The teacher didn't seem much interested, and Paul could not understand why Donaldson had insisted on this second narrative. Was it possible that the compulsively neat journalist had done so in order that the meeting would satisfy his passion for symmetry, or was it his feeling that Paul's story was a necessary token of reciprocity for the teacher's statement?

More likely, Paul concluded, Donaldson simply didn't want the man to know that Paul was involved in helping the police with the investigation.

The crystalline eyes of the ebony cat glittered, her back rose in a high arch, and her tail streamed in a rhythmical art-nouveau curve across her legs. Alice insisted that he buy her without haggling over the price, overriding the protests of economy he was prone to raise in the final week of their vacation.

The cat formed the handle of a magnifying glass on display in a shop of Gray's Antique Mall that specialized in objects glorifying the feline image. Alice had an even more expansive concept of crime collecting than Paul. Since he had studied the investigations of Edgar Allan Poe into the real-life murder of the Hoboken cigar sales-girl Mary Cecilia Rogers, she couldn't understand how he could regard his library as complete without a "black cat" as a symbol of one of Poe's most famous stories. There was no resisting her mastery in such matters, and Paul, in the end, surrendered his credit card to the proprietor.

The fact was that he was in uncharacteristically low spirits, and Alice knew why. She decided to bring the matter out into the open.

"Stop moping at once. I know what's getting to you. We're leaving on Wednesday, and you're beginning to get the idea that you won't see the end of this business. Shouldn't I worry a bit about what's happened to your sense of values? The only thing that can make you happy at this point is for this madman to knock off three to five more women in the next few days so you can fly home content with the thought that you haven't missed anything." Seeing that he looked a little offended, she added in consolation, "It seems to me that you've done your best to put the investigation on the right course. It's not your fault if the police haven't tracked the man down yet. What did he say: 'Catch me when you can'? That seems to leave the time schedule wide open, and Scotland Yard doesn't seem to be in any hurry to satisfy his request."

Paul knew she was only half serious, but nonetheless he couldn't help defending the police. "I'm sure they're doing what they can, according to their own lights. It seems to me that there's an administrative schism hampering their work. From the beginning I've felt Warren has listened to me with an open mind, but this fellow Higgins is another story. He just can't swallow the notion that ricin could be used in an unofficial murder. He probably thinks there's never been a Molotov cocktail thrown by anyone but a Russian soldier. That's a glib comparison, I know, but there's no dealing with a man whose preconceptions can't be budged an inch.

"At my last meeting I felt I began to grab at least a corner of his attention, but he really had no choice but to listen to me then. It was that damn letter, you see. He tends to think it's a fake, they both do in fact, but neither feels he can entirely dare to be wrong. They're not going to publicize it for the time being, but they don't quite know how to deal with the fact that the correspondent, crank though he may be, has given them precisely the same warning as I. Come to think of it, that's a disconcerting point only if they're convinced I'm sane."

Alice wrinkled her nose in an imitation of disdain. "I have no idea what's on their minds," she said, "but if you keep trying to persuade me they've treated you sensibly, even I'll begin to doubt your sanity. I refuse to forget that if it weren't for your sharp eyes and unwillingness to be bowled over by my brilliant arguments, they would never have had an inkling that Margaret Sanders had been murdered. What would they have then to investigate? The murder of a policewoman. They probably would have speculated forever about the possibility that she had unwittingly stumbled across some spy activity in the course of her work or at least that some high-strung foreign agent had thought she had. Smug as those two men must be, I'm sure they can't credit the Ripper letter for the discovery of the link between the two cases. In the first place, you tell me they think it's a fraud, and they may well be right for all we know. Even if there is a chance that it's genuine, how can we tell whether the murderer would have revealed himself if you hadn't already blown the whistle on him? I just can't understand why they're showing little gratitude."

Paul tried to slow her down. "You're not being entirely fair, you know. I think Warren has been more than courteous. I've even felt some warmth break through the official veneer from time to time. And at the last meeting, I had the impression (I guess all professors have to feel that way) that they both were genuinely interested in what I had to say."

"If they're so interested, why do they go through this ridiculous charade of separating you from the other witnesses and of insisting that you not even learn their names? If they won't give you any facts to feed on, how are you supposed to help them further?"

Paul spread out a hand in a gesture of helplessness. "I suppose that's just the point. We all recognize that there's not much more I can do for them. They must be tired by now of my postmortem commentary. That seems to be about all I've been able to do so far. Perhaps I suffer under the curse of the crime historian: I can analyze and reappraise after the fact, but when it comes to tracking down a killer or trying to predict where and whom he will strike next, I am hopeless."

For a moment he thought that Alice had stopped listening. She had paused at a booth featuring a collection of cameos of all varieties, stone, shell, and lava. She had already amassed a considerable cameo hoard of her own, many of them bearing the images of heroic women and swans. She wore them, self-consciously but quite successfully, as emblems of her forcefulness and beauty. It was not only the cameo display that made him fear she had tired of the conversation, but a new hazard awaited in the very next booth: an array of vintage clothes of the flapper era.

However, it was dangerous to underrate the capacity of Alice's intricate mind. Replacing on the counter a cameo she had been examining through the jeweler's glass, she turned full face to Paul and said:

"You know I can't stand these self-criticism sessions. I think many of the ideas you've come up with have been forward looking. I hope you haven't forgotten that it was you that predicted that the police chemists would find ricin in Margaret Sanders's body. Nevertheless, in this century of Margaret Thatcher, I hope you won't resent a little hint from your wife."

Although Paul was used to hearing the unexpected from Alice, it was a part of their marital pact that he would always profess surprise. "Don't tell me that deductions have been germinating while you were giving Leda and her manly pet the once-over."

Alice led him to a side aisle of the mall and lowered her voice. She always whispered when she had something interesting to say, even if they were alone in a restaurant or were talking on the telephone. He strained to catch her words. Her new idea had been taking shape since last night, when he returned from the newspaper office and gave her a brief summary of the schoolteacher's story. One of the phrases that the man had used wasn't exactly accurate, she had thought at the time, and it had been bothering her ever since. Perhaps it was something Paul should talk about with the police. Paul listened to her with great attention.

It was not until 9:00 that evening that they returned to the hotel. A telephone message was waiting for Paul at the hall porter's desk. It was from Warren, but Paul didn't recognize the number. He called from their room, Alice's ear close to his. They were taken aback when a voice at the other end answered, "Madame Tussaud's." Putting aside his first thought that he had, as the macabre result of misdialing, obtained the wrong number, Paul asked for Inspector Warren. The operator without hesitation told him that Warren was expecting his call and that she would put him on directly.

In less than a minute the Pryes heard Warren's voice. "Oh, Prye, I'm so glad you're returned. Would it be terribly inconvenient for you to join me here as soon as possible?" Paul resisted the impulse to ask whether it was not rather late for a tour of the Chamber of Horrors. Instead he simply said he would come immediately. He was glad he had not attempted a joke or even asked any question, for Warren volunteered: "The pattern has resumed. We've had a 'double event.'"

•

For almost a century Madame Tussaud's had refused to display a model of Jack the Ripper in the Chamber of Horrors. It was the feeling of the management, maintained despite the disappointment expressed by many visitors, that any attempted likeness of Jack the Ripper "would be completely imaginary," since "no one had caught a glimpse of his figure, or even a likely figure, let alone a face." For many years, though, one of the Ripper's victims had been displayed in the Chamber, waiting on the corner of a Victorian street for a customer. Finally, however, in this centennial year, Madame Tussaud's had bowed to popular demand and the Ripper now stood by the side of his victim. His featureless face was averted from the viewers, who could observe, however, his black hair curling on the nape of his neck beneath a deerstalker cap.

Paul had been unaware of the attentions Madame Tussaud's was lavishing on the Ripper during the tourist season. Near the new waxwork exhibit was a collection of Ripper items from the archives of the museum, including a blown-up reproduction of one of the Ripper's letters and a newspaper poster advertising an article about one of his fresh outrages. Also on display were a number of the famous illustrations of the crimes from contemporary periodicals, such as *Punch* and the *Penny Illustrated Paper*. Included in the collection was *Punch*'s horrifying image of Crime as a white-shrouded knife-wielding ghost that the magazine dubbed the "Nemesis of Neglect." Completing the special installation was a series of crudely illustrated ha'penny broadsheets, and Victorian photographs of the slums of Whitechapel.

Inspector Warren and Constable Garson accompanied

Paul Prye silently through the exhibition. They then met privately in one of the administrative offices of the museum. Warren, in the cogent fashion Paul had found so impressive at their first meeting, laid out the principal facts of the first of the two new attacks.

The victim was Yvonne Lascombes, a twenty-three-year-old French stenographer on holiday with a male friend. About 3:00 that afternoon they paid a visit to Madame Tussaud's, including the Chamber of Horrors. They had lingered quite a while in the special exhibition devoted to Jack the Ripper, about whom they had read a good deal this summer in Parisian newspapers. At about 4:15 they left the museum in the midst of a heavy stream of tourists. Just as they turned west toward Baker Street, Lascombes felt a sudden sharp pain in her right thigh. In a spontaneous reaction (she had been in London for several days and had been following the stories of the umbrella murders), she turned sharply around, scanning the street for a sign of her possible assailant. The street was thick with pedestrians, none of whom displayed any unusual haste. As to umbrellas, they were a common enough sight that afternoon, since a hard, wind-driven rain was falling without let-up. When she confessed her fear to her companion, he hailed a policeman, who had the good sense to bring them quickly to a hospital. Warren's latest report was that a preliminary examination had disclosed a deep telltale puncture in the young woman's thigh. She remained in the hospital with a very high fever and only fitful consciousness; there was grave concern for her condition.

The second attack apparently took place about fifteen minutes later, only a short distance away. Betty Fenning, forty-three, a housewife, was walking down Baker Street after a visit to her sister. She was just about to enter the underground station when she heard a sharp crack and shortly thereafter felt a slight stinging sensation in her back. She, too, had read of the ricin murders, but bent on getting home in time to prepare dinner, she didn't give her experience a second thought. By the time she reached home, however, the soreness in her back seemed worse, and she told her husband what had happened. He called the police, who brought Mrs. Fenning to the hospital for medical examination. On admittance, her back showed the trace of a very superficial puncture; it was observed that she was wearing a slicker and a woolen sweater. It was hoped that she had escaped serious injury, but further tests were proceeding.

Paul's pencil worked furiously as he filled the last few pages of his increasingly dramatic notebook. When Warren finished his account of the Baker Street attack, he was quiet for a few moments, as if waiting for Paul to absorb the full force of the new developments. Then he said:

"In short, your prophecy of yesterday is fulfilled. And yet, it seems to me we are presented with fresh enigmas. Perhaps your views would be enlightening."

Paul, still struggling to adjust his normally deliberate thought processes to the rapidity of the day's developments, asked, "The whole business is getting so far beyond me you'll have to tell me what puzzles you most."

Inspector Warren obliged, his smile temporarily extinct. "Why would he try to bring off a double event? I know you will tell me that it was because he's copying the Ripper, but couldn't he make his point without such slavish imitation? I'm particularly struck by the fact that in his strange compulsion to perpetrate the second attack immediately after the stabbing of Mlle. Lascombes, he was willing for the first time to diverge from his established pattern."

"In what way?" Paul asked.

"I assume that you'll agree that this remarkable exhibition I've called you here to view would meet your definition of a Jack the Ripper 'shrine' (your term from Thuggee vocabulary escapes me for the moment). I'm therefore only applying your own theory when I observe that Betty Fenning was the only one of his victims who was not set upon either while or after she was visiting a site dedicated to the Ripper. And I note as a second point of special interest in the Fenning attack that the murderer unaccountably changed his previous technique—firing the pellet, as in the bungled Kostov attempt, instead of stabbing with the umbrella. How are we to account for those variations so late in the game?"

Paul felt the need of an introductory disclaimer. "I'm flattered that you're still interested in consulting my opinion, because I don't see that, with all my theorizing, I've really accomplished much. From what you tell me, one of these new victims, Mlle. Lascombes, may be in critical condition. The other, if she's escaped, can thank her good luck rather than us. It's true that to a certain extent I predicted the double event, but I can hardly take pride in detective work whose only merit consists of producing a body count.

"As a professor, I must admit, though, that these regrets don't prevent me from finding particular significance in today's attacks. I am now convinced more than ever that the umbrella man has planned from the outset to match the Ripper's crimes one by one until the entire series is run out. The double event teaches us that our murderer is indeed of the conservative school that attributes only five crimes to the Ripper and that therefore, as Umbrella Jack's letter promised, today's double event finds its proper place in the sequence.

"You've raised an important point in asking why the double event had to be paralleled so slavishly. Why, for example, could not the ricin murderer have continued methodically to claim single victims day by day until he had arrived at the magical number of five? I think perhaps to have at least a shadow of an answer it may be necessary to guess what the original double event meant for Jack the Ripper himself. The usual explanations have never completely satisfied me. We are told that on the night of August 30, 1888, the Ripper's blood lust ran so strong that it could not be slaked by one victim. A variant of this explanation was advanced by one of Jack's own letters: that he had to prematurely interrupt his mutilations of the first body because of worry that he would be caught by the night patrolman and that, therefore, he immediately stalked off in pursuit of another victim on whom he could 'operate' at more leisure. It may be that there is something in these ideas, but I think they address themselves to only one side of the Ripper's psyche. Blood lust he had in abundance, but particularly if we are to concede that at least some of his letters are genuine, he also appears to have been motivated to a large degree by bravado and a compulsive self-glorification. If he indeed wrote the first "Jack the Ripper" letter, it is perhaps not coincidental that it was dispatched only shortly before he attempted and carried off the double event—his most convincing proof of the futility of Scotland Yard's investigative and defensive measures.

"As we look back through crime history, we again and again encounter 'double events' as evidence of an attempt by a criminal to surpass his own past accomplishments and those of his rivals. If, as I've asked before, you will pardon me for drawing on American experience, I could point to the famous Coffeyville raid of the Dalton Gang in 1892, in which they attempted to outdo Jesse James by becoming the first to rob two banks simultaneously in the same town. Or if you'd prefer an example closer at hand, there's the final exploit of the English train robbers Poole and Nightingale. Their double event took place on New Year's night of 1849, when they robbed the Plymouth-London mail train and then reboarded the train for a second attempt when it returned through Bristol.

"Now the trouble with double events, and the essence of their challenge, is that they are terribly hard to bring off with success. The Dalton Gang was annihilated by armed citizens at Coffeyville, and Poole and Nightingale were arrested in a first-class car in possession of incriminating objects, including a ludicrous pair of false mustaches. Jack the Ripper was luckier, but only as a result of split-second timing. If he had lingered a few moments longer at the scene of the second murder, he would have been taken by the policeman whose beat passed through Mitre Square. It should therefore be perfectly understandable if our murderer took the double event as not only his greatest challenge but his greatest risk. Some of the strange departures you've noted he took from his usual procedure may be explainable precisely on that ground: he felt a compulsion to attempt a double killing, but, like those jumpers in the horse shows we like to watch on television when we're here, he may have shied at the most hazardous barrier."

Inspector Warren, who had listened with patience, broke in for the first time. "I'm not sure that I quite follow you in that. He did strike twice and escape unscathed."

Paul nodded. "That's of course correct, as far as it takes us. But I think we see a sense of strain, a need to cut corners to come through to safety. As you pointed out, only the first of his two victims had visited the Ripper exhibition; the second appears to have been chosen at random from pedestrians in the neighborhood. To me the arbitrary choice of the second victim seems rooted in the murderer's concern for his own safety. He could hope with impunity to strike one of the Madame Tussaud visitors as she emerged from the museum in a crowd of departing tourists. This was precisely the sort of thing he had done before in the two earlier crimes. But to have attacked two women at the museum entrance would have multiplied the chances of his being spotted, and he was not willing to take that risk. Instead, an unrelated victim who was just a short distance away on Baker Street had to make do.

"Another possibility has occurred to me, but here I am treading on thin ice and I would have to urge the point for your comment with great tentativeness."

"This is no moment for academic scruples," Warren interjected. "What do you have in mind?"

"Well, I was struck as you were by the modification in the mode of attack. I wonder whether the firing of the second pellet through the air might not reflect the same desire of the killer to get through the second attack as soon as possible and to escape from the scene. Let me ask you this, though: Has it occurred to you that, if I am right that the double event was a part of the murderer's original planning, he might have modified the mechanism of the umbrella to permit the double loading and ejection of pellets? Perhaps if he did, the modification was not thoroughly tested and the second pellet was ejected with less force than would have been required for it to drive deeply enough into the victim's body to have lethal effect."

Warren's answer was noncommittal. "I have no useful response to give you on that point, Professor Prye. We simply haven't any evidence of the nature of the ejection mechanism that was used in the Markov murder or in the recent attacks. Even if your speculation is not well

founded, and the murderer found an opportunity to re-
load the device after he stabbed Mlle. Lascombes, it remains strange that he chose to fire the pellet at Mrs.
Fenning through the air; he must have known of the
failure of the Kostov assassination attempt. Of course, we
must constantly recognize the limits of our own knowledge. There may have been a number of successful as-
sassinations by this means of which we are unaware."

Warren and Prye talked on for more than an hour
about the Markov and Kostov attacks and their parallels
and dissimilarities to the new cases. It was only when
they had completed their exchange on that subject that
Paul noticed that Constable Garson was adding to his voluminous notes. Perhaps the implied flattery of this
ongoing record gave him new courage, for he opened a
new avenue of discussion.

"I'd be much surprised if I haven't just about outlived
my usefulness to you tonight. But I have an additional
thought, perhaps even less easy to substantiate than
what we've been talking about so far. The thought is this:
A few days ago you challenged me to find a pattern in
these crimes, and I think we've seen one asserting itself
with the commission of these new crimes. But what I'm
beginning to wonder is whether within that pattern there
is not a subdesign, an arabesque that may have thus far
escaped our notice."

Warren said nothing, but his silence seemed to encour-
age Paul to go on. Paul sprawled in his chair as if to demonstrate that he wanted to develop the point at leisure.

When he had finished, he was gratified by Warren's
frankness. "That is a remarkable notion, Professor Prye. I
will undertake the indicated inquiries at once, and of
course, if we turn up anything useful, I may wish to call
upon your assistance." As a last sign of admiration, War-

ren added, "If you don't mind my asking, how precisely did the thought come to you?"

Paul gave the credit where it was due.

"It was really the result of a question Alice asked today, while we were in Gray's Antique Mall, of all places."

Warren mused, "She must be a remarkable woman."

Alice would be thrilled, Paul reflected. He had long half suspected that she was an Irene Adler in search of a Sherlock Holmes.

•

Over their nightcaps, Alice said, "I suppose I'll read your brilliant deductions in tomorrow morning's papers."

Paul had treated himself to a very tall scotch. With regret, she shook the last drops from the traveling container. Oh well, it made little sense to replenish the supply. They were going home Wednesday. Paul downed a generous portion straight before he answered.

"Actually, I expect to see only a sketchy account of the attacks. There's no doubt left we're dealing with a copycat murderer whose compulsion is so strong that it is stirred by crimes of a century ago—"

Alice interrupted him. "But he takes his weapon from one of the most bizarre crimes of this era. And even if Jack the Ripper is his principal model, is it really so strange that he can still inspire emulation, the way he's become the toast of the town this summer?"

Paul was not inclined to debate the point. "The fact remains, Alice, that the umbrella man, like the copycat breed in general, must live on publicity like a vampire on blood. Warren's quite concerned about this. Late as it was when we left Madame Tussaud's, he went directly to an emergency meeting of the London press association to plead for restraint in the reporting of the new crimes. He didn't tell me the details of the proposal he was to make, but it was my strong suggestion that all speculations as to the Ripper pattern of the crimes be suppressed. If I am not mistaken, I will be surprised to see any mention of the French victim's having visited the Ripper exhibition."

Alice was pessimistic about the likelihood of Warren's mission succeeding. "The journalists may play by the Yard's rules—that is, except the ones that specialize in photos of big bosoms. But how is Warren counting on the umbrella man to cooperate? Won't he make his own publicity? Until these two attacks, I didn't know whether to believe that Umbrella Jack's letter was authentic, but now I'd say the odds are it was. Warren declined to release the letter to the press and you kept your mouth shut. Good for you both. Do you think the murderer will put up with that kind of neglect very long? If I were he, I'd just pop off another epistle, but this time I'd address it to one of the London newspapers. Isn't that what Jack the Ripper did?"

Paul nodded, and Alice continued.

"And I think the monster knows quite a lot about this town. When he addresses his new letter, my bet would be that he chooses a paper that doesn't brood long and hard on what news is fit to print."

In bed the conversation went on and threatened to last through the night. A double worry, fueled by the headlong rush of events, preyed on Paul's mind. Part of his distress Alice had identified—the increasing consciousness of their Wednesday return to America, with the mystery still unresolved and his first campaign as detective come to nothing. A second related concern had cropped up more recently: that the murderer was himself under the pressure of an impending departure and was driven to complete his criminal cycle with breathtaking speed. It was a strange and unprecedented race between hunter and hunted, both pursued not by the hound of heaven but by the dates on their airplane tickets.

"There's one murder left, I'm sure of it," Paul was saying. "He'll attempt it soon, at the rate he's going; perhaps even tomorrow. And if he's not stopped, it's bound to be the worst."

Alice asked for an explanation. He reminded her of the unspeakable butchery of Mary Kelly, the atrocity that capped the Ripper's crimes; after he had sated himself on these final horrors he disappeared without a trace to become a never-ending legend and enigma.

"The umbrella man's 'Mary Kelly' is next," Paul said with assurance. "He plans something more spectacular for her, and more horrible."

Alice was puzzled. "But how could he do that? It seems to me that in this respect he's limited by his choice of weapon. A ricin death is dreadful, but we know its features and its cause. The Ripper, crude as he was, had this advantage: there are endless variations in the outrages that can be perpetrated by knife or blunt instrument on the human body. And he worked up to the full range of ferocity in his last crime."

"You're right, and it's for that reason that some of the Ripper researchers think there was something special about Mary Kelly, that somehow her murder was the pivot on which the whole series of crimes turned, the goal toward which the Ripper had always been moving along the paths of his dark design."

Alice was not in a mood to give up easily. "Well, let's assume for the moment that the ricin inhibits him, that the final attack must in method pretty much resemble the others. What else could he do to imitate the Kelly murder?"

Paul was silent for a few moments. "I've been thinking about that ever since I left Madame Tussaud's, and the best I can manage is a couple of ideas. To accomplish his ghoulish dissection of Mary Kelly, the Ripper had to ensure that he would be left in undisturbed possession of the corpse for a period of several hours. This had not happened before: previously he had had to work quickly so that he could escape from the scene of the crime.

"Now he had to hit on a murder site where he need not fear the sound of a bobby's tread, and it really wasn't hard for him to make the necessary arrangements. He merely followed Mary Kelly into her room, where he murdered and dismembered her in perfect solitude. This was the only Ripper murder to be committed indoors, and there was good reason for the change of scene. If the umbrella man has some special horror planned for his last victim, he may decide at last to come in from the streets where all his past attacks have taken place. And it's possible that even if the last murder is to be no more or less horrific than the others, his preoccupation with the pattern of the Ripper crimes may itself drive him indoors.

"So one possible innovation we might expect is a change of locale." He came to a full stop, and then added, "There's another feature of the Kelly crime he might want to imitate as well."

Alice had not said anything for a while, so Paul gently shook her shoulder to see whether she was still awake. Taking his hand in hers, she said, "I may be too tired to argue, Paul, but not sleepy enough to drop off just yet. What's the other possible twist he could borrow from the Ripper's last crime?"

"The most dramatic aspect of the Kelly murder, I think, was its timing. The Ripper killed Mary in the early hours of Lord Mayor's Day, and must have felt a special thrill at scaring the hell out of all the merrymakers. It's just possible that if our murderer is determined to push his rivalry to the limit, he'll want his last crime to form part of some public event."

Alice half rose on an elbow and turned to him. "What an incredible finale that would be, if these most secret of crimes should go public. Do you know whether there are any holidays that are to be celebrated here in the next week?"

Paul eased her pillow under her head as if he regretted to be disturbing her rest. This late-night murder talk was getting to be worse than wine or caffeine.

"I don't know of any holidays, but you know how many times we've blundered about such things before." Their most recent fiasco in that line had been to plan to be in Paris on May Day. The whole city was closed up tight. Fortunately, they had been able to escape to London on an early-morning flight.

Now they remembered that experience and joked a little about the crazy-quilt pattern of European holidays. In a little while the conversation petered out.

It must have been past 3:00 A.M. when Alice spoke again.

"Paul, I'm not getting a wink of sleep. It's partly that you've got me thinking about the umbrella man, but that's not all. I've started worrying about getting home in a few days and all the things we'll have to do to straighten up the house and get ready for the fall term. I know it's awfully selfish of me, but I wish we didn't have to give the whole of our last few days here to this case. There are many things I'd like to do and I hope I don't have to do them all alone. We haven't been to the show at the Royal Academy, and you promised to let me replace your disgraceful Harris tweed at Harrod's. We also have some theater tickets, you know, and I hope that Inspector Warren is not going to ruin our last evenings with new unscheduled meetings."

Paul had completely lost track of their theater schedule, and asked what they still had left to see. Alice had the details at her fingertips: "Tomorrow night (or I should say tonight) there's the Noel Coward revival at the Haymarket. On Tuesday—our last night—we finish up in grand style with Glenda Jackson's new play. I've forgotten Monday for the moment. Oh, yes, Monday I'm sacrificing to you. Isn't it the last big event at your festival?"

Paul suddenly sat bolt upright. He cupped the back of his head with his left hand and stared into space as though trying to pick out a detail in the wallpaper design that was dimly illumined by the lights of Piccadilly.

"What has gotten into you?" Alice asked, punching his chest to claim some attention.

Without responding he rolled around, catching her in a tight embrace and burrowing his lips into her shoulder.

"What is it?" she repeated.

All she got in return were some nonsense sounds muffled by her shoulder. What a time, she thought, for the man to be talking baby talk.

She listened more attentively, and two syllables detached themselves from his ecstatic gibberish.

Lulu.

· 10 ·

Paul Prye, as a student of the literature of crime, was familiar with the writings of the German playwright Frank Wedekind. In the last decade of the nineteenth century, Wedekind was working in Paris on his masterpiece, two plays about Lulu, an expressionist femme fatale. Lulu was a symbol of the amoral sex drive that becomes corrupted and distorted when subjected to the demands and pressures of society. In the first play, *Earth Spirit*, Lulu appears at the height of her powers as the destroyer of three middle-class lovers. The sequel, however, reflects a crucial change in the author's scheme of his heroine's career. Wedekind spent the first half of 1894 in London, where the Ripper's crimes were still very much in the mind of public and police; it was in that year that Sir Melville Macnaghten of Scotland Yard wrote his famous memorandum on the principal suspects in the case. When he returned to Paris, Wedekind decided to work the Ripper murders into the fabric of Lulu's story. The second play, *Pandora's Box*, traces the fall of his heroine from a glamorous courtesan to a whore making her debut on the streets of London; in the last scene she and Countess Geschwitz, her lesbian worshiper, are murdered by her nemesis and male counterpart, Jack the Ripper.

The Wedekind plays formed the basis of *Lulu*, an opera by Alban Berg, but the third act, depicting the Ripper murders, was left unfinished at the composer's death. Only in 1979 was the opera completed by other hands and given its first full performance by the Paris Opera. Paul Prye had never seen the work in any version, though he knew it well from records, and he had been looking forward with sharp anticipation to Monday's performance at the music festival.

What exactly was the "festival"? Paul had not paid much attention to the credits in the programs he had bought at the earlier events they had attended. Now, after turning on the bedlamp and blurting out a hasty explanation to Alice, he sprang onto the floor, shunning his slippers in a dash to his suitcase. Here in a pocket compartment he had compulsively stored theater programs together with tour brochures, museum stubs, and other mementoes of the trip. He found the *Moses and Aaron* program toward the middle of his collection.

The full name of the sponsor of the music festival was the Society for Twentieth Century Theatre Music. The TCT, to use its somewhat arbitrary abbreviation, was a joint venture of East and West Germany, one of the first fruits of the cultural accords recently reached between the two countries in spite of the disapproval of the Soviet Union. Operated from twin headquarters in Leipzig and Hamburg, the company had embarked, amid wide acclaim, on its first international tour devoted to the works of the German and Austrian Expressionists. The crown of its London festival was its celebrated performance of the complete *Lulu*, which was being presented in a fund-raising gala performance on Monday as an appendage to the TCT's three-week run.

Paul started to summarize the program note for Alice. "Bring me some decaf," she told him from bed, "and there's a chance I'll catch the drift." He did her bidding and she listened as she sipped. Her eyes were brightening but her brow was stern. Her first comments were cautious; he knew, though, that she was trying to bridle her own excitement as much as his.

"We shouldn't go head over heels about this. I think we were both at least half asleep when your thunderbolt struck. I don't know how many times—it's usually just after dawn—I seem to awaken with a brilliant discovery about art history. When the sun's up, I'm left face to face with my shimmering thought. Nine times out of ten, it's either foolishness, or someone else has already published it, or both.

"In these early hours of shaking loose of sleep (the Greeks have a better word: the 'hypnopompic' hours), you can't even talk of wishful thinking, it's more like wishful dreaming. We've hoped so that this dreadful business would come to an end before we leave, and now you've come up with a wonderful climax, a kind of operatic setting of Alfred Hitchcock's *The Man Who Knew Too Much:* the cymbals will clash while the umbrella strikes home. God, I'd love you to be right. Yet I have this persistent doubt; it whispers to me that you've made the murderer in your own image. I'm supposed to summon up in my mind's eye a homicidal opera fan who thinks of *Lulu* as Jack the Ripper's opera. Isn't he really a minor character?"

Paul gave her that tolerant look she couldn't abide much before noon. "Minor he is to most operagoers but, I can assure you, not to the umbrella man. This is where his whole design has been moving. We're near the end, and for once I think we can be on the scene ahead of time."

Alice threw him a new challenge. "Do you mean he'd never have begun at all if he couldn't have counted on such a gaudy finale, an umbrella flashing behind the curtain of an upper box?"

The rejoinder stymied Paul for a moment. "You've found a delicate spot. I'm not absolutely certain that I must accept that premise. Did he have *Lulu* in mind before he began or did it occur to him when he was in midcourse? I'm going to leave the issue open for the moment, except that I feel confident that by the time he wrote his first letter to Scotland Yard he'd seen his plan through to the end."

Alice turned from critic to ally. "I suppose we could find out when the publicity for the festival was first released. That might give us some idea as to the earliest possible date he could have mapped out the full series of attacks in the trail of the Ripper. Couldn't Inspector Warren look into it? You really should call him at once." She pointed to the phone. Alice had the habit of providing graphic illustration to her suggestions. Perhaps her index finger had unconsciously assumed the function of the lighted arrow that guided the audience through her slide lectures.

Paul could not locate Warren either at home or at the Yard. When, close to noon, the inspector at last returned his call, it was obvious at once that he was not in a very good mood. The truce he thought he'd worked out with the press had been broken before it was formed. Before his evening meeting began, an envelope had been left on the front doorstep of one of London's less scrupulous newspapers. It contained another typed letter from the self-styled Umbrella Jack. Warren read Prye the contents:

> The double event was right on schedule. Where's your famous police? They dont seem to think your readers would like to see my letters. Maybe you dont agree, so I send this to you. Mary Kelly's the last, and very soon.
>
> Umbrella Jack

The letter had been published in full in the early-morning edition under a flaunting "exclusive" headline. What was worse, the newspaper's front-page editorial railed against Scotland Yard for suppressing the murderer's previous correspondence.

When Warren had calmed down, Paul took courage and tried out his Lulu theory. The detective, as usual, let him proceed without interruption. By the time Paul came to his summation, he'd come under the spell of his own oratory.

"In short, everything fits. The time: the new letter says 'very soon' and the opera performance is only two days off. The occasion: Mary Kelly was killed on a great city holiday, and the umbrella murderer chooses a gala wind-up of a music festival. The place: for the first time our man moves indoors for the kill and dramatically outdoes the Ripper. While Jack chose the lonely room of a pros-titute, his modern rival strikes out at a thronged theater in the Strand. Inspector Warren, if you'll take a chance on my being right, I think we've got him at last.''

Warren's answer gave him all he could have hoped for. "The point is rather that I can't afford to assume that you're wrong. The events have a dreadful way of bearing out your prophecies. We will make necessary arrange-ments at the theater. I know we can count on your coop-eration.''

They turned to another subject. Paul cupped his hand over the speaker; when Alice had left for Scotland she had wanted a surprise, and perhaps she would have one yet. Warren was making progress.

Paul inquired as to the fate of Friday's victims. The news was mixed. The condition of Mlle. Lascombe con-tinued to worsen, but Mrs. Fenning would probably be released from the hospital later in the day.

On Sunday it was reported that the young French-woman had died.

•

The Pryes spent a quiet weekend. There was nothing they could do about the umbrella murders except to wait for Monday night to prove Paul right or wrong. It was odd how they were able to put aside any thoughts of the case in the busy rounds of their last days in London. Strangely, they almost felt that the murders were already in the past and had added a new chapter to the crime annals by which Paul theorized they had been inspired.

They had never enjoyed Noel Coward as much as in Saturday night's performance. What had struck them be-fore as artificiality now seemed, in the light of their experience of the last two weeks, to address admirably a clamorous need they felt from time to time to put the less pleasant facts of life at a distance. Sunday (after they adjusted to the morning's disturbing news of the death of Mlle. Lascombes) was a peaceful day. In the afternoon they made their first visit to the Dulwich Gallery to see the Poussins and Tiepolos and were glad to find that they could once again look at paintings without the intrusion of associations of violence.

When they woke up on Monday morning, the Pryes found themselves in a tacit conspiracy against their rising tension. Perhaps they had taken a cue from their three teenage children, who shared the habit of producing exaggerated yawns whenever they were nervous. Fetching breakfast, making half-hearted gestures toward straightening the room, or doing nothing in particular, Paul and Alice floated back and forth across the carpet like bathrobed ghosts and by 10:00 had not made any firm plans for the day, an unheard-of phenomenon during their trips to London.

Later that morning, Paul received the telephone call he had been expecting. Warren was on the line: "We think we may have found it. Would it be convenient for you to meet us at the warehouse?" He gave Paul an address that meant nothing to him, adding his assurance that it was was only a short taxi ride from the hotel.

Paul's cab stopped in a street not far from Millbank. He paid the driver distractedly, for his eye was on the sign of the establishment. The sign boldly jutted out from the red brick of the building, roaring the name of the business, VROOM! Beneath the name was pictured, full front, a Pop Art Hell's Angel bearing down on the viewer. A smaller placard to the right of the entrance advertised in more modest letters MOPED AND MOTORCYCLE

RENTALS RATES BY THE YEAR, DAY OR HOUR. It also noted encouragingly that "any license" was "acceptable."

Paul was met in the sales office by Inspector Warren, who was flanked by Constable Garson and another man Paul did not know. Warren greeted him cheerfully. "How good of you to come. This gentleman is the assistant manager of the agency"—Warren could not bring himself to pronounce *VROOM!*—"Mr. Philip Watkins. He has been most cooperative, and we are very grateful to him. Mr. Watkins, we'd like to have another view, if you don't mind."

They passed through the rear door of the office into the rental warehouse. In several close ranks traversing the entire length of the warehouse floor and separated by narrow and barely passable aisles were motorcycles, scooters, and mopeds of every make and description—Honda, Vespa, Garelli, Harley-Davidson, Kawasaki, Yamaha. Although the Japanese dominated the inventory, they seemed to have adapted to the local environment, for most of the models were painted the respectable black that had been de rigeur in London taxicabs until the recent color explosion.

As they proceeded single file up one of the aisles, their path was blocked by a lone motorcycle that had been headed out of one of the ranks. If Paul did not know it had been placed there for his inspection, he could have indulged the fancy that it had been cast out by its neighbors, a pariah among motorcycles, because it did not resemble the others in the slightest. It was painted, or perhaps resprayed, a deep red with black streaks.

Warren gave him a few minutes to look it over, and then asked, "Well, what is your opinion? Could that be the celebrated motorcycle of Commercial Street?"

Paul nodded slightly as he answered. "It could be the same; the colors and design are similar, no question about it. But I couldn't swear to it; the radiation of the stripes from a point behind the headlight is just as I remember it. I have no idea how many similar motorcycles there are in London, or in this warehouse, for that matter."

"There are none on this floor, and very few even of solid crimson, that we have seen for ourselves. We are fortunate that the man, in this respect at least, had a certain flair. He had another trait that helps us further: a passion for economy. Mr. Watkins has been kind enough to review his journal of rentals. He has verified that this motorcycle was rented on Thursday, 18 August, the day of the walking tour. Not only that, it was rented on an hourly basis, having been picked up at 1:00 P.M. and returned about four hours later. Have I got that right, Mr. Watkins?"

"Exactly, Inspector," the nervous assistant manager answered, mopping his perspiring brow.

"What did the customer look like? And was there a record made of his name and driver's license number?" Paul asked in rapid-fire sequence.

Inspector Warren held up his hand as a warning to Watkins not to answer. "I think that takes us a little beyond the area where we think you can be of assistance, Professor Prye. I can tell you that Mr. Watkins has given us extremely useful information, and that we are making appropriate inquiries."

Paul was offended by Warren's sudden return to official secrecy after all the facts and theories they had exchanged over the past week. But when they were seated together in the police car with Garson at the wheel, Warren promptly repaired the slight breach. He had not wanted to speak openly before Watkins, but now told Prye what he had learned about the man who had rented the motorcycle. Why hadn't he used his own motorcycle? Good question. Perhaps he didn't own one. But then again, perhaps it was just the low cunning so common in those who aren't very bright. He may have thought that if anything went wrong, and the numbers were taken down by a bystander, a rental license plate would be harder to trace to him.

Dropping him off at the hotel, Warren grasped Paul's hand with another of his characteristic flare-ups of warmth. "I shall see you and Mrs. Prye at the theater tonight. I'm particularly looking forward to meeting Mrs. Prye. I have long suspected she is the real detective in your family—rather like the wife of Inspector Bucket."

Damn the man, Paul thought, he's full of surprises. He's even read *Bleak House*.

·

For once Alice had made no objection to arriving at the theater early. But it had not been easy to find a cab even on Piccadilly because a blinding rain was falling, with no sign of moderating. Warren had asked them to arrive at 6:30, an hour before curtain, and they were at least twenty minutes late. As they drove along the Strand toward the theater, the Pryes saw no visible sign of a heavy police presence. Warren knew his job.

In the outer lobby they were met by Detective Constable Garson, who extended his hand toward them. Paul thought it was the beginning of a handshake, but he was wrong; Garson took possession of their umbrella, which he said he would entrust to the attendant. He walked in the direction of the cloakroom, and the Pryes looked after him. A line of early arrivals, some headed for the buffet bars and others simply taking refuge from the foul weather, had begun to form before the cloakroom and seemed to be moving very slowly although the counter was staffed by three attendants. During the course of the week, theaters and other places of public accommodation had posted signs requiring the deposit of umbrellas, but the checking process here was obviously working with special deliberation. It looked like a security checkpoint in an airport. Alice whispered to Paul that the attendants must be CID men giving the umbrellas a close inspection as they were handed across the counter. Paul did not reply, for Garson was coming back to take them to the theater manager's office, where Warren had said he would be waiting for them.

The room was along a ground-floor corridor that led past the theater's bookstore and gift shop. Garson opened the door without knocking; he stood aside to let the Pryes enter. As he did so, Paul's eye fell first on Inspector Warren, who strode to the door to receive them. Despite his recently expressed pleasure at the opportunity to meet Alice, he seemed businesslike, almost to the point of rudeness, when he took her hand. He murmured rapidly, "You are a remarkable woman. I've heard so much about you from Professor Prye."

Paul looked over Warren's shoulder and was stunned by the turnout. It was as if he had presented himself at the registration desk of the first annual reunion of the Jack the Ripper walking tour. He nodded hello to Frank Collins, the "Limping Man" he'd interviewed at Donaldson's office, James Holloway from Birmingham, and, of course, Gladys Hunter. Smiling at her, Alice whispered to Paul didactically, "If your eyes ever travel up from her legs, I trust you'll notice that the hair is wispy and the jaw far too strong." Many other walkers had answered Warren's call: two of the Dutch cadets, the suburban lady—who'd given over her tweeds for silk—and even the Swedish couple. A jittery little man Paul didn't recognize was introduced to him as the assistant curator of the Black Museum, whose European holiday had been cut short on orders from the Yard.

By the time the Pryes made their rounds, it was close to 7:00. Warren asked Garson to escort Mrs. Prye to her seat, for their work was about to begin.

Around the walls the police had installed, at eye level, four closed-circuit television monitors that were trained on the street entrance to the outer lobby, the lobby bar, the cloakroom, and the queue that was being shepherded to go past the lone ticket taker in a single file. Beginning at 6:30, Warren had assigned each member of the group to observe one of the monitor screens. Paul was added to the contingent poised to watch the queue that had formed to surrender their tickets; the camera was hidden in the ceiling slightly behind the ticket taker and gave them an unobstructed downslanting view of the face of each theatergoer.

It was now 7:00 and the queue moved forward toward the screen. Paul began to shake his head without interruption. Occasionally a facial trait would cause him to squint, but only for an instant, and without disrupting the regular swing of his head. After a while he grinned foolishly at the memory of a similar gesture he had often made as a child. He had stood in the schoolyard during recess, shaking his head in rapid oscillation, while a classmate displayed for his inspection a pack of baseball cards; then the motion of his head would be accompanied by the sotto voce refrain: "Got it; got it; got it." Now his headshake meant "No, that's not him. I'm sure of it."

Because the police had stationed only a single ticket taker at the door, to give the watchers a better view of the entrants, the theater filled slowly. By 7:45, though, the last stragglers were being seated. The observation posts in the manager's office were still manned, but Warren released Prye and the Swedish couple, who were anxious to see the opera.

When Paul joined Alice, he told her that the walkers had not spotted the umbrella man.

Alice was frustrated. "Are you sure he couldn't have slipped by you?"

Paul shook his head. "That's very unlikely."

Alice turned a palm upward in a gesture of defeat. "Then it means that the man's not in the theater?"

Paul opened his program and answered without looking up. "Not at all. It means that he's not in the audience."

•

There was no point in asking him to explain. He was determined to be enigmatic tonight, and in any event, the house lights had already dimmed. The conductor made his way to the pit amid scattered applause; then the curtain rose on a scene Alice knew from the pages of Paul's dog-eared volume of Wedekind's plays. There was the animal trainer at the entrance to a circus tent sneering at the feeble passions of drawing-room theater and offering instead his menagerie of the beasts in man. At his command, a potbellied roustabout ducked into the tent and brought forward in his arms a "snake," the singer who was to play Lulu. God, how awful, Alice complained inwardly; these Expressionists can't even read Genesis right. Eve was *not* the serpent!

Alice elbowed Paul and hoped he could see her scowl. "Don't blame me," he whispered, "for the excesses of your adored nineteenth century."

Excesses there were aplenty in the first two acts. Alice had found the action of the original Wedekind plays quaint and stilted in the translation Paul had urged on her some years ago, but seeing it unroll before her she was forced to take a closer look and didn't like what she saw. She'd often accused Paul of being more of a feminist than she was, but now she was repelled by Wedekind's femme fatale. What was she but a construct of male fantasy, this embodiment of elemental force that drove all men within her ambit to distraction but seemed to feel so little herself? She had a God-given power, one of her lovers sang, to turn people around her into criminals without having any notion of what she was doing. No, Alice corrected herself, it was not wholly true that Lulu had no passion: She could not let Dr. Schön escape her clutches, but it was not love or sex that spurred her, only the iron need of possession, no more ennobling than the snarl of a bitch in the manger. At the feet of Lulu—this serial "killer" of men moved not by her own lust but by the lust of her victims—the corpses piled up during the first two acts. Her husband, Dr. Goll, had a fatal stroke when he broke in upon a painter's amorous pursuit of Lulu; then the painter, now her spouse, cut his throat after learning of her continuing liaison with Dr. Schön; and finally she shot Schön with his own revolver instead of following his order to commit suicide. It was a *ronde* of rejected love that had become a dance of death.

On most theater occasions Alice and Paul were untiring promenaders, but tonight during both intervals they kept their seats and barely tucked in their knees as their row emptied in a stream to the stalls bar. Patrons who strolled toward the lobby for a smoke were turned back by the ushers without explanation, and many of them stood willfully blocking the aisles and grumbling of the growing power of antismoker malice. Paul continued to read the libretto and Alice despaired of catching his attention. These fits of scholarly detachment came on him at odd times. The third act was soon to begin, and how could he remain so calm? So little time, it seemed to her, remained to test his final theory that had been backed to the hilt by Warren and his well-hidden forces, and yet her husband sat there studying the libretto, his eyes shooting back and forth between the bilingual columns to test his woefully weak German. She could not understand how Paul, usually so high-strung, could look for all the world as if he'd lost all interest in what might come.

"What's the last act like?" she finally asked.

"I've not seen it before. The orchestral music of the final scene is absolutely bloodcurdling, but it's hard to get used to hearing Berg's murder music sung."

"How ridiculous," Alice rejoined. "What is most of Italian opera but warbled homicide?" She suddenly turned serious. "Paul, what's going to happen? Where am I to look? You won't tell me, though you know, or you think you know."

Paul read on without lifting his eyes. "We'll just have to wait and see. I could be wrong. It might have been what you said, wishful dreaming."

So that was it, she thought. Typical macho stuff, unworthy of Paul. He had so much at stake now that he was withdrawing just when the wheel was beginning to spin. She leaned over and whispered encouragingly, "It is an ingenious idea however it works out. Keep the details to yourself if you must, but don't give up now. Make the umbrella man prove you wrong."

The curtain rose on the first scene of Act 3. Lulu and her latest lover, Dr. Schön's son Alwa, were shown in their luxurious Paris apartments entertaining guests with gambling and banqueting. At the end of the scene Lulu fled in men's clothes, just before the arrival of the police to arrest her as the escaped murderess of Schön.

Alice, who always placed words before music, saw nothing much new here. Lulu was nothing but a transvestite Manon Lescaut.

But then the curtain rose again on the final scene. Lulu, now living in a depressing London attic with Alwa and her mysterious ancient protector Schigolch, was about to embark on her first night as a prostitute. As if to mock the weather and the Pryes' secret quest, the rain was heard falling on the attic roof, and Schigolch announced that it was "beating a tattoo." Alice was fascinated by the strange irrelevance of the decrepit surroundings and of Lulu's new calling. The costumes, sets, and the program notes might proclaim her a would-be whore starving in a garret, but the stage action and opera tradition pointed in another direction. Lulu was presiding over a salon of varied admirers as if she were a caricature of the Marschallin from *Rosenkavalier*, drawn by a parodist with dreadful taste. As the scene opened, Lulu's two lovers, Schigolch and Alwa, were in full possession of her shabby realm, but their domination was to be challenged by a stream of visitors.

Alice was startled by the first client to enter. He was a professor, clean-shaven, with sharp features like a fowl, and a friendly smile. He wore a top hat and carried a dripping umbrella in his hand.

Alice craned her neck over to Paul. He was still reading his libretto with the aid of a pen flashlight.

The professor kissed Lulu lightly on the forehead, and like a trained prizefighter, she returned a solid kiss on the mouth. They retired to her bedroom; he reemerged and left the apartment. Then the adoring Countess Geschwitz arrived, bringing a portrait of Lulu that she had preserved like a holy icon.

With the next visitor, a crescendo of violence began to mount. It was a black customer, who refused to abide by the house rule of payment in advance; he got into a fight with Alwa, struck him over the head with a bottle, and fled. Schigolch, badly shaken, hid the body and took off for the pub. The two women were left alone on the stage.

Lulu went to the door and admitted a new client—her last.

Paul had closed his libretto, and both the Pryes bent forward to gaze at Jack the Ripper in person. He was a thick-set man with jaunty movements. His face was pale, and beneath high, arching brows his enflamed eyes were fixed on the ground. He had a drooping mustache, scanty beard, and matted side-whiskers, and his hands had been painted a fiery stage-red. His first words to Lulu were gallant: "I think you have a pretty mouth." She told him she got it from her mother, but then proceeded to hard bargaining. Would he spend the night with her? She'd ask very little. He was not enthusiastic, he said he must go home; besides, if he slept there overnight, someone would empty his pockets. Lulu began to beg him to stay, pleading with her destroyer. At last he agreed, and she took a lamp to show him to her room. Jack made her put it aside; they needed no light, for the moon was shining.

Both the Pryes stared after him when he followed Lulu into the bedroom. A few chilling moments passed, and then, though braced for what they knew was coming, they were startled by Lulu's death cry: "No! No! No, no!" Countess Geschwitz ran to her aid, but the Ripper anticipated her. Stooping, he wrenched the door open and plunged a blood-stained knife into her body. He had performed before their eyes Wedekind's "double event." The opera ended as the dying countess vowed eternal devotion to Lulu.

Alice tensely waited for the curtain calls. One by one the singers appeared—first Lulu's two lovers, then the top-hatted professor and the black client. They withdrew, and the apron of the stage was empty again. Then from the wings walked a grim-faced Jack the Ripper. He made two perfunctory bows and was gone. Finally, the side curtains parted once more and his two victims made their entrance. They smiled and waved their arms in response to a warm ovation.

The audience was enthusiastic and called the third-act cast back many times, At last the applause died away and the theater began to empty out.

"What do we do now?" Alice asked.

Paul took her hand as he answered: "We wait here. *La commedia non é finita.*"

•

The soprano who had sung Lulu took her final bow, entrusted her floral tributes to an attendant waiting in the wings, and returned to her dressing room, glad that the evening and the run were over. She had never really liked *Lulu,* despite the wonders it had worked for her career.

When she opened her dressing-room door, the same scene lay before her as after every one of the performances in which she had a role, major or minor. On her table before the mirror was a vase filled with twelve red roses, never a flower more or less, and always just beginning to unfold their secret beauties.

And, of course, he was there. The stage manager of the TCT. Strange how she never seemed to think of him by name anymore. For a few months—it had been more than a year ago—she had blundered unthinking and out of boredom into . . . could you call it an affair? The word was ridiculously inappropriate, it had much too much weight for any relation you could have with such a fatuous person, such a dim shadow of a man. For want of anything better to do she had formed the short-lived habit of dining with him after theater hours, of sleeping with him when they had not drunk too much, and then she'd passed on to new attachments—a German tenor, a Hungarian music critic, and a minor Polish official with a mysterious expense account. It seemed to her, looking back, that she'd simply changed her schedule or her itinerary, that was all, and in the course of change the stage manager had been left behind.

He was a rather tall man, just under six feet, but his shoulders slumped, depriving him of some of his height.

She'd never found his face appealing. His high cheek-bones overmatched the tiny slanting eyes that would come close to disappearing altogether when he'd smile his subservient smile, anxious but failing to please. Why smile at all with a mouth like that? For the smile pulled wide his fleshy lips and disclosed small, eroded stumps of teeth unevenly spaced, which looked as if they belonged to a predatory fish that had worn them down in the gnawing of its prey.

He was there again and she could not ignore him. She spoke to him in Czech.

"Karel, it's sweet of you to have brought me flowers. I've told you not to do so, but you pay me no attention. It is all over between us; you've known that all these months and I have no words left that would make it clearer. Still, we can work together, I shall always regard you as a friend, and I know you would never want to make our collaboration in the Theatre uncomfortable for either of us. It is not that I'm ungrateful for your devotion; it's touching, such a show of constancy. Still, these attentions must stop, you just have to be realistic."

The stage manager said nothing. He did not even smile, and she thanked God for that. He didn't even seem to be looking at her as she spoke. His eyes would dart from side to side as if seeking an object to fix upon, but then they would swing back into a steady forward gaze. But he was still not looking at her as she spoke; he seemed to pick out a spot on the wall behind her head. What a hangdog look the man had, she thought; it was, if anything, worse than his smile.

She couldn't stand the silence that had risen like a wall between them, so she spoke again.

"Karel, I just am in no state tonight to deal with heavy emotions. This damn opera is too much for me. Two acts of portraying a morbid and degenerate whore were quite enough for me all these years, and now some idiot had to dream up this Grand Guignol finale. I will be frank with you, Karel: I've never fancied Jack the Ripper as my leading man."

If she'd been playing for sympathy or attempting to lead him away from thoughts of their "past," it was obvious she was having no success. She'd never seen the man at such a loss for words. Ordinarily he would greet her with cascades of speech, praise for her performance and her beauty, projects for a splendid night in town that only became more ambitious with their continued rejection. Tonight, he seemed unaccountably nervous. Discrete beads of sweat started all over his face, standing firmly in place without combining or running down the taut skin of his cheeks. A nervous tic she had never seen before pulled at the corner of his left eye. She began to feel he had come tonight to tell her something decisive but could not find a beginning. She talked to him again, afraid she was babbling but determined to fill the void between them that was oppressing her.

"It is a dreadful finale that should not have been staged. But never have I found it so horrible as here in London, in the midst of these new crimes that have been committed in the Ripper's name. Have you read the news reports? How foolish of me to have asked this of you of all people, who read everything, and, if you'll pardon the comment, have always seemed to me to have a penchant for the lurid! You will forgive me, Karel, we are after all old friends. I couldn't help but think that somewhere in the city, who knows, perhaps in the audience, is a man who is thirsty for the blood of Lulu—for my life's blood."

He still stood there unmoving, by the side of his gift of roses. He really looked terribly sad, as if he had suffered an irretrievable loss of which he was becoming increasingly aware. The twitch at the edge of his eye had stopped and tears began to well up. The singer really didn't know what to do with him this evening.

"I tell you what, Karel," she said in a consoling voice into which she put some of the thrilling vibrato her fans loved, "you can take me back to the hotel tonight—don't misunderstand me, I mean to the lobby bar. We'll have a drink together to ward off the effects of this torrential downpour, and there we'll toast the festival and part as good friends."

He still said nothing, but seemed to muster courage; for the first time he drew his eyes down from the wall and directed them full on her face. A hint of the smile she despised followed.

"What a strange companion you'll be," she continued, "for you persist in this uncustomary silence. But perhaps a drink will bring you round. Wait here a moment. It won't take me long to change."

When she reemerged from behind a screen in a flamboyant dress not remarkably different from Lulu's last apparel, he had not moved. But she noticed something new.

"You've certainly come prepared," she said. "When in England, do as the English do; you're just the image of Neville Chamberlain. Why bring it here, though, to my room? Is the roof leaking? I suppose not, or you would not hold it furled."

The stage manager did not smile any longer. Instead, to her utter astonishment and horror, he stiffened his arm and lunged at her. But before he could reach her, he was overwhelmed by an avalanche of blue.

He didn't try to break free. Instead, using his weapon for the last time, he drove the tip of the umbrella deep into the flesh of his own thigh.

It was very late when Paul returned to the hotel. He had put Alice into a cab, but Warren had asked him to stay at the theater, saying that there were some points on which he wanted to have his views.

When Paul opened the door, a familiar slim arm shot out; it was offering him a glass of scotch. Alice had decided the night's melodrama had justified her in replacing their stock.

She first wanted to know the details of Warren's operations at the theater. Who knew of the police presence? And was the screening of the audience purely diversionary? Paul told her that all measures had been planned with the secret knowledge and cooperation of the London theater management. The police were admitted to the theater before dawn and quickly set up the monitoring devices. It had been Paul's theory that the probable intended victim was Lulu herself: what more dramatic consummation of the crimes could be imagined than to murder in real life the character whom Berg's Jack the Ripper killed in the make-believe of the opera? The screening operation was mounted in earnest, for no one could be sure yet who the murderer was. Nevertheless, their principal conjecture was that the attack would occur backstage, and elaborate plans for an ambush were made. Police officers were hidden, following the second interval, in recesses of Lulu's dressing room and in the two adjoining rooms; immediately prior to the fall of the final curtain, Slapak was seen entering the dressing room, and the police were in readiness for a sudden response.

Was Slapak aware of the police activity in the lobby? The television monitoring had been carried on as unobtrusively as possible, but it was considered not unlikely that a hint of the operation might filter through to the staff or company of the TCT. It was hoped that, if this happened, the result would not be unfavorable. Perhaps the competitive instinct in the killer would be stirred further by the thought of bringing off a backstage murder while the front of the house swarmed with police.

One of the fine points of Slapak's planning had escaped their notice. He had been able to bring his umbrella into the theater building without fear of detection—among the props of the opera production.

For hours they sat talking about Karel Slapak, the stage manager of the TCT who had revealed himself as the umbrella murderer.

Alice was exhilarated by the arrest but frustrated that its perfect timing made it impossible to determine how the murderer would have proceeded.

"I can't figure out what was in his mind. If he intended to come off scot free, it didn't make any sense to attack the prima donna with the umbrella. She was the only one of his victims who knew him. The ricin works so slowly that she would have certainly had time to identify him to the police. Am I going wrong somewhere, Paul? Is it possible that he didn't intend to get away, and that perhaps it was always his plan to be caught so that he could enjoy his celebrity to the fullest?"

Paul was tired enough to have an open mind. "Anything's possible, I suppose. But I think he intended to escape unscathed. After all, Jack the Ripper vanished into thin air, and Slapak could hardly claim to have surpassed him if he ended up in the arms of the police. Still, the point you make about ricin is unanswerable. It is a clumsy weapon to use against a victim who knows you unless you have an infallible escape plan."

"Then why did he pick ricin as his weapon?"

"We've been struggling with that problem from the beginning. I think that the same competitive instinct that drove him to best Jack the Ripper in the centennial year caused him to try outdoing the original umbrella murderer by using an ostensibly inaccessible poison for his own selfish purposes. Having begun with ricin, he had to use it to the very end. It became his signature, as Jack's mutilations had branded his crimes. Unless the poisoned umbrella was seen to have a role in the murder of the soprano then, if he was indeed planning to escape still anonymous, there would have been nothing to tie the last murder into his series and to prove he had completed his full string."

Alice's head had lolled onto one shoulder but she was still listening intently. "Well, it seems to me, Paul, you have painted him into a corner. He must use ricin, but if he does his victim will identify him to the police. You're surely not going to tell me that he had a helicopter conveniently poised on the theater roof?"

"No, the man was cooler than that. He intended to leave London at leisure, with the rest of the theater troupe, after grieving with them decorously over the death of a leading lady. His solution was quite different, and it is perhaps wrong to speak of it as a solution, for it was to be the very essence of the last crime. He had no intention that the singer would die of ricin poisoning. He had something much more violent in mind and much more personal. His last crime had to be different from the others if it was to rival the night of horrors in which Jack the Ripper coolly dismembered Mary Kelly.

"Even in this crucial respect Slapak had a precedent at hand—and a very modern precedent at that. I don't know whether you remember, Alice, that when we were going through our F. Tennyson Jesse game of speculating on the motives of Margaret Sanders's attacker, you suggested to me in jest that perhaps it was an act of terrorism directed against tourists unduly interested in the monuments of crime. I think that the events have proved that your insight was brilliant but that you had the reality of the crime exactly reversed. What we seem to be dealing with here is a case of a *murderer* who is morbidly preoccupied with crime history. Do you remember the Crimmins case?''

"Alice Crimmins?" Alice looked puzzled, wondering why he'd find any relevance in the cause célèbre of the New York City housewife who'd been accused of murdering her children.

Paul, in his weariness, had not noticed the ambiguity. "No, I was referring to Craig Crimmins. He was the Metropolitan Opera stagehand who murdered a female violinist during an intermission. You'll recall that he forced her at knifepoint to a sixth-floor roof and then, after an apparent struggle, threw her off. Her body was found below on a steel platform in a cooling tower in the opera building.

"The murder took place in 1980, and you'll remember it received an enormous amount of newspaper coverage. Slapak seems to have traveled to New York in the course of his work; you'll remember what the schoolteacher told us of the beginnings of his conversation with Margaret Sanders. And even if he wasn't there in 1980, he can hardly have missed reports of the case, particularly with his obvious immersion in true crime."

Alice had been listening with a deepening frown. "And you think that Slapak had planned to reenact the Metropolitan Opera murder?"

Paul was prepared for her doubts. "In this case I can tell you that not only do I think so, but that Inspector Warren agrees. To give him credit, he was the first to talk of identifying a pattern in these crimes, though I don't suppose any of us thought we'd end up with the complexities we've uncovered. One of the reasons he asked me to stay was so that we could explore together the hidden geography of the theater building. We found it to be a maze of staircases and skylights. We will never know precisely where Slapak would have led her. But I feel sure that if we had not anticipated him, her broken body would have been found somewhere in the depths of that building. Perhaps the body would also have shown signs of sexual assault, strangulation, or even mutilation—God knows how far he would have pressed the imitation of Mary Kelly's death. I think that before he left he would have thrown the ricin umbrella down after her. Paradoxically, his final murder would have at last yielded up the secret of this infamous weapon."

Alice tapped her knee to emphasize a new objection. "Still, I don't understand what he wanted the police to believe when they found the umbrella, and presumably also detected traces of ricin in her body. The fall itself would so obviously have been the cause of death; wouldn't the police have wondered about the redundancy of the murderer's weapon?"

Paul had to leave the point open. "I don't know what he expected the police to conclude had happened. I think he hoped they'd have theorized that the singer, when attacked with the umbrella, had struggled with him or had begun calling for help and that he had to use more violent means to effect his escape. It is possible, though, that he did not intend to leave the murder scenario to the imagination of Scotland Yard. I am convinced, and must confess that I never doubted from the start, that he was indeed the author of the Umbrella Jack letters. It would have been quite in keeping with his boastful character for him to send off a last letter crowing about the opera murder and giving some fictional account about the circumstances that led to his change of course."

Alice still couldn't reconcile herself to the thought that so many mysteries would remain if Slapak kept to his stubborn silence. "Doesn't it bother you," she asked, "that when all is said and done, we may still be unable to fathom the man's motives? It seems that all along he must have planned to cap the crimes with the murder of a woman who had rejected him. But are we to take this to mean that had he and the singer lived happily ever after, those three other women would never have died? Was the whole Jack the Ripper pattern just a ruse to put us off the trail of the truth—that he did not hate women so much that he was impelled to kill at random, but that instead random murders camouflaged a plan of revenge against the one woman who had wronged him?"

Paul had expected the question. Alice was right to ask it, because it was much more interesting than any of the details they had discussed before. He said, "That's the final riddle, and ironically, it's the same question that is still being asked about Jack the Ripper. Many have wondered whether there was not more than a little method in his madness, whether the pattern of prostitute murders did not divert his pursuers from some more specific target of his malice. It is this kind of doubt that gave us the startling proposition that all the murders were nothing but an elaborate cover-up for a midwife's botched abortion. More to the point, though, are the other theories I've mentioned to you, that the Ripper was driven from the beginning by a plan of revenge against Mary Kelly. The Sickert theory, that she was eliminated as an inconvenient witness of a disgraceful marriage, is only the latest variant. For years before this new notion saw the light of day, people found other reasons to read the first four crimes as milestones on the way to the discovery and punishment of Mary Kelly.

"In the case of Slapak, we have this advantage at least, that we know revenge and jealousy lay at or near the root of the opera attack. But I, for one, cannot conclude from this that the earlier crimes are to be dismissed as 'camouflage.' Too much vainglory is evidenced by the whole sequence to convince me that Slapak was not powerfully motivated in each of the crimes, including the last, by a desire to copy and indeed supplant the most famous of all serial murderers."

"What does this do then to the murder-motive classification of F. Tennyson Jesse?" Alice asked with a smile.

Paul acknowledged a palpable hit. "I suppose it means that, charming as I shall always regard her writing to be, it may be time, in light of the bizarre experience of the most recent decades, to put aside the neat compartments into which she thought criminal conduct could be divided and analyzed. Instead, I find that one clear result of this most unusual stay in London has been to drive me back to Dostoevski."

Paul rummaged about in his suitcase and took out the copy of *The House of the Dead* that he had purchased the previous afternoon at Foyle's. He turned to a marked page and read to Alice:

> I am trying to make our criminals come under different categories; is this possible? Reality is so infinitely diverse that it eludes the most ingenious deductions of abstract thought; it does not admit of bold and precise classifications.

Alice's questions about the umbrella man were far from exhausted, but her mind darted away to a fresh subject: the surprise that Paul had withheld from her.

"Tell me about the other man they've arrested. Where do you figure he fits in? No, since you've insisted on being so mysterious, you'd better start at the beginning. What made you suspect there might have been a 'second man'?"

Paul was bent on being generous, though there was no better way to irritate Alice. "I must have had a glimmer of the idea for quite a while, but it was, of course, something you said that clinched the point. You'll remember the 'hint' you gave me at Gray's Mall. It had struck you that something the schoolteacher said at Donaldson's office wasn't accurate. In his account of the incident on Commercial Street, he remarked that the reckless driving of the motorcyclist had thrown all of us into a panic. That was almost true, but not completely. Most of us were panicked, but not the man I saw attacking Margaret Sanders. He did not fall or lose his poise in the slightest; instead, he stabbed her at precisely the moment when the confusion of the others would make it least likely that he'd be observed.

"I'd always wondered about the crucial detail of the murderer's planning: How could he know in advance when it would be possible for him to strike without being noticed, and, indeed, how could he have known that it would ever be possible to attack covertly and escape? The arrival of the motorcycle and the chaos it caused seemed providential, and he was able to take advantage of them with the split-second timing of an athlete. I'd always thought this was curious, and to me the instantaneous and unerring response was particularly impressive since I seem to have such slow and muddled responses to sudden sights and sounds. Though the oddness of the favoring circumstance the cyclist provided him never stopped bothering me, I had half explained it away. Perhaps, I thought, the murderer set out on the walking tour intending to strike only if the right opportunity presented itself. I didn't change my mind on this point even when I became convinced the man had set out to copy the series of the East End murders. After all, he wasn't under any desperate compulsion to kill on the day of my walking tour; there were plenty of Ripper walks scheduled during his stay, not to mention all the other places and events associated in some way with the Ripper murders. It was clear to me that the murderer combined a strong homicidal urge with a high degree of cunning and calculation—one might almost say prudence. I think the same can be said of Jack the Ripper."

Alice asked him how her "hint" had helped if he'd been as puzzled by the killer's poise as she was. He paused a moment to indulge a satisfied smile. It was a rare experience for him to hold her spellbound, and he savored it. Her mind was so active it had the habit of operating many of its circuits simultaneously; now he had her full attention. She had planted her feet on an ottoman and clasped her knees as she waited for him to continue. Where had he seen that pose before? Of course; it was the elf (now grown beautiful) who watched the Fairy-Feller wield his ax.

"It isn't that your point was completely new," he replied. "But you urged it so persuasively that I could no longer escape the force of the necessary conclusion: *the murderer hadn't been startled by the motorcycle because he knew it was coming and precisely when and where.* He'd arranged for it to come, and the diversion it would cause was to provide cover for his attack.

"So that was the birth of my 'second man,' or perhaps I should say his confirmation, for I'd already seen another sign of his hand at work, or, at least, his voice."

"You mean as the man who called Lord Whitman's secretary for admission to the Black Museum," Alice volunteered.

"Precisely. I had with some misgivings attributed the discrepancy to Mr. Clark's self-assurance and his impatience with our unscheduled interview. But the fact remained that two members of the walking tour insisted that the killer spoke with a European accent. The teacher thought, in fact, it was Balkan, while Mr. Clark was sure he was English, and an uneducated Londoner to boot.

"Your hint suggested to me I'd done Clark an injustice. Perhaps his recollection was accurate, and the man who spoke to him was not the 'J. L. Ventra' who signed the register of the museum and stabbed Policewoman Sterling in Victoria Street.

"Final proof was provided by the 'double event.' Here we had for the first time two attacks committed in an incredibly short interval. It struck us all as unlikely that the murderer, usually so cautious, would have stabbed Mlle. Lascombes, then calmly turned the corner into Baker Street and attacked Mrs. Fenning. Then there was the unaccountable change to the ineffectual firing of the umbrella device instead of the universally lethal stabbing. My first tack, when I spoke to Warren at Madame Tussaud's, was to clutch at straws: perhaps the murderer's clumsiness in the second attack was due to an untested double loading of the device and to his haste to flee. But the inspector wasn't convinced and neither was I. Before I left the museum I broached the new theory: that a second man had been in the picture from early on. He had driven the motorcycle, placed the call to Mr. Clark, and made the unsuccessful attack on Mrs. Fenning with a second poisoned umbrella. I suggested the police look for the motorcycle, and this morning they found it."

He told Alice for the first time of his visit to VROOM!, and then filled in the details of the arrest of the second man at the theater at the very moment when Karel Slapak was overpowered.

It had been easy to locate the accomplice. He had

signed for the motorcycle in his own name, Sam Tutchin (perhaps the agency was, after all, scrupulous about demanding presentation of licenses despite the permissive tone of its advertisement). He was a local stagehand at the theater. Constable Garson had taken him in charge while he was busy with his mates disassembling the modular blocks that supported the back wall of the set for the murder scene of *Lulu*. Garson's voice was almost obliterated by the resounding clash made by the interlocking modules as they were stacked in the rear of the stagehouse. Nevertheless, Tutchin heard him without difficulty. It was almost as if he had been waiting with resignation for his appearance.

Tutchin had readily confessed his involvement in the crimes. He was a slow-witted man, and the reaction of Warren and his colleagues had been sympathetic. Paul had no doubt that they believed him.

The story he told would almost have been amusing if it had not turned into a nightmare. The visiting stage manager Slapak had been very friendly to the crew from the day he arrived to make plans for the run. After a while, he seemed to single Tutchin out from the group; they would have brown-bag lunches together and talk about everything under the sun: problems of reduced employment in the theater business, English politics, sports and the 1988 Olympics, soccer hooliganism, and cars and motorcycles. The man seemed to Tutchin to be mad about motorcycles and was delighted when the stagehand told him he sometimes drove them (though he couldn't afford to own one himself).

In time, Slapak started to ask Tutchin for little favors. For example, he'd ask whether on his way to work he'd pick him up a pack of a brand of English cigarettes he particularly liked. Whenever Tutchin did an errand for him, Slapak would give him an unreasonably large tip, never less than ten pounds.

Then one day (when the festival run had just begun), Slapak requested another service. He told him he was a great admirer of the British police, that he'd always longed to visit the Museum of Scotland Yard. It was hard to get admitted, and he'd heard it was even harder if you were foreign. He'd be very grateful, he said, exhibiting a twenty-pound note, if Tutchin would place a call for him. Tutchin agreed, and Slapak gave him a note providing the telephone number of Lord Whitman's office and instructions as to what he should say.

The next request was much odder, and Tutchin had hesitated for a moment; he had been persuaded, however, by an offer of a hundred pounds and expenses. Slapak told him he had a friendly grudge against a member of the cast who had got drunk one night in Leipzig and driven a car through Slapak's garage door. He had a wonderful idea for revenge. He knew the singer was going on a walking tour the next day, and he thought there was no better way of getting even than by having some wild cyclist scare the wits out of the man. He thought Tutchin was just the man for the job. It would be perfectly simple and wouldn't get Tutchin into any trouble. Slapak told him the exact place at which the "scare" should be brought off and had calculated when the group would arrive there; he had taken the tour himself the week before and knew the route precisely. As it turned out, though, Tutchin had had to improvise. The rain had caused the group's progress to slacken, and he had had to follow them at a discreet distance for a long time before he could find the right moment for his frightening maneuver.

Then the news stories about the ricin murders of Sterling and Sanders had exploded on television and in the papers. Tutchin told the police that the report of Sanders having been stabbed with an umbrella on an East End walking tour had stunned him. All his original qualms about the motorcycle "scare" returned to him with new force, and he had the chilling fear that he had been an unwitting accomplice to Slapak in the Sanders murder, that he had provided cover for the umbrella assault. He said he had confronted Slapak with his suspicion, threatening to expose him. Warren was inclined to believe (and Paul agreed) that Tutchin was claiming after the fact more insight than he was capable of. More likely, Slapak had planned from the outset that, when the first two murders were revealed (if not by discovery on the part of the police, then through his triumphant letters to Scotland Yard), he would terrorize Tutchin by telling him how he had duped him into serving as an accessory in the Sanders murder. Perhaps, for good measure, he intended to spell out for Tutchin his even subtler role in preparing the way for Slapak's attack on Policewoman Sterling. The point of these revelations would have been to convince the stagehand how dark the case looked against him as a conspirator and to win not only his silence but his cooperation in the use Slapak still had for him. And how did Slapak intend the involuntary partnership in crime to have ended for Tutchin? With the murder of the stagehand, possibly, but Paul Prye thought it more in keeping with Slapak's vanity for him to have planned on leaving Tutchin to face the police alone after his own escape; the stagehand's final service would be to pay inarticulate tribute, in his confession, to the genius of the modern Jack the Ripper.

This reasoning made Paul suspect that it was Slapak who had approached Tutchin with the news of the unknowing accomplice's role in the murders, and that Tutchin had not taken the initiative in this confrontation, as he now claimed. In any event, the two men spoke, and what Slapak told him threw Tutchin into a panic. The stage manager said he was a foreign agent and had now disposed (with Tutchin's help) of two enemies of his regime. However, it was necessary for him to disguise the purpose of his attacks and to provide himself an iron-clad alibi. Therefore, under penalty of disclosing Tutchin's role in the previous crimes (perhaps he had threatened him with worse), the theater hand was to simulate a similar attack on a random woman pedestrian at a moment when Slapak would be visibly engaged in work at the theater. Tutchin refused; he wouldn't get more deeply involved, and he certainly was not going to kill someone to save Slapak, or himself, for that matter. But Slapak had renewed his threats and added persuasion. The pedestrian would come to no harm. It was necessary only that the attempt be identifiable as a ricin attack. He would provide a weaker dose of ricin, and if Tutchin fired from at least six feet away the pellet would lodge itself in a superficial layer of skin. In a panic, Tutchin had yielded. He did as he was told. Slapak had furnished him an umbrella, which he had returned with great relief an hour after the attack. The news of the "double event" had left Tutchin thunderstruck. He had been living in a trance ever since, and no handshake, no kiss he had ever known was so welcome as Constable Garson's tap on his shoulder.

"Poor man," Alice said when Paul finished the story. "What will happen to him?"

Paul shook his head. "I don't know. I'm glad I don't have to make the decision. To punish him severely would make a mockery of the deterrence theory, but on the other hand, he is partly responsible for the deaths of two people." He added judiciously, "I can't see how he can be blamed for more than gullibility in calling Lord Whitman's office."

Alice had a final reservation. "It seems to work out very well, but doesn't it add still another riddle to the enigma of Slapak? Doesn't a man who takes such obvious pleasure in killing usually act alone? I mean, isn't the pleasure a private thing?"

Paul smiled. "The point's a good one. But the twentieth century may come to be remembered as the age of the loss of privacy. If it's left us in so many of life's intimacies, why not in murder as well? You'll remember the ghastly case of the Hillside Strangler in California, where the serial rape-murders turned out to be the work of a pair of cousins. Perhaps a new era began with Leopold and Loeb."

In a moment, Paul had a more charitable afterthought. "Come to think of it, maybe it's nothing new at all, if Walter Sickert's son is right, and Jack the Ripper really was Sir William Gull and was assisted by a sadistic coachman. Maybe the privacy of Victorian sex crimes has been overrated."

•

With great discipline, the Pryes finished packing Wednesday morning before they read the newspaper. On page one they learned that Karel Slapak had at last done something original: he had become the first poisoned-umbrella suicide. The report stated that he had died in the early hours without having said a word to the authorities. The prima donna was quoted at length. She had spurned his affections, she said, but had never been able to end his dogged attachment to her. He was an odd man, outgoing in company when he wanted to be, almost charismatic, she would say, but beneath the veneer of social charm she had always detected a loneliness, or kind of depression. She felt sorry for him in spite of all.

"What typically operatic tripe!" Alice said. "To her Slapak's just a male version of Turandot. In opera a bloodthirsty princess can order hundreds of suitors beheaded, but just because she falls for the tenor, we're supposed to love her in the end."

Another article on the case pleased Alice more. Inspector Warren was quoted as acknowledging the assistance of Professors Paul and Alice Prye of New York City. She pointed out Warren's comment to Paul.

He had obviously expected the public praise. "Oh, yes. He told me that, now that the rule of anonymity had served its purpose, he'd have something nice to say."

Alice liked the ring of Warren's tribute but was suspicious. "Would it be wrong for me to ask whether it was Warren's idea to give us equal billing?"

Paul dodged the question. "Why do you insist on depriving our marriage of all its mystery?"

"I desist forever from curiosity, except for one more question: Does Higgins love us as much as Warren does?"

Paul doubted it.

"I know we've convinced him that Slapak's the murderer. How could his skepticism survive the events backstage? But when I spoke last to Warren to say good-bye, he told me that Higgins was still searching for a Bulgarian connection."

•

When the captain switched off the seat-belt sign, Paul pushed his seat back. He heard the agonizing crunch of a knee. As he turned around to apologize, he encountered a florid, beefy face suffused with intense hostility. Wherever I look, thought Paul, there's another candidate for my bookshelves.

A few moments passed.

"Alice," he said.

"Yes, dear."

"Do you think I'll hold up?"

"What in the world are you talking about?"

"I mean do you suppose I'll last long—to a ripe old age?"

"Of course you will. You come from good stock. But

when we get home, you'll have to wean yourself away from the *patisseries* we've become used to, and you simply must stop inventing excuses to avoid the Exercycle."

Paul didn't acknowledge her words but continued to muse in silence. Alice began to wonder whether she had responded too flippantly. "What's on your mind, Paul? Have you been feeling all right?"

"I'm feeling fine," he answered, with an unaccountably wistful look. "But do you think that with luck I could live another twenty-two years?"

"I'll be seriously displeased with you if you don't. You'd only be sixty-five. You're good for another forty years at least."

A smile of relief at last appeared on Paul's features. "I hope you're right. And if you are, when the year 2010 rolls around, would you come back to London with me for the Crippen centennial?"